A DAY IN OLD ATHENS

A PICTURE OF ATHENIAN LIFE

BY

WILLIAM STEARNS DAVIS

PROFESSOR OF ANCIENT HISTORY IN THE
UNIVERSITY OF MINNESOTA

———•◦◦❋◦◦•———

ALLYN AND BACON

Boston   New York   Chicago

PREFACE.

THIS little book tries to describe what an intelligent person would see and hear in ancient Athens, if by some legerdemain he were translated to the fourth century B.C. and conducted about the city under competent guidance. Rare happenings have been omitted and sometimes, to avoid long explanations, probable matters have been stated as if they were ascertained facts; but these instances are few, and it is hoped no reader will be led into serious error.

The year 360 B.C. has been selected for the hypothetical time of this visit, not because of any special virtue in that date, but because Athens was then architecturally almost perfect, her civic and her social life seemed at their best, the democratic constitution held its vigor, and there were few outward signs of the general decadence which was to set in after the triumph of Macedon.

I have endeavored to state no facts and to make no allusions, that will not be fairly obvious to a reader who has merely an elementary knowledge of Greek annals, such information, for instance, as may be gained through a good secondary school history of ancient times. This naturally has led to comments and descriptions which more advanced students may find superfluous.

The writer has been under a heavy debt to the numerous and excellent works on Greek " Private Antiquities " and "Public Life" written in English, French, or German, as well as to the various great Classical Encyclopaedias and Dictionaries, and to many treatises and monographs upon the topography of Athens and upon the numerous phases ill

of Attic culture. It is proper to say, however, that the material from such secondary sources has been merely supplementary to a careful examination of the ancient Greek writers, with the objects of this book kept especially in view. A sojourn in modern Athens, also, has given me an impression of the influence of the Attic landscape upon the conditions of old Athenian life, an impression that I have tried to convey in this small volume.

I am deeply grateful to my sister, Mrs. Fannie Davis Gifford, for helpful criticism of this book while in manuscript ; to my wife, for preparing the drawings from Greek vase-paintings which appear as illustrations; and to my friend and colleague, Professor Charles A. Savage, for a kind and careful reading of the proofs. Thanks also are due to Henry Holt and Company for permission to quote material from their edition of Von Falke's " Greece and Borne."

W. S. D.
UNIVERSITY OF MINNESOTA,
MINNEAPOLIS, MINNESOTA.
May, 1914.

CONTENTS.

v

Contents

Chapter XX. The Temples and Gods of Athens.

Chapter XXI. The Great Festivals of Athens.

MAPS, PLANS, AND ILLUSTRATIONS.

A Day in Old Athens

A DAY IN OLD ATHENS.

CHAPTER I.

THE PHYSICAL SETTING OF ATHENS.

1. The Importance of Athens in Greek History. — To three ancient nations the men of the twentieth century owe an incalculable debt. To the Jews we owe most of our notions of religion; to the Komans we owe traditions and examples in law, administration, and the general management of human affairs which still keep their influence and value; and finally, to the Greeks we owe nearly all our ideas as to the fundamentals of art, literature, and philosophy, in fact, of almost the whole of our intellectual life. These Greeks, however, our histories promptly teach us, did not form a single united nation. They lived in many " city-states " of more or less importance, and some of the largest of these contributed very little directly to our civilization. Sparta, for example, has left us some noble lessons in simple living and devoted patriotism, but hardly a single great poet, and certainly never a philosopher or a sculptor. When we examine closely, we see that the civilized life of Greece, during the centuries when she was accomplishing the most, was peculiarly centered at Athens. Without Athens, Greek history would lose three quarters of its significance, and modern life and thought would become infinitely the poorer.

2. Why the Social Life of Athens is so Significant. — Because, then, the contributions of Athens to our own life are so important, because they touch (as a Greek would say) upon almost every side of " the true, the beautiful, and the good,"

A Day in Old Athens

it is obvious that the outward conditions under which this Athenian genius developed deserve our respectful attention. For assuredly such personages as Sophocles, Plato, and Phidias were not isolated creatures, who developed their genius apart from, or in spite of, the life about them, but rather were the ripe products of a society, which in its excellences and weaknesses presents some of the most interesting pictures and examples in the world. To understand the Athenian civilization and genius it is not enough to know the outward history of the times, the wars, the laws, and the lawmakers. We must see Athens as the average man saw it and lived in it from day to day, and then perhaps we can partially understand how it was that during the brief but wonderful era of Athenian freedom and prosperity, 1 Athens was able to produce so many men of commanding genius as to win for her a place in the history of civilization which she can never lose.

3. The Small Size and Sterility of Attica. — Attica was a very small country according to modern notions, and Athens the only large city therein. The land barely covered some 700 square miles, with 40 square miles more, if one includes the dependent island of Salamis. It was thus far smaller than the smallest of our American " states " (Rhode Island = 1250 square miles), and was not so large as many American counties. It was really a triangle of rocky, hill-scarred land thrust out into the JSgean Sea, as if it were a sort of continuation of the more level district of Bceotia. Yet small as it was, the hills inclosing it to the west, the seas pressing it from the northeast and south, gave it a unity and isolation all its own. Attica was not an island;

1 That era may be assumed to begin with the battle of Marathon (490 B.C.), and it certainly ended in 322 B.C., when Athens passed decisively under the power of Macedonia ; although since the battle of Chae-roneia (338 B.C.) she had done little more than keep her liberty on sufferance-

The Physical Setting of Athens

3

but it could be invaded only by sea, or by forcing the resistance which could be offered at the steep mountain passes towards Bceotia or Megara. Attica was thus distinctly separated from the rest of Greece. Legends told how, when the half-savage Dorians had forced themselves southward over the mainland, they had never penetrated

SKETCH MAP OF
ATTICA

SCALE OF MILES

into Attica; and the Athenians later prided themselves upon being no colonists from afar, but upon being " earth-sprung," — natives of the soil which they and their twenty-times grandfathers had held before them.

This triangle of Attica had its peculiar shortcomings and virtues. It was for the most part stony and unfertile. Only a shallow layer of good soil covered a part of its hard foundation rock, which often in turn lay bare on the sur-

face. The Athenian farmer had a sturdy struggle to win a scanty crop, and about the only products he could ever raise in abundance for export were olives (which seemed to thrive on scanty soil and scanty rainfall) and honey, the work of the mountain bees.

4. The Physical Beauty of Attica. — Yet Attica had advantages which more than counterbalanced this grudging of fertility. All Greece, to be sure, was favored by the natural beauty of its atmosphere, seas, and mountains, but Attica was perhaps the most favored portion of all. Around her coasts, rocky often and broken by pebbly beaches and little craggy peninsulas, surged the deep blue Egeau, the most glorious expanse of ocean in the world. Far away spread the azure water, 1 — often foam-crested and sometimes alive with the dolphins leaping at their play, — reaching towards a shimmering sky line where rose "the isles of Greece," masses of green foliage, or else of tawny rock, scattered afar, to adapt the words of Homer, "like shields laid on the face of the glancing deep."

Above the sea spread the noble arch of the heavens, — the atmosphere often dazzlingly bright, and carrying its glamour and sparkle almost into the hearts of men. The Athenians were proud of the air about their land. Their poets gladly sung its praises, as, for example, Euripides, 2 when he tells how his fellow countrymen enjoy being —

Ever through air clear shining brightly As on wings uplifted, pacing lightly.

5. The Mountains of Attica.—The third great element, besides the sea and the atmosphere of Athens, was the mountains. One after another the bold hills reared them-

1 The peculiar blueness of the water near Attica is probably caused by the clear rocky bottom of the sea, as well as by the intensity of the sunlight. 2 Medea: 829.

selves, cutting short all the plainlands and making the farmsteads often a matter of slopes and terraces. Against the radiant heavens these mountains stood out boldly, clearly; revealing all the little gashes and seams left from that long forgotten day when they were flung forth from the bowels of the earth. None of these mountains was very high: Hymettus, the greatest, was only about 3500 feet; but rising as they often did from a close proximity to the sea, and not from a dwarfing table-land, even the lower hills uplifted themselves with proud majesty.

These hills were of innumerable tints according to their rocks, the hue of the neighboring sea, and the hour of the day. In spring they would be clothed in verdant green, which would vanish before the summer heats, leaving them rosy brown or gray. But whatever the fundamental tone, it was always brilliant; for the Athenians lived in a land where blue sky, blue sea, and the massive rock blent together into such a galaxy of shifting color, that, in comparison, the lighting of almost any northern or western landscape would seem feeble and tame. The Athenians absorbed natural beauty with their native air.

6. The Sunlight in Athens. — The Athenian loved sunshine, and Helios the Sun God was gracious to his prayers. In the Athens of to-day it is reckoned that the year averages 179 days in which the sun is not concealed by clouds one instant; and 157 days more when the sun is not hidden more than half an hour. 1 Ancient Athens was surely not more cloudy. Nevertheless, despite this constant sunshine and a southern latitude, Athens was striken relatively seldom with semitropical heat. The sea was a good friend,

1 The reason for these many clear days is probably because when the moist west and

southwest winds come in contact with the dry, heated air of the Attic plain, they are at once volatilized and dispersed, not condensed (as in northern lands); therefore the day resolves itself into brilliant sunshine.

bringing tempering breezes. In the short winter there might be a little frost, a little snow, and a fair supply of rain. For the rest of the year, one golden day was wont to succeed another, with the sun and the sea breeze in ever friendly rivalry. The climate saved the Athenians from being obliged to wage a stern warfare with nature as did the northern peoples. Their life and civilization could be one developed essentially " in the open air"; while, on the other hand, the bracing sea breeze saved them from that enervating lethargy which has ruined so many southern folk. The scanty soil forced them to struggle hard to win a living; unless they yielded to the constant beckoning of the ocean, and sought food, adventure, wealth, and a great empire across the seas.

7. The Topography of the City of Athens. — So much for the land of Attica in general; but what of the setting of the city of Athens itself? The city lay in a plain, somewhat in the south central part of Attica, and about four miles back from the sea. A number of mountains came together to form an irregular rectangle with the Saronic Gulf upon the south. To the east of Athens stretched the long gnarled ridge of Hymettus, the wildest and grayest mountain in Attica, the home of bees and goatherds, and (if there be faith in pious legend) of innumerable nymphs and satyrs. To the west ran the lower, browner mountains, yEgaleos, across which a road (the " Sacred Way ") wound through an easy pass towards Eleusis, the only sizable town in Attica, outside of Athens and its harbors. To the rear of the plain rose a noble pyramid, less jagged than Hymettus, more lordly than ^Egaleos; its summits were fretted with a white which turned to clear rose color under the sunset. This was Pentelicus, from the veins whereof came the lustrous marble for the master sculptor. Closer at hand, nearer the center of the plain, rose a small and very isolated hill, —

Lycabettus, whose peaked summit looked down upon the roofs of Athens. And last, but never least, about one mile southwest of Lycabettus, upreared a natural monument of much greater fame, — not a hill, but a colossal rock. Its shape was that of an irregular oval; it was about 1000 feet long, 500 feet wide, and its level summit stood 350 feet above the

plain. This steep, tawny rock, flung by the Titans, one might dream, into the midst of the Attic plain, formed one of the most famous sites in the world, for it was the Acropolis of Athens. Its full significance, however, must be explained later. From the Acropolis and a few lesser hills close by, the land sloped gently down towards the harbors and the Saronic Bay. These were the great features of the outward setting of

Athens. One might add to them the long belt of dark green olive groves winding down the westward side of the plain, where the Cephisus (which alone among Attic rivulets did not run dry in summer) ran down to the sea. There was also a shorter olive belt west of the city, where the weaker Ilissus crept, before it lost itself amid the thirsty fields.

Sea, rock, and sky, then, joined together around Athens as around almost no other city in the world. The landscape itself was adjusted to the eye with marvelous harmony. The colors and contours formed one glorious model for the sculptor and the painter, one perpetual inspiration for the poet. Even if Athens had never been the seat of a famous race, she would have won fame as being situated in one of the most beautiful localities in the world. Rightly, therefore, did its dwellers boast of their city as the " Violet-crowned " (lostephanos).

8. 360 B.C. —The Year of the Visit to Athens. — This city let us visit in the days of its greatest outward glory. We may select the year 360 B.C. At that time Athens had recovered from the ravages of the Peloponnesian War, while the Macedonian peril had not as yet become menacing. The great public buildings were nearly all completed. No signs of material decadence were visible, and if Athens no longer possessed the wide naval empire of the days of Pericles, her fleets and her armies were still formidable. The harbors were full of commerce; the philosophers were teaching their pupils in the groves and porticoes; the democratic constitution was entirely intact. With intelligent vision we will enter the city and look about us.

CHAPTER II. THE FIRST SIGHTS IN ATHENS.

9. The Morning Crowds bound for Athens. — It is very early in the morning. The sun has just pushed above the long ridge of Hymettus, sending a slanting red bar of light across the Attic plain, and touching the opposite slopes of ./Egaleos with livid fire. Already, however, life is stirring outside the city. Long since, little market boats have rowed across the narrow strait from

Salamis, bringing the island farmers' produce, and other farmers from the plain and the mountain slopes have started for market. In the ruddy light the marble temples on the lofty Acropolis rising ahead of these hurrying rustics are standing out clearly; the spear and helmet of the great brazen statue of the Athena Pro-machos are flashing from the noble citadel, as a kind of day beacon, beckoning onward toward the city. From the Peiraeus, the harbor town, a confused hum of mariners lading and unlading the vessels is even now rising, but we cannot turn ourselves thither. Our route is to follow the farmers bound for market.

The most direct road from the Peiraeus to Athens is hidden indeed, for it leads between the towering ramparts of the " Long Walls," two mighty barriers which run parallel almost four miles from the inland city to the harbor, giving a guarded passage in wartime and making Athens safe against starvation from any land blockade; but there is an outside road leading also to Athens from the western farmsteads, and this we can conveniently follow. Upon this

A Day in Old Athens

route the crowd which one meets is certainly not aristocratic, but it is none the less Athenian. Here goes a drover, clad in skins, his legs wound with woolen bands in lieu of stockings; before him and his wolf-like dog shambles a flock

of black sheep or less manageable goats, bleating and baaing as they are propelled toward market. After him there may come an unkempt, long-bearded farmer flogging on a pack ass or a mule attached to a clumsy cart with solid wheels, and laden with all kinds of market produce. The roadway, be it said, is not good, and all carters have their troubles; there-

PEASANT GOING TO MARKET.

fore, there is a deal of gesticulating and profane invocation of Hermes and all other gods of traffic; for, early as it is, the market place is already filling, and every delay promises a loss. There are still other companies bound toward the city: countrymen bearing cages of poultry; others engaged in the uncertain calling of driving pigs; swarthy Oriental sailors, with rings in their ears, bearing bales of Phoenician goods from the Peiraeus; respectable country gentlemen, walking gravely in their best white mantles and striving to avoid the mud and contamination; and perhaps also a small company of soldiers, just back from foreign service, passes, clattering shields and spear staves.

10. The Gate and the Street Scenes. — The crowds grow denser as everybody approaches the frequented "Peiraeus

The First Sights in Athens

Gate," for nearly all of Attica which lies within easy reach of Athens has business in the Market Place every morning. On passing the gate a fairly straight way leads through the city to the market, but progress for the multitude becomes slow. If it is one of the main thoroughfares, it is now very likely to be almost blocked with people. There are few late risers at Athens ; the Council of Five Hundred, 1 the huge Jury Courts, and the Public Assembly (if it has met to-day 2) are appointed to gather at sunrise. The plays in the theater, which, however, are given only on certain festivals, begin likewise at sunrise. The philosophers say that "the man who would accomplish great things must be up while yet it is dark." Athenians, therefore, are always awake and stirring at an hour when men of later ages and more cold and foggy climes will be painfully yawning ere getting out of bed.

The Market Place attracts the great masses, but by no means all; hither and thither bevies of sturdy slave girls, carrying graceful pitchers on their heads, are hurrying towards the fountains which gush cool water at most of the street corners. Theirs is a highly necessary task, for few or no houses

1 The "Boule," the great standing committee of the Athenian people to aid the magistrates in the government.

2 In which case, of course, the regular courts and the Council would hardly meet.

AT THE STREET FOUNTAIN.
A Day in Old Athens

have their own water supply ; and around each fountain one can see half a dozen by no means slatternly maidens, splashing and flirting the water one at another, while they wait their turn with the pitchers, and laugh and exchange banter with the passing farmers' lads. Many in the street crowds are rosy-cheeked schoolboys, walking decorously, if they are lads of good breeding, and blushing modestly when they are greeted by their fathers' acquaintances. They do not loiter on the way. Close behind, carrying their writing tablets, follow the faithful 'pedagogues,' the body-servants appointed to conduct them to school, give them informal instruction, and, if need be, correct their faults in no painless manner. Besides the water maids and the schoolboys, from the innumerable house doors now opening the respective masters are stepping forth — followed by one, two, or several serving varlets, as many as their wealth affords. All these join in the crowd entering from the country. " Athenian democracy " always implies a goodly amount of hustling and pushing. No wonder the ways are a busy sight !

11. The Streets and House Fronts of Athens. — Progress is slower near the Market Place because of the extreme narrowness of the streets. They are only fifteen feet wide or even less, — intolerable alleys a later age would call them, — and dirty to boot. Sometimes they are muddy, more often extremely dusty. Worse still, they are contaminated by great accumulations of filth ;

for the city is without an efficient sewer system or regular scavengers. Even as the crowd elbows along, a house door will frequently open, an ill-favored slave boy show his head, and with the yell, " Out of the way ! " slap a bucket of dirty water into the street. There are many things to offend the nose as well as the eyes of men of a later race. It is fortunate indeed that the Athenians are otherwise a healthy folk, or

they would seem liable to perpetual pestilence; even so, great plagues have in past years harried the city.

The first entrance to Athens will thus bring to a stranger, full of the city's fame and expectant of meeting objects of beauty at every turn, almost instant disappointment. The narrow, dirty, ill-paved streets are also very crooked. One can readily be lost in a labyrinth of filthy little lanes the moment one quits the few main thoroughfares. High over head, to be sure, the red crags of the Acropolis may be towering, crowned with the red, gold, and white tinted marble of the temples, but all around seems only monotonous squalor. The houses seem one continuous series of blank walls; mostly of one, occasionally of two stories, and with flat roofs. These walls are usually spread over with some dirty gray or perhaps yellow stucco. For most houses, the only break in the street walls are the simple doors, all jealously barred and admitting no glance within. There are usually no street windows, if the house is only one story high. If it has two stories, a few narrow slits above the way may hint that here are the apartments for the slaves or women. There are no street numbers. There are often no street names. " So-and-so lives in such-and-such a quarter, near the Temple of Heracles; " that will enable you to find a householder, after a few tactful questions from the neighbors; and after all, Athens is a relatively small city 2 (as great cities are reckoned), very

1 The most fearful thereof was the great plague of 430 B.C. (during the Peloponnesian War), which nearly ruined Athens.

2 Every guess at the population of Athens rests on mere conjecture; yet, using the scanty data which we possess, it seems possible that the population of all Attica at the height of its prosperity was about 200,000 free persons (including the metics — resident foreigners without citizenship); and a rather smaller number of slaves—say 150,000 or less. Of this total of some 350,000, probably something under one half resided in the city of Athens during times of peace, the rest in the outlying farms and villages. Athens may be imagined as a city of about 150,000 — possibly a

closely built, and her regular denizens do not feel the need of a directory.

So the crowd elbows its way onward: now thinning, now gaining, but the main stream always working towards the Market Place.

12. The Simplicity of Athenian Life. — It is clear we are entering a city where nine tenths of what the twentieth century will consider the "essential conveniences" of life are entirely lacking; where men are trying to be civilized — or, as the Greeks would say, to lay hold upon "the true, the beautiful, and the good," without even the absolute minimum of those things which people of a later age will believe separate a " civilized man" from a "barbarian." The gulf between old Athens and, for instance, new Chicago, is greater than is readily supposed. 1 It is easy enough to say that the Athenians lacked such things as railways, telephones, gas, grapefruit, and cocktails. All such matters we realize were not known by our fathers and grandfathers, and we are not yet so removed from them that we cannot transport ourselves in imagination back to the world of say 1820 A.D. ; but the Athenians are far behind even our grandfathers. When we investigate, we will find conditions like these — houses absolutely without plumbing, beds without sheets, rooms as hot or as cold as the outer air, only far more drafty. We must cross rivers without bridges; we must fasten on our clothes (or rather our "two pieces of cloth") with two pins

instead of with a row of buttons; we must wear sandals without stockings (or go barefoot) ; must warm ourselves over a pot of ashes; judge plays or lawsuits on a cold winter morning sitting in the open air; we must

trifle more. During serious wars there would be of course a general removal into the city.

1 See the very significant comment on the physical limitations of the old Athenian life in Zimmern's The Greek Commonwealth, p. 209.

study poetry with very little aid from books, geography without real maps, and politics without newspapers; and lastly," we must learn how to be civilized without being comfortable !" 1

Or, to reverse the case: we must understand that an Athenian would have pronounced our boasted "civilization " hopelessly artificial, and our life so dependent on outward material props and factors as to be scarcely worth the living. He would declare himself well able to live happily under conditions where the average American or Englishman would be cold, semi-starved, and miserable. He would declare that his woe or happiness was retained far more under his own control than we retain ours, and that we are worthy of contemptuous pity rather than of admiration, because we have refined our civilization to such a point that the least accident, e.g. the suspension of railroad traffic for a few days, can reduce a modern city to acute wretchedness.

Probably neither the twentieth century in its pride, nor the fourth century B.C. in its contempt, would have all the truth upon its side. 2 The difference in viewpoint, however, must still stand. Preeminently Athens may be called the " City of the Simple Life." Bearing this fact in mind, we may follow the multitude and enter the Market Place; or, to use the name that stamps it as a peculiarly Greek institution, — the Agora.

1 Zimmern, ibid.

2 The mere matter of climate would of course have to come in as a serious factor. The Athenian would have found his life becoming infinitely more complex along the material side when he tried to live like a kalos-k'agathos — i.e. a "nobleand good man," or a "gentleman," — in a land where the thermometer might sink to 15° below zero Fahrenheit (or even lower) from time to time during the winter.

CHAPTER III. THE AGORA AND ITS DENIZENS.

13. The Buildings around the Agora. — Full market time! J The great plaza of the Agora is buzzing with life. The contrast between the dingy, dirty streets and this magnificent public plaza is startling. The Athenians manifestly care little for merely private display, rather they frown upon it; their wealth, patriotism, and best artistic energy seem all lavished upon their civic establishments and buildings.

The Agora is a square of spacious dimensions, planted here and there with graceful bay trees. Its greatest length runs north and south. Ignoring for the time the teeming noisy swarms of humanity, let our eyes be directed merely upon the encircling buildings. The place is almost completely inclosed by them, although not all are of equal elegance or pretension. Some are temples of more or less size, like the temple of the " Paternal Apollo " near the southwestern angle; or the " Metroon," the fane of Cybele " the Great Mother of the Gods," upon the south. Others are governmental buildings ; somewhat behind the Metroon rise the imposing pillars of the Council House, where the Five Hundred are deliberating on the policy of Athens; and hard by that is the Tholos, the "Bound House," with a peaked, umbrella-shaped roof, beneath which the sacred public hearth fire is ever kept burning, and where the presiding Committee of the Council 2 and certain high officials

1 Between nine and twelve A.M.

* This select committee was known technically as the Prytanes. 16

take their meals, and a good deal of state business is transacted. The majority of these buildings upon the Agora, however, are covered promenades, porticoes, or stose.

The stoae are combinations of rain shelters, shops, picture galleries, and public offices. Turn under the pillars of the "Royal Stoa" upon the west, and you are among a whispering, nudging, intent crowd of listeners, pushing against the barriers of a low court. Long rows of jurors are sitting on their benches; the " King Archon " is on the president's stand, and some poor wight is being arraigned on a charge of " Impiety " l ; while on the walls behind stand graved the ancient laws of Draco and Solon.

Cross the square, and on the opposite side is one of the most magnificent of the porticoes, the " Painted Porch " (Stoa Poikile), a long covered walk, a delightful refuge alike from sun and rain. Almost the entire length of the inner walls (for it has columns only on the side of the Agora) is covered with vivid frescoes. Here Polygnotus and other master painters have spread out the whole legendary story of the capture of Troy and of the defeat of the Amazons; likewise the more historical tale of the battle of Marathon. Yet another promenade, the " Stoa of Zeus," is sacred to Zeus, Giver of Freedom. The walls are not frescoed, but hung with the shields of valiant Athenian warriors.

In the open spaces of the plaza itself are various altars, e.g. to the " Twelve Gods," and innumerable statues of local

A WAYSIDE HERM.

1 The so-called " King Archon " had special cognizance of most cases involving religious questions; and his court was in this stoa.

worthies, as of Harmodius and Aristogeiton, the tyrant-slayers ; while across the center, cutting the Market Place from east to west, runs a line of stone posts, each surmounted with a rude bearded head of Hermes, the trader's god; and each with its base plastered many times over with all kinds of official and private placards and notices.

14. The Life in the Agora. — So much for the physical setting of the Agora: of far greater interest surely are the people. The whole square is abounding with noisy activity. If an Athenian has no actual business to transact, he will at least go to the Agora to get the morning news. Two turns under the " Painted Porch " will tell him the last rumor as to the foreign policy of Thebes: whether it is true that old King Agesilaus has died at Sparta; whether corn is likely to be high, owing to a failure of crops in the Euxine (Black Sea) region ; whether the " Great King " of Persia is prospering in his campaign against Egypt. The crowd is mostly clad in white, though often the cloaks of the humbler visitors are very dirty, but there is a sprinkling of gay colors,— blue, orange, and pink. Everybody is talking at once in melodious Attic; everybody (since they

are all true children of the south) is gesticulating at once. To the babel of human voices is added the wheezing whistle of donkeys, the squealing of pigs, the cackle of poultry. Besides, from many of the little factories and workshops on or near the Agora a great din is rising. The clamor is prodigious. Criers are stalking up and down the square, one bawling out that Andocides has lost a valuable ring and will pay well to recover it; another that Pheidon has a desirable horse that he will sell cheap. One must stand still for some moments and let eye and ear accustom themselves to such utter confusion.

15. The Booths and Shops in the Agora. — At length out of the chaos there seems to emerge a certain order.

The major part of the square is covered with little booths of boards and wicker work, very frail and able to be folded up, probably every night. There are little lanes winding amid these booths; and each manner of huckster has its own especial " circle " or section of the market. " Go to the wine," "to the fish," "to the myrtles" (i.e. the flowers), are common directions for finding difficult parts of the Agora. Trade is mostly on a small scale, —the stock of each vender is distinctly limited in its range, and Athens is without " department stores." Behind each low counter, laden with its wares, stands the proprietor, who keeps up a din from leathern lungs: " Buy my oil !" " Buy charcoal ! " " Buy sausage!" etc., until he is temporarily silenced while dealing A CARPENTER. with a customer.

In one " circle " may be found onions and garlic (a favorite food of the poor) ; a little further on are the dealers in wine, fruit, and garden produce. Lentils and peas can be had either raw, or cooked and ready to eat on the spot. An important center is the bread market. The huge cylindrical loaves are handed out by shrewd old women with proverbially long tongues. Whosoever upsets one of their delicately balanced piles of loaves is certain of an artistic tongue lashing. Elsewhere there is a pottery market, a clothes market, and, nearer the edge of the Agora, are " circles," where objects of real value are sold, like jewelry,

chariots, good furniture. In certain sections, too, may be seen strong-voiced individuals, with little trays swung by straps before them, pacing to and fro, and calling out, not foods, but medicines, infallible cure-alls for every human distemper. Many are the unwary fools who patronize them.

16. The Flower and the Fish Venders. — Two circles attract especial attention, the Myrtles and the Fish. Flowers and foliage, especially when made up into garlands, are absolutely indispensable to the average Greek. Has he a great family festival, e.g. the birth of a son, then every guest should wear a crown of olives; is it a wedding, then one of flowers. 1 Oak-leaves do

the honors for Zeus; laurel for Apollo; myrtle for Aphrodite (and is not the Love-Goddess the favorite ?). To have a social gathering without garlands, in short, is impossible. The flower girls of Athens are beautiful, impudent, and not at all prudish. Around their booths press bold-tongued youths, and not too discreet sires ; and the girls can call everybody familiarly by name. Very possibly along with the sale of the garlands they make arrangements (if the banquet is to be of the less respectable kind) to be present in the evening themselves, perhaps in the capacity of flute girls.

More reputable, though not less noisy, is the fish market. Athenians boast themselves of being no hearty "meat eaters " like their Boeotian neighbors, but of preferring the more delicate fish. No dinner party is successful without a seasonable course of fish. The arrival of a fresh cargo from the harbor is announced by the clanging of a bell, which is likely to leave all the other booths deserted, while a crowd elbows around the fishmonger. He above all others com-

The Greeks lacked many of our common flowers. Their ordinary flowers were white violets, narcissus, lilies, crocuses, blue hyacinths, and roses ("the Flower of Zeus")- The usual garland was made of myrtle or ivy, and then entwined with various flowers.

mands the greatest flow of billingsgate, and is especially notorious for his arrogant treatment of his customers, and for exacting the uttermost farthing. The " Fish " and the " Myrtles " can be sure of a brisk trade on days when all the other booth keepers around the Agora stand idle.

All this trade, of course, cannot find room in the booths of the open Agora. Many hucksters sit on their haunches on the level ground with their few wares spread before them. Many more have little stands between the pillars of the stoae; and upon the various streets that converge on the market there is a fringe of shops, but these are usually of the more substantial sort. Here are the barbers' shops, the physicians' offices (if the good leech is more than an itinerant quack), and all sorts of little factories, such as smithies, where the cutler's apprentices in the rear of the shop forge the knives which the proprietor sells over the counter, the slave repositories, and finally wine establishments of no high repute, where wine may not merely be bought by the skin (as in the main Agora), but by the pot-ful to be drunk on the premises.

17. The Morning Visitors to the Agora. — The first tour of inspection completed, several facts become clear to the visitor. One is the extraordinarily large proportion of men among the moving multitudes. Except for the bread women and the flower girls, hardly one female is to be found among the sellers. Among the purchasers there is not a single reputable lady. No Athenian gentlewoman dreams of frequenting the Agora. Even a poor man's wife prefers to let her spouse do the family marketing. As for the " men folk," the average gentleman will go daily indeed to the Agora, but if he is really pretentious, it will be merely to gossip and to meet his friends; a trusted servant will attend to the regular purchasing. Only when an important dinner party is on hand will the master take pains to order

for himself. If he does purchase in person, he will never carry anything himself. The slaves can attend to that ; and only the slaveless (the poorest of all) must take away their modest rations of boiled lentils, peas, beans, onions, and garlic, usually in baskets, though yonder now is a soldier who is bearing off a measure of boiled peas inside his helmet.

Another thing is striking. The average poor Athenian seems to have no purse. Or rather he uses the purse provided by nature. At every booth one can see unkempt buyers solemnly taking their small change from their mouths. 1 Happy the people that has not learned the twentieth century wisdom concerning microbes ! For most Athenians seem marvelously healthy.

Still one other fact is brought home constantly. " Fixed prices " are absolutely unknown. The slightest transaction involves a war of bargaining. Wits are matched against wits, and only after a vast deal of wind do buyer and seller reach a fair compromise. All this makes retail trade in the Agora an excellent school for public affairs or litigation.

18. The Leisured Class in Athens. — Evidently Athens, more than many later-day cities, draws clear lines between the workers and the " gentlemen of leisure." There is no distinction of dress between the numerous slaves and the humbler free workers and traders; but there is obvious distinction between the artisan of bent shoulders who shambles out of yonder pungent tannery, with his scant garments girded around him, and the graceful gentleman of easy gestures and flowing drapery who moves towards the Tholos. There is great political democracy in Athens, but not so much social democracy. "Leisure," i.e. exemption from

A wealthier purchaser would, of course, have his own pouch, or more probably one carried for him by a slave.

every kind of sordid, money-getting, hard work, is counted the true essential for a respectable existence, and to live on the efforts of others and to devote oneself to public service or to letters and philosophy is the open satisfaction or the private longing of every Athenian.

A great proportion of these, therefore, who frequent the Agora are not here on practical business, unless they have official duties at the government offices. 1 But in no city of any age has the gracious art of doing nothing been brought to such perfection. The Athenians are an intensely gregarious people. Everybody knows everybody else. Says an orator, "It is impossible for a man to be either a rascal or an honest man in this city without your all knowing it." Few men walk long alone; if they do keep their own company, they are frowned on as " misanthropes." The morning visit to the Agora " to tell or to hear some new thing " 2 will be followed by equally delightful idling and conversation later in the day at the Gymnasia, and later still, probably, at the dinner-party. Easy and unconventional are the personal greetings. A little shaking out of the mantle, an indescribable flourish with the hands. A free Greek will despise himself for " bowing," even to the Great King. To clasp hands implies exchanging a pledge, something far more than mere salutation.

" Chaire, Aristomenes!"

" Chaire, Cleandros !"

Such is the usual greeting, using an expressive word which can mean equally well " hail! " and " farewell! "

19. Familiar Types around the Agora. — These animated, eager-faced men whose mantles fall in statuesque folds prefer obviously to walk under the Painted Porch, or the blue

1 To serve the state in any official capacity (usually without any salary attached to the office) would give the highest satisfaction to any Greek. The desire for participation in public affairs might be described as a mania. 2 Acts of the Apostles, 17:21.

roof of heaven, while they evolve their philosophies, mature their political schemes, or organize the material for their orations and dramas, rather than to bend over desks within close offices. Around the Athenian Agora, a true type of this preference, and busy with this delightful idleness, half a century earlier could have been seen a droll figure with " indescribable nose, bald head, round body, eyes rolling and twinkling with good humor," scantily clad, — an incorrigible do-nothing, windbag, and hanger-on, a later century might assert, — yet history has given to him the name of Socrates.

Not all Athenians, of course, make such justifiable use of their idleness. There are plenty of young men parading about in long trailing robes, their hair oiled and curled most effeminately, their fingers glittering with jewels, — " ring-loaded, curly-locked coxcombs," Aristophanes, the comic poet, has called them, — and they are here only for silly display. Also there are many of their elders who have no philosophy or wit to justify their continuous talking; nevertheless, all considered, it must be admitted that the Athenians make a use of their dearly loved " leisure," which men of a more pragmatic race will do well to consider as the fair equivalent of much frantic zeal for "business." Athenian "leisure" has already given the world Pericles, Thucydides, ^Eschylus, Sophocles, Euripides, Socrates, and Plato, not to name such artists as Phidias, whose profession cannot exempt them from a certain manual occupation.

20. The Barber Shops.—This habit of genteel idleness naturally develops various peculiar institutions. For example, the barber shops are almost club rooms. Few Hellenes at this time shave their beards, 1 but to go with unkempt whiskers and with too long hair is most disgrace-

1 Alexander the Great (336-323 B.C.) required his soldiers to be shaved (as giving less grasp for the enemy!), and the habit then spread generally through the whole Hellenic world.

ful. The barber shops, booths, or little rooms let into the street walls of the houses, are therefore much frequented. The good tonsors have all the usual arts. They can dye gray hair brown or black; they can wave or curl their patrons' locks (and an artificially curled head is no disgrace to a man). Especially, they keep a good supply of strong perfumes ; for many people will want a little scent on their hair each morning, even if they wish no other attention. But it is not an imposition to a barber to enter his shop, yet never move towards his low stool before the shining steel mirror. Anybody is welcome to hang around indefinitely, listening to the proprietor's endless flow of talk. He will pride himself on knowing every possible bit of news or rumor: Had the Council resolved on a new fleet-building program ? Had the Tyrant of Syracuse's " four " the best chance in the chariot race in the next Olympic games ? The garrulity of barbers is already proverbial.

" How shall I cut your hair, sir ? " once asked the court tonsor of King Archelaus of Macedon.

" In silence," came the grim answer.

But the proprietor will not do all the talking. Everybody in the little room will join. Wits will sharpen against wits; and if the company is of a grave and respectable sort, the conversation will grow brisk upon Plato's theory of the " reality of ideas," upon Euripides's interpretation of the relations of God to man, or upon the spiritual symbolism of Scopas's bas-reliefs at Halicarnassus.

The barber shops by the Agora then are essential portions of Athenian social life. Later we shall see them supplemented by the Gymnasia; — but the Agora has detained us long enough. The din and crowds are lessening. People are beginning to stream homeward. It lacks a little of noon according to the "time-staff" (gnomon), a simple sun dial which stands near one of the porticoes, and we will now follow some Athenian gentleman towards his dwelling.

CHAPTER IV. THE ATHENIAN HOUSE AND ITS FURNISHINGS.

21. Following an Athenian Gentleman Homeward. — Leavin g the Agora and reentering the streets the second impression of the residence districts becomes more favorable. There are a few bay trees planted from block to block; and ever and anon the monotonous house walls recede, giving space to display some temple, like the Fane of Hephaestos 1 near the Market Place, its columns and pediment flashing not merely with white marble, but with the green, scarlet, and gold wherewith the Greeks did not hesitate to decorate their statuary.

At street corners and opposite important mansions a Hermes-bust like those in the plaza rises, and a very few houses have a couple of pillars at their entrances and some outward suggestion of hidden elegance.

We observe that almost the entire crowd leaving the Agora goes on foot. To ride about in a chariot is a sign of undemocratic presumption; while only women or sick men will consent to be borne in a litter. We will select a sprucely dressed gentleman who has just been anointed in a barber's shop and accompany him to his home. He is neither one of the decidedly rich, otherwise his establishment would be exceptional, not typical, nor is he of course one of the hard-working poor. Followed by perhaps two clean and capable serving lads, he wends his way down several of the narrow lanes that lie under the northern brow

of the Acropolis. 1 Before a plain solid house door he halts and cries Pai! Pai! ["Boy ! Boy !"]. There is a rattle of bolts and bars. A low-visaged foreign-born porter, whose business it is to show a surly front to all unwelcome visitors, opens and gives a kind of salaam to his master; while the porter's huge dog jumps up barking and pawing joyously.

As we enter behind him (carefully advancing with right foot foremost, for it is bad luck to tread a threshold with the left) we notice above the lintel some such inscription as " Let no evil enter here !" or " To the Good Genius," then a few steps through a narrow passage bring us into the Aula, the central court, the indispensable feature of every typical Greek house.

22. The Type and Uses of a Greek House. — All domestic architecture, later investigators will discover, falls into two great categories — of the northern house and the southern house. The northern house begins with a single large room, " the great hall," then lesser rooms are added to it. It gets its light from windows in the outer walls, and it is covered by a single steep roof. The southern (Greek and Oriental) house is a building inclosing a rectangular court. The rooms, many or few, get their light from this court, while they are quite shut off from the world outside. All in all, for warm climates this style of house is far more airy, cool, comfortable than the other. The wide open court becomes the living room of the house save in very inclement weather.

Socrates is reported to have uttered what was probably the average sensible view about a good house. 2 The good house, he thought, should be cool in summer, and warm in winter, convenient for the accommodation of the family and its possessions. The central rooms should therefore be

1 This would be a properly respectable quarter of the city, but we do not know of any really "aristocratic residence district" in Athens.

lofty and should open upon the south, yet for protection in summer there should be good projecting eaves (over the court) and again the rooms on the northern exposure should be made lower. All this is mere sense, but really the average male Athenian does not care a great deal about his dwelling. He spends surprisingly little money beautifying it. Unless he is sick, he will probably be at home only for sleeping and eating. The Agora, the Public Assembly, the Jury Courts, the Gymnasium, the great religious festivals consume his entire day. " I never spend my time indoors," says Xenophon's model Athenian, " my wife is well able to run the household by herself." 1 Such being the case, even wealthy men have very simple establishments, although it is at length complained (e.g. by Demosthenes) that people are now building more luxurious houses, and are not content with the plain yet sufficient dwellings of the great age of Pericles. 2

23. The Plan of a Greek House. — The plan of a Greek house naturally varies infinitely according to the size of its land plot, the size of the owner's family, his own taste, and wealth. It will usually be rectangular, with the narrower side toward the street; but this is not invariable. In the larger houses there will be two courts (aulce), one behind the other, and each with its own circuit of dependent chambers. The court first entered will be the Andronitis (the Court of the Men), and may be even large enough to afford a considerable promenade for exercise. Around the whole of the open space run lines of simple columns, and above the opening swings an awning if the day is very hot. In the very center rises a small stone altar with a statue of Zeus the Protector (Zeus Herkelos), where the father of the

1 Xenophon, Economics, VII. 3.

2 Very probably in such outlying Greek cities as Syracuse, Taras (Tarentum), etc., more elegant houses could be found than any at this time in Athens.

family will from time to time offer sacrifice, acting as the priest for the household. Probably already on the altar there has been laid a fresh garland; if

GARDEN

not, the newcomers

at all four sides open the various chambers, possibly twelve in all. They really are cells or compartments rather than rooms, small and usually lighted only by their doors. Some

are used for storerooms, some for sleeping closets for the male slaves and for the grown-up sons of the house, if there are any. Dark, ill ventilated, and most scantily furnished, it is no wonder the average Athenian loves the Agora better than his chamber.

The front section of the house is now open to us, but it is time to penetrate farther. Directly behind the open court is a sizable chamber forming a passage to the inner house. This chamber is the Andron, the dining hall and probably the most pretentious room in the house. Here the guests will gather for the dinner party, and here in one corner smokes the family hearth, once the real fire for the whole household cooking, but now merely a symbol of the domestic worship. It is simply a little round altar sacred to Hestia, the hearth goddess, 1 and on its duly rekindled flame little " meat offerings and drink offerings " are cast at every meal, humble or elaborate.

In the rear wall of the Andron facing the Andronitis is a solid door. We are privileged guests indeed if we pass it. Only the father, sons, or near male kinsmen of the family are allowed to go inside, for it leads into the Gynceconitis, the hall of the women. To thrust oneself into the Gynse-conitis of even a fairly intimate friend is a studied insult at Athens, and sure to be resented by bodily chastisement, social ostracism, and a ruinous legal prosecution. The Gynseconitis is in short the Athenian's holy of holies. Their women are forbidden to participate in so much of public life that their own peculiar world is especially reserved to them. To invade this world is not bad breeding; it is social sacrilege.

In the present house, the home of a well-to-do family, the Gynseconitis forms a second pillared court with adjacent rooms of substantially the same size and shape as the Andronitis. One of the rooms in the very rear is proclaimed by the clatter of pots and pans and the odor of a frying

1 Who corresponds to the Roman goddess Vesta.

The Athenian House and Its Furnishings 31

turbot to be the kitchen; others are obviously the sleeping closets of the slave women. On the side nearest to the front of the house, but opening itself upon this inner court, is at least one bed chamber of superior size. This is the Thalamos, the great bedroom of the master and mistress, and here are kept all the most costly furnishings and ornaments in the house. If there are grown-up unmarried daughters, they have another such bedroom (anti-thalamos) that is much larger than the cells of the slave girls. Another special room is set apart for the working of wool, although this chief occupation of the female part of the household is likely to be carried on in the open inner court itself, if the weather is fine. Here, around a little flower bed, slave girls are probably spinning and embroidering, young children playing or quarreling, and a tame quail is hopping about and watching for a crumb. There are in fact a great many people in a relatively small space; everything is busy, chattering, noisy, and confusing to an intruding stranger.

24. Modifications in the Typical Plan. — These are the essential features of an Athenian house. If the establishment is a very pretentious one, there may be a small garden in the rear carefully hedged against intruders by a lofty wall. 1 More probably the small size of the house lot would force simplifications in the scheme already stated. In a house one degree less costly, the

Gynseconitis would be reduced to a mere series of rooms shut off in the rear. In more simple houses still there would be no interior section of the house at all. The women of the family would be provided for by a staircase rising from the main hall to a second story, and here a number of upper chambers would give the needful seclusion. 2 Of course as one goes down

1 Such a luxury would not be common in city houses ; land would be too valuable.

2 Houses of more than two stories seem to have been unknown in Athens. The city lacked the towering rookeries of tenements (insula)

the social scale, the houses grow simpler and simpler. Small shops are set into the street wall at either side of the entrance door, and on entering one finds himself in a very limited and utterly dingy court with a few dirty compartments opening thence, which it would be absurd to dignify by the name of "rooms." Again one ceases to wonder that the male Athenians are not " home folk " and are glad to leave their houses to the less fortunate women!

25. Rents and House Values. — Most native Athenians own their houses. Houses indeed can be rented, usually by the foreign traders and visitors who swarm into the city; and at certain busy seasons one can hire "lodgings " for a brief sojourn. Eents are not unreasonable, 8 % or 8|% of the value of the house being counted a fair annual return. But the average citizen is also a householder, because forsooth houses are very cheap. The main cost is probably for the land. The chief material used in building, sun-dried brick, is very unsubstantial, 1 and needs frequent repairs, but is not expensive. Demosthenes the Orator speaks of a "little house" (doubtless of the kind last described) worth only seven minse [about $126.00], and this is not the absolute minimum. A very rich banker has had one worth 100 minse [about $1800.00], and probably this is close to the maximum. The rent question is not therefore one of the pressing problems at Athens.

26. The Simple yet Elegant Furnishings of an Athenian Home. — These houses, even owned by the lordly rich, are surprisingly simple in their furnishings. The accumulation of heavy furniture, wall decorations, and bric-a-brac which will characterize the dwellings of a later age, would be

which were characteristic of Rome ; sometimes, however, a house seems to have been shared between several families.

This material was so friable and poor that the Greek burglar was known as a " Wall-digger." It did not pay him to pick a lock ; it was simpler for him to quarry his way through the wall with a pickax.

utterly offensive to an Athenian — contradicting all his ideas of harmony and " moderation." The Athenian house lacks of course bookcases and framed pictures. It probably too lacks any genuine closets. Beds, couches, chairs (usually backless), stools, footstools, and small portable tables,— these alone seem in evidence. In place of bureaus, dressers, and cupboards, there are huge chests, heavy and carved, in which most of the household gear can be locked away. In truth, the whole style of Greek household life expresses that simplicity on which we have already commented. Oriental carpets are indeed met with, but they are often used as wall draperies or couch covers rather than upon the floors. Greek costume (see p. 43) is so simple that there is small need for elaborate chests of drawers, and a line of pegs upon the wall cares for most of the family wardrobe.

All this is true; yet what furniture one finds is fashioned with commendable grace. There is a marked absence of heavy and unhealthful upholstery; but the simple bed (four posts sustaining a springless cushion stuffed with feathers or wool) has its woodwork adorned with carving which is a true mean betwixt the too plain 1 and the too ornate; and the whole bed is given an elegant effect by the magnificently embroidered scarlet tapestry which overspreads it.

The lines of the legs of the low wooden tables which are used at the dinner parties will be a lesson (if we have time to study them) upon just proportion and the value of subtle curves. Moreover, the different household vessels, the stone and bronze lamps, the various table dishes, even the common pottery put to the humblest uses, all have a beauty, a chaste elegance, a saving touch of deft ornamentation, which transforms them out of " kitchen ware" into works of art. Those black water pots covered with red-clay figures which the serving maids are bearing so carelessly into the scullery at the screaming summons of the cook will be some day perchance the pride of a museum,

and teach a later age that costly material and aristocratic uses are not needful to make an article supremely beautiful. Of course the well-to-do Athenian is proud to possess certain "valuables." He will have a few silver cups elegantly chased, and at least one diner's couch in the andron will be made of rare imported wood, and be inlaid with gilt or silver. On festival days the house will be hung with brilliant and elaborately wrought tapestries which will suddenly emerge from the great chests. Also, despite frowns and criticisms, the custom is growing of decorating one's walls with bright-lined frescoes after the manner of the Agora colonnades. In the course of a few generations the homes of the wealthier Greeks will come to resemble those of the Romans, such as a later age has resurrected at Pompeii.

CHAPTER V. THE WOMEN OF ATHENS.

27. How Athenian Marriages are Arranged. — Over this typical Athenian home reigns the wife of the master. Public opinion frowns upon celibacy, and there are relatively few unmarried men in Athens. An Athenian girl is brought up with the distinct expectation of matrimony. 1 Opportunities for a romance almost never will come her way; but it is the business of her parents to find her a suitable husband. If they are kindly people of good breeding, their choice is not likely to be a very bad one. If they have difficulties, they can engage a professional " matchmaker," a shrewd old woman who, for a fee, will hunt out an eligible young man. Marriage is contracted primarily that there may be legitimate children to keep up the state and to perpetuate the family. That the girl should have any will of her own in the matter is almost never thought of. Very probably she has never seen " Him," save when they both were marching in a public religious procession, or at some rare family gathering (a marriage or a funeral) when there were outside guests. Besides she will be "given away" when only about fifteen, and probably has formed no intelligent opinion or even prejudices on the subject.

If the young man (who will marry at about thirty) is independent in life, the negotiations will be with him directly. If he is still dependent on the paternal allowance, the two

1 The vile custom of exposing unwelcome female babies probably created a certain preponderance of males in Attica, and made it relatively easy to marry off a desirable young girl.

35

sets of parents will usually arrange matters themselves, and demand only the formal consent of the prospective bridegroom. He will probably accept promptly this bride whom his father has selected; if not, he risks a stormy encounter with his parents, and will finally capitulate. He has perhaps never seen " Her," and can only hope things are for the best; and after all she is so young that his friends tell him that he can train her to be very useful and obedient if he will only take pains. The parents, or, failing them, the guardians, adjust the dowry—the lump sum which the bride will bring with her towards the new establishment. 1 Many maxims enjoin "marry only your equal in fortune." The poor man who weds an heiress will not be really his own master; the dread of losing the big dowry will keep him in perpetual bondage to her whims.

28. Lack of Sentiment in Marriages.—Sometimes marriages are arranged in which any sentiment is obviously prohibited. A father can betroth his daughter by will to some kinsman,

who is to take her over as his bride when he takes over the property. A husband can bequeath his wife to some friend who is likely to treat her and the orphan children with kindness. Such affairs occur every day. Do the Athenian women revolt at these seemingly degrading conditions, wherein they are handed around like slaves, or even cattle ? —According to the tragic poets they do. Sophocles (in the Tereus) makes them lament,

" We women are nothing;—happy indeed is our childhood, for then we are thoughtless; but when we attain maidenhood, lo! we are driven away from our homes, sold as merchandise, and compelled to marry and say ' All's well.'"

Euripides is even more bitter in his Medea: —

1 The dowry was a grcat protection to the bride. If her husband divorced her (as by law he might), the dowry must be repaid to her guardians with 18 per cent, interest.

Surely of creatures that have life and wit, We women are of all things wretchedest, Who first must needs, as buys the highest bidder, Thus buy a husband, and our body's master. 1

29. Athenian Marriage Rites. — However, thus runs public custom. At about fifteen the girl must leave her mother's fostering care and enter the house of the stranger. The wedding is, of course, a great ceremony; and here, if nowhere else, Athenian women can surely prepare, flutter, and ordain to their heart's content. After the somewhat stiff and formal betrothal before witnesses (necessary to give legal effect to the marriage), the actual wedding will probably take place, — perhaps in a few days, perhaps with a longer wait till the favorite marriage month Gamelion [January]. 2 Then on a lucky night of the full moon the bride, having, no doubt tearfully, dedicated to Artemis her childish toys, will be decked in her finest and will come down, all veiled, into her father's torchlit aula, swarming now with guests. Here will be at last that strange master of her fate, the bridegroom and his best man (paranymphos). Her father will offer sacrifice (probably a lamb), and after the sacrifice everybody will feast on the flesh of the victim ; and also share a large flat cake of pounded sesame seeds roasted and mixed with honey. As the evening advances the wedding car will be outside the door. The mother hands the bride over to the groom, who leads her to the chariot, and he and the groomsman sit down, one on either side, while with torches and song the friends go with the car in jovial procession to the house of the young husband.

"Ho, Hymen! Ho, Hymen ! Hymenaeos ! lo ! "

So rings the refrain of the marriage song; and all the

1 Way's translation.

2 This winter month was sacred to Hera, the marriage guardian.

doorways and street corners are crowded with onlookers to shout fair wishes and good-natured raillery.

At the groom's house there is a volley of confetti to greet the happy pair. The bride stops before the threshold to eat a quince. 1 There is another feast, — possibly riotous fun and hard drinking. At last the bride is led, still veiled, to the perfumed and flower-hung marriage chamber. The doors close behind the married pair. Their friends sing a merry rollicking catch outside, the Epithalamium. The great day has ended. The Athenian girl has experienced the chief transition of her life.

30. The Mental Horizon of Athenian Women. — Despite the suggestions in the poets, probably the normal Athenian woman is neither degraded nor miserable. If she is a girl of good ancestry and the usual bringing up, she has never expected any other conditions than these. She knows that her parents care for her and have tried to secure for her a husband who will be her guardian and solace when they are gone. Xenophon's ideal young husband, Ischomachus, says he married his wife at the age of fifteen. 2 She had been " trained to see and to hear as little as

possible "; but her mother had taught her to have a sound control of her appetite and of all kinds of self-indulgence, to take wool and to make a dress of it, and to manage the slave maids in their spinning tasks. She was at first desperately afraid of her husband, and it was some time before he had " tamed " her sufficiently to discuss their household problems freely. Then Ischomachus made her join with him in a prayer to the gods that " he might teach and she might learn all that could conduce to their joint happiness "; after which they took admirable counsel together, and her tactful and ex-

1 The symbol of fertility.

2 See Xenophon's "The Economist," VII ff. The more pertinent passages are quoted in W. S. Daris's Readings in Ancient History, vol. I, pp. 265-271.

perienced husband (probably more than twice her age) trained her into a model housewife.

31. The Honor paid Womanhood in Athens. — Obviously from a young woman with a limited intellectual horizon the Athenian gentleman can expect no mental companionship ; but it is impossible that he can live in the world as a keenly intelligent being, and not come to realize the enormous value of the "woman spirit" as it affects all things good. Hera, Artemis, Aphrodite, above all Pallas-Athena,— city-warder of Athens, — who are they all but idealizations of that peculiar genius which wife, mother, and daughter show forth every day in their homes ? An Athenian never allows his wife to visit the Agora. She cannot indeed go outside the house without his express permission, and only then attended by one or two serving maids; public opinion will likewise frown upon the man who allowed his wife to appear in public too freely 1 ; nevertheless there are compensations. Within her home the Athenian woman is within her kingdom. Her husband will respect her, because he will respect himself. Brutal and harsh he may possibly be, but that is because he is also brutal and harsh in his outside dealings. In extreme cases an outraged wife can sue for divorce before the archon. And very probably in ninety-nine cases out of a hundred the Athenian woman is contented with her lot: partly because she knows of nothing better; partly because she has nothing concrete whereof to complain.

Doubtless it is because an Athenian house is a "little oasis of domesticity," tenderly guarded from all insult, — a miniature world whose joys and sorrows are not to be

1 Hypereides, the orator, says, " The woman who goes out of her own home ought to be of such an age that when men meet her, the question is not' Who is her husband ?' but ' "Whose mother is she?' " Pericles, in the great funeral oration put in his mouth by Thucydides, says that the best women are those who are talked of for good or ill the very least

shared by the outer universe, — that the Athenian treats the private affairs of his family as something seldom to be shared, even with an intimate friend. Of individual women we hear and see little in Athens, but of noble womanhood a great deal. By a hundred tokens, delightful vase paintings, noble monuments, poetic myths, tribute is paid to the self-mastery, the self-forgetfulness, the courage, the gentleness "of the wives and mothers who have made Athens the beacon of Hellas"; and there is one witness better than all the rest. Along the "Street of the Tombs," by the gate of the city, runs the long row of stelse (funeral monuments), inimitable and chaste memorials to the beloved dead; and here we meet, many times over, the portrayal of a sorrow too deep for common lament, the sorrow for the lovely and gracious figures who have passed into the great Mystery. Along the Street of the Tombs the wives and mothers of Athens are honored not less than the wealthy, the warriors, or the statesmen.

32. The Sphere of Action of Athenian Women. — Assuredly the Athenian house mother cannot match her husband in discussing philosophy or foreign politics, but she has her own home problems and confronts them well. A dozen or twenty servants must be kept busy. Prom her, all

the young children must get their first education, and the girls probably everything they are taught until they are married. Even if she does not meet many men, she will strive valiantly to keep the good opinion of her husband. If she has shapely feet and hands (whereon great stress is laid in Hellas), she will do her uttermost to display them to the greatest advantage 1 ; and she has, naturally, plenty of other vanities (see p. 49). Her husband has turned over to her the entire management of the household. This means

1 The custom of wearing sandals instead of shoes of course aided the developing of beautiful feet.

that if he is an easy-going man, she soon understands his home business far better than he does himself, and really has him quite at her mercy. Between caring for her husband's wants, nursing the sick slaves, acting as arbitress in their inevitable disputes, keeping a constant watch upon the storeroom, and finally in attending to the manufacture of nearly all the family clothing, she is not likely to rust in busy idleness, or sit complaining of her lot. At the many great public festivals she is always at least an onlooker and often she marches proudly in the magnificent processions. She is allowed to attend the tragedies in the theater. 1 Probably, too, the family will own a country farm, and spend a part

of the year thereon. Here she will be allowed a delightful freedom of movement, impossible in the closely built city. All in all, then, she will complain of too much enforced activity rather than of too much idleness.

Nevertheless our judgment upon the Athenian women is mainly one of regret. Even if not discontented with their

1 Not the comedies —they were too broad for refined women. But the mere fact that Athenian ladies seem to have been allowed to attend the tragedies is a tribute to their intellectual capacities. Only an acute and intelligent mind can follow Eschylus, Sophocles, and Euripides.

SPINNING.

lot, they are not realizing the full possibilities which Providence has placed within the reach of womanhood, much less the womanhood of the mothers of the warriors, poets, orators, and other immortals of Athens. One great side of civilization which the city of Athens might develop and realize is left unrealized. This civilization of Athens is too masculine ; it is therefore one sided, and in so far it does not realize that ideal "Harmony" which is the average Athenian's boast.

CHAPTER VI. ATHENIAN COSTUME.

33. The General Nature of Greek Dress. — In every age the important kingdom of dress has been reserved for the peculiar sovereignty of woman. This is true in Athens, though not perhaps to the extent of later ages. Still an Athenian lady will take an interest in "purple and fine linen" far exceeding that of her husband, and where is there a more fitting place than this in which to answer for an Athenian, the ever important question " wherewithal shall I be clothed" ?

Once again the Athenian climate comes in as a factor, this time in the problem of wardrobe. Two general styles of garment have divided the allegiance of the world, — the clothes that are put on and the clothes that are wrapped around. The former style, with its jackets, trousers, and leggins, is not absolutely unknown to the Athenians,— their old enemies, the Persians, wear these 1 ; but such clumsy, inelegant garments are despised and ridiculed as fit only for the "Barbarians" who use them. They are not merely absurdly homely; they cannot even be thrown off promptly in an emergency, leaving the glorious human form free to put forth any noble effort. The Athenians wear the wrapped style of garments, which are, in final analysis, one or two large square pieces of cloth flung skilfully around the body and secured by a few well-placed

iThe Persians no doubt learned to use this style of garment during their life on the cold, windy steppes of Upper Asia, before they won their empire in the more genial south.

pins. This costume is infinitely adjustable; it can be expanded into flowing draperies or contracted into an easy working dress by a few artful twitches. It can be nicely adjusted to meet the inevitable sense of " beauty " bred in the bone of every Athenian. True, on the cold days of midwinter the wearers will go about shivering; but cold days are the exception, warm days the rule, in genial Attica. 1

This simplicity of costume has produced certain important results. There are practically no tailors in Athens, only cloth merchants, bleachers, and dyers. Again fashions (at least in the actual cut of the garments) seldom change. A cloak that was made in the days of Alcibiades (say 420 B.C.) can be worn with perfect propriety to-day (360 B.C.) if merely it has escaped without severe use or moth holes. It may be more usual this year to wear one's garments a little higher or a little more trailing than formerly; but that is simply a matter for a shifting of the pins or of the girdle.

As a result, the Athenian seldom troubles about his " spring " or " winter " suit. His simple woolen garments wear a very long time; and they have often been slowly and laboriously spun and woven by his wife and her slave girls. Of course even a poor man will try to have a few changes of raiment, — something solid and coarse for every day, something of finer wool and gayer color for public and private festivals. The rich man will have a far larger wardrobe, and will pride himself on not being frequently seen in the same dress ; yet even his outfit will seem very meager to the dandies of a later age.

34. The Masculine Chiton, Himation, and Chlamys. — The

lr rhe whole civilization of Athens was, of course, based on a climate in which artificial heat would be very little needed. A pot of glowing charcoal might be used to remove the chill of a room in the very coldest weather. Probably an Athenian would have regarded a climate in which furnace heat was demanded nearly eight months in the year as wholly unfit for civilized man.

essential garments of an Athenian man are only two — the chiton and the himation. The chiton may be briefly described as an oblong of woolen cloth large enough to wrap around the body somewhat closely, from the neck down to just above the knees. The side left open is fastened by fibulae — elegantly wrought pins perhaps of silver or gold; in the closed side there is a slit for the arm. There is a girdle, and, if one wishes, the skirt of the chiton may be pulled up through it, and allowed to hang down in front, giving the effect of a blouse. The man of prompt action, the soldier, traveler, worker, is " well girded," — his chiton is drawn high, but the deliberate old gentleman who parades the Agora, discussing poetry or statecraft, has his chiton falling almost to a trailing length. Only occasionally short sleeves are added to this very simple garment; they are considered effeminate, and are not esteemed. If one's arms get cold, one can protect them by pulling up the skirt, and wrapping the arms in the blouse thus created.

An Athenian gentleman when he is in the house wears nothing but his chiton; it is even proper for him to be seen wearing nothing else upon the streets, but then more usually he will add an outer cloak, — his himation.

The himation is even simpler than the chiton. It is merely a generous oblong woolen shawl. There are innumerable ways of arranging it according to the impulse of the moment; but usually it has to be worn without pins, and that involves wrapping it rather tightly around the body, and keeping one of the hands confined to hold the cloak in place. That is no drawback, however, to a genteel wearer. It proclaims to the world that he does not have to work, wearing his hands for a living; therefore he can keep them politely idle. 1 The adjustment of the himation is a work

iWorkiugmen often wore no himation, and had a kind of chiton (an exomis) which was especially arranged to leave them with free use of their arms.

of great art. A rich man will often have a special slave whose business it is to arrange the hang and the folds before his master moves forth in public; and woe to the careless fellow if the effect* fails to display due elegance and dignity!

There is a third garment sometimes worn by Athenians. Young men who wish to appear very active, and genuine travelers, also wear a chlamys, a kind of circular mantle or cape which swings jauntily over their shoulders, and will give good protection in foul weather.

There are almost no other masculine garments. No shirts (unless the chiton be one), no underwear. In their costume, as in so many things else, the Athenians exemplify their oft-praised virtue of simplicity.

35. The Dress of the Women. — The dress of the women is like that of the men, but differs, of course, in complexity. They also have a chiton, 1 which is more elaborately made, especially in the arrangement of the blouse ; and probably there is involved a certain amount of real sewing 2 ; not merely of pinning.

Greater care is needed in the adjustment of the " zone " (girdle), and half sleeves are the rule with women, while full sleeves are not unknown. A Greek lady again cannot imitate her husband, and appear in public in her chiton only. A himation, deftly adjusted, is absolutely indispensable whenever she shows herself outside the house.

These feminine garments are all, as a rule, more elaborately embroidered, more adorned with fringes and tassels, than those of the men. In arranging her dress the Athenian lady is not bound by the rigid precepts of fashion.

1 This robe was sometimes known by the Homeric name of peplos.

3 Probably with almost all Greek garments the main use of the needle was in the embroidery merely, or in the darning of holes and rents. It was by no means an essential in the real manufacture.

Every separate toilette is an opportunity for a thousand little niceties and coquetries which she understands exceedingly well. If there is the least excuse for an expedition outside the house, her ladyship's bevy of serving maids will have a serious time of it. While their mistress cools herself with a huge peacock-feather fan, one maid is busy over her hair; a second holds the round metallic mirror before her; a third stands ready to extend the jewel box whence she can select finger rings, earrings, gold armlets, chains for her neck and hair, as well as the indispensable brooches whereon the stability of the whole costume depends. When she rises to have her himation draped around her, the directions she gives reveal her whole bent and character. A dignified and modest matron will have it folded loosely around her entire person, covering both arms and hands, and even drawing it over her head, leaving eyes and nose barely visible. Younger ladies will draw it close around the body so as to show the fine lines of their waists and shoulders. And in the summer heat the himation (for the less prudish) will become a light shawl floating loose and free over the shoulders, or only a kind of veil drawn so as to now conceal, now reveal, the face.

Children wear miniature imitations of the dress of their elders. Boys are taught to toughen their bodies by refraining from thick garments in cold weather. In hot weather they can frequently be seen playing about with very little clothing at all!

36. Footwear and Head Coverings. — Upon his feet the Athenian frequently wears nothing. He goes about his home barefoot; and not seldom he enjoys the delight of running across the open greensward with his unsandaled feet pressing the springing ground; but normally when he walks abroad, he will wear sandals, a simple solid pair of open soles tied to his feet by leather thongs passing between

the toes. For hard country walking and for hunting there is something like a high leather boot, 1 though doubtless these are counted uncomfortable for ordinary wear. As for the sandals, simple as they are, the Attic touch of elegance is often upon them. Upon the thongs of the sandals there is usually worked a choice pattern, in some brilliant color or even gilt.

The Athenians need head coverings even less than footgear. Most of them have thick hair ; baldness is an uncommon affliction ; everybody is trained to walk under the full glare of Helios with little discomfort. Of course certain trades require hats, e.g. sailors who can be almost identified by their rimless felt caps. Genteel travelers will wear wide-brimmed hats ; but the ladies, as a rule, have no headgear besides their tastefully arranged hair, although they will partly atone for the lack, by having a maid walk just behind them with a gorgeously variegated parasol.

37. The Beauty of the Greek Dress. — Greek costume, then, is something fully sharing in the national characteristics of harmony, simplicity, individuality. It is easy to see how admirably this style of dress is adapted to furnish ever ready models and inspiration for the sculptor. 2 Unconventional in its arrangement, it is also unconventional in its color. A masculine crowd is not one unmitigated swarm of black and dark grays or browns, as with the multitudes of a later age. On the contrary, white is counted theoretically the most becoming color on any common occasion for either sex; 3 and on festival days even grave and elderly men will appear with chitons worked with brilliant em-

1 Actors, too, wore a leather boot with high soles to give them extra height — the cothurnus.

2 " The chiton became the mirror of the body," said the late writer, Achilles Tatius.

8 No doubt farmers and artisans either wore garments of a non-committal brown, or, more probably, let their originally white costume get utterly dirty.

broidery along the borders, and with splendid hiraatia of some single clear hue—violet, red, purple, blue, or yellow. As for the costume of the groom at a wedding, it is far indeed from the " conventional black " of more degenerate days. He may well wear a purple-edged white chiton of fine Milesian wool, a brilliant scarlet himation, sandals with blue thongs and clasps of gold, and a chaplet of myrtle and violets. His intended bride is led out to him in even more dazzling array. Her white sandal-thongs are embroidered with emeralds, rubies, and pearls. Around her neck is a necklace of gold richly set, — and she has magnificent golden armlets and pearl eardrops. Her hair is fragrant with Oriental nard, and is bound by a purple fillet and a chaplet of roses. Her ungloved fingers shine with jewels and rings. Her main costume is of a delicate saffron, and over it all, like a cloud, floats the silvery tissue of the nuptial veil.

38. Greek Toilet Frivolities. — From the standpoint of inherent fitness and beauty, this Athenian costume is the noblest ever seen by the world. Naturally there are ill-advised creatures who do not share the good taste of their fellows, or who try to deceive the world and themselves as to the ravages of that arch-enemy of the Hellene, — Old Age. Athenian women especially (though the men are not without their follies) are sometimes fond of rouge, false hair, and the like. Auburn hair is especially admired, and many fine dames bleach their tresses in a caustic wash to obtain it. The styles of feminine hair dressing seem to change from decade to decade much more than the arrangements of the garments. Now it is plaited and crimped hair that is in vogue, now the more beautiful " Psyche-knots" ; yet even in their worst moods the Athenian women exhibit a sweet reasonableness. They have not yet fallen into the clutches of the Parisian hairdresser.

The poets, of course, ridicule the foibles of the fair sex. 1 Says one: —

The golden hair Nikylla wears

Is hers, who would have thought it ?

She swears 'tis hers, and true she swears For I know where she bought it !

And again: —

You give your cheeks a rosy stain, With washes dye your hair; But paint and washes both are vain To give a youthful air. An art so fruitless then forsake, Which, though you much excel in, You never can contrive to make Old Hecuba young Helen.

But enough of such scandals! All the best opinion — masculine and feminine — frowns on these follies. Let us think of the simple, dignified, and aesthetically noble costume of the Athenians as not the least of their examples to another age.

1 Translated in Falke's Greece and Rome (English translation, p. 69). These quotations probably date from a time considerably later than the hypothetical period of this sketch ; but they are perfectly proper to apply to conditions in 360 B.C.

CHAPTER VII. THE SLAVES.

39. Slavery an Integral Part of Greek Life. — An Athenian lady cares for everything in her house, — for the food supplies, for the clothing, yet probably her greatest task is to manage the heterogeneous multitude of slaves which swarm in every wealthy or even well-to-do mansion. 1

Slaves are everywhere: not merely are they the domestic servants, but they are the hands in the factories, they run innumerable little shops, they unload the ships, they work the mines, they cultivate the farms. Possibly there are more able-bodied male slaves in Attica than male free men, although this point is very uncertain. Their number is the harder to reckon because they are not required to wear any distinctive dress, and you cannot tell at a glance whether a man is a mere piece of property, or a poor but very proud and important member of the " Sovereign Demos [People] of Athens."

No prominent Greek thinker seems to contest the righteousness and desirability of slavery. It is one of the usual, nay, inevitable, things pertaining to a civilized state. Aristotle the philosopher puts the current view of the case very clearly. "The lower sort of mankind are by nature slaves, and it is better for all inferiors that they should be under the rule of a master. The use made of slaves and of tame animals is not very different; for both by their bodies

1 The Athenians never had the absurd armies of house slaves which characterized Imperial Rome ; still the numbers of their domestic servants were, from a modern standpoint, extremely large. 61

minister to the needs of life." The intelligent, enlightened, progressive Athenians are naturally the " masters"; the stupid, ignorant, sluggish minded Barbarians are the "inferiors." Is it not a plain decree of Heaven that the Athenians are made to rule, the Barbarians to serve ? — No one thinks the subject worth serious argument.

Of course the slave cannot be treated quite as one would treat an ox. Aristotle takes pains to point out the desirability of holding out to your " chattel" the hope of freedom, if only to make him work better; and the great philosopher in his last testament gives freedom to five of his thirteen slaves. Then again it is recognized as clearly against public sentiment to hold fellow Greeks in bondage. It is indeed done. Whole towns get taken in war, and those of the inhabitants who are not slaughtered are sold into slavery. 1 Again, exposed children, whose parents have repudiated them, get into the hands of speculators, who raise them " for market." There is also a good deal of kidnapping in the less civilized parts of Greece like ^Etolia. Still the proportion of genuinely Greek slaves is small. The great majority of them are " Barbarians," men born beyond the pale of Hellenic civilization.

40. The Slave Trade in Greece. — There are two great sources of slave supply: the Asia Minor region (Lydia and Phrygia, with Syria in the background), and the Black Sea region, especially the northern shores, known as Scythia. It is known to innumerable heartless " traders " that human flesh commands a very high price in Athens or other Greek cities. Every little war or raid that vexes those barbarous countries so incessantly is followed by the sale of the unhappy captives to speculators who ship them on, stage by stage, to Athens. Perhaps there is no war; the

1 For example, the survivors, after the capture of Melos, iu the Pelopon-nesian War.

supply is kept up then by deliberate kidnapping on a large scale, or by piracy. 1 In any case the arrival of a chain gang of fettered wretches at the Peiraeus is an everyday sight. Some of these creatures are submissive and tame (perhaps they understand some craft or trade); these can be sold at once for a high price. Others are still doltish and stubborn. They are good for only the rudest kind of labor, unless they are kept and trained at heavy expense. These brutish creatures are frequently sold off to the mines, to be worked to death by the contractors as promptly and brutally as one wears out a machine ; or else they become public galley slaves, when their fate is practically the same. But we need not follow such horrors.

The remainder are likely to be purchased either for use upon the farm, the factory, or in the home. There is a regular " circle" at or near the Agora for traffic in them. They are often sold at auction. The price of course varies with the good looks, age, 2 or dexterity of the article, or the abundance of supply. "Slaves will be high" in a year when there has been little warfare and raiding in Asia Minor. "Some slaves," says Xenophon, "are well worth two minse [$36.00] and others barely half a mina [$9.00] ; some sell up to five minse [$90.00] and even for ten [$180.00]. Nicias, the son of Nicaretus, is said to have given a talent [over $ 1000.00] for an overseer in the mines." 3 The father of Demosthenes owned a considerable factory. He had thirty-two sword cutters worth about five minae each, and twenty couch-makers (evidently less skilled) worth together 40 minae [about $720.00]. A girl who is

1 A small but fairly constant supply of slaves would come from the seizure of the persons and families of bankrupt debtors, whose creditors, especially in the Orient, might sell them into bondage.

2 There was probably next to no market for old women ; old men in broken health would also be worthless. Boys and maids that were the right age for teaching a profitable trade would

fetch the most.

» Xenophon, Memorabilia, ii. 5, § 2.

handsome and a clever flute player, who will be readily hired for supper parties, may well command a very high price indeed, say even 30 minae [about $540.00].

41. The Treatment of Slaves in Athens. — Once purchased, what is the condition of the average slave ? If he is put in a factory, he probably has to work long hours on meager rations. He is lodged in a kind of kennel; his only respite is on the great religious holidays. He cannot contract valid marriage or enjoy any of the normal conditions of family life. Still his evil state is partially tempered by the fact that he has to work in constant association with free workmen, and he seems to be treated with a moderate amount of consideration and good camaraderie. On the whole he will have much less to complain of (if he is honest and industrious) than his successors in Imperial Rome.

In the household, conditions are on the whole better. Every Athenian citizen tries to have at least one slave, who, we must grant, may be a starving drudge of all work. The average gentleman perhaps counts ten to twenty as sufficient for his needs. We know of households of fifty. There must usually be a steward, a butler in charge of the storeroom and cellar, a marketing slave, a porter, a baker, a cook, 1 a nurse, perhaps several lady's maids, the indispensable attendant for the master's walks (a graceful, well-favored boy, if possible), the pedagogue for the children, and in really rich families, a groom, and a mule boy. It is the business of the mistress to see that all these creatures are kept busy and reasonably contented. If a slave is reconciled to his lot, honest, cheerful, industrious, his condition is not miserable. Athenian slaves are allowed a surprising amount of liberty, so most visitors to the city complain. A slave may be flogged most cruelly, but he cannot be put to

1 Who, however, could not be trusted to cook a formal dinner. For such purpose an expert must be hired.

death at the mere whim of his master. He cannot enter the gymnasium, or the public assembly; but he can visit the temples. As a humble member of the family he has a small part usually in the family sacrifices. But in any case he is subject to one grievous hardship: when his testimony is required in court he must be " put to the question" by torture. On the other hand, if his master has wronged him intolerably, he can take sanctuary at the Temple of Theseus, and claim the privilege of being sold to some new owner. A slave, too, has still another grievance which may be no less galling because it is sentimental. His name (given him arbitrarily perhaps by his master) is of a peculiar category, which at once brands him as a bondman: Geta, Manes, Dromon, Sosias, Xanthias, Pyrrhias, — such names would be repudiated as an insult by a citizen.

42. Cruel and Kind Masters. — Slavery in Athens, as everywhere else, is largely dependent upon the character of the master ; and most Athenian masters would not regard crude brutality as consistent with that love of elegance, harmony, and genteel deliberation which characterizes a well-born citizen. There do not lack masters who have the whip continually in their hands, who add to the raw stripes fetters and branding, and who make their slaves unceasingly miserable; but such masters are the exception, and public opinion does not praise them. Between the best Athenians and their slaves there is a genial, friendly relation, and the master will put up with a good deal of real impertinence, knowing that behind this forwardness there is an honest zeal for his interests.

Nevertheless the slave system of Athens is not commendable. It puts a stigma upon the glory of honest manual labor. It instills domineering, despotic habits into the owners, cringing subservience into the owned. Even if a slave becomes freed, he does not become an Athenian citizen; he is only a "metic," a resident foreigner, and his old master, or some other Athenian, must be his patron and representative in every kind of legal business. It is a notorious fact that the mere state of slavery robs the victim of his self-respect and manhood. Nevertheless nobody dreams of abolishing slavery as an institution, and the Athenians, comparing themselves with other communities, pride themselves on the extreme humanity of their slave system.

43. The "City Slaves" of Athens. — A large number of nominal " slaves " in Athens differ from any of the creatures we have described. The community, no less than an individual, can own slaves just as it can own warships and temples. Athens owns " city slaves " (Demosioi) of several varieties. The clerks in the treasury office, and the checking officers at the public assemblies are slaves; so too are the less reputable public executioners and torturers; in the city mint there is another corps of slave workmen, busy coining "Athena's owls" — the silver drachmas and four-drachma pieces. But chiefest of all, the city owns its public police force. The " Scythians " they are called from their usual land of origin, or the " bowmen," from their special weapon, which incidentally makes a convenient cudgel in a street brawl. There are 1200 of them, always at the disposal of the city magistrates. They patrol the town at night, arrest evil-doers, sustain law and order in the Agora, and especially enforce decorum, if the public assemblies or the jury courts become tumultuous. They have a special cantonment on the hill of Areopagus near the Acropolis. " Slaves" they are of course in name, and under a kind of military discipline; but they are highly privileged slaves. The security of the city may depend upon their loyal zeal. In times of war they are auxiliaries. Life in this police force cannot therefore be burdensome, and their position is envied by all the factory workers and the house servants.

CHAPTER VIII. THE CHILDREN.

44. The Desirability of Children in Athens. — Besides the oversight of the slaves the Athenian matron has naturally the care of the children. A childless home is one of the greatest of calamities. It means a solitary old age, and still worse, the dying out of the family and the worship of the family gods. There is just enough of the old superstitious "ancestor worship" left in Athens to make one shudder at the idea of leaving the "deified ancestors" without any descendants to keep up the simple sacrifices to their memory. Besides, public opinion condemns the childless home as not contributing to the perpetuation of the city. How Corinth, Thebes, or Sparta will rejoice, if it is plain that Athens is destroying herself by race suicide! So at least one son will be very welcome. His advent is a day of happiness for the father, of still greater satisfaction for the young mother.

45. The Exposure of Infants. — How many more children are welcome depends on circumstances. Children are expensive luxuries. They must be properly educated and even the boys must be left a fair fortune. 1 The girls must always have good dowries, or they cannot " marry according to their station." Public opinion, as well as the law, allows a father (at least if he has one or two children already) to exercise a privilege, which later ages will pronounce one of the foulest blots on Greek civilization. After the birth of a child there is an anxious day or two for the poor young

1 The idea of giving a lad a " schooling " and then turning him loose tc» earn his own living in the world was contrary to all Athenian theory and practice.

mother and the faithful nurses. — Will he ' nourish' it ? Are there boys enough already ? Is the disappointment over the birth of a daughter too keen ? Does he dread the curtailment in family luxuries necessary to save up for an allowance or dowry for the little stranger? Or does the child promise to be puny, sickly, or even deformed ? If any of these arguments carry adverse weight, there is no appeal against the father's decision. He has until the fifth day after the birth to decide. In the interval he can utter the fatal words " Expose it! " The helpless creature is then put in a rude cradle, or more often merely in a shallow pot and placed near some public place; e.g. the corner of the Agora, or near a gymnasium, or the entrance to a temple. Here it will soon die of mere hunger and neglect, unless rescued. If the reasons for exposure are evident physical defects, no one will touch it. Death is certain. If, however, it seems healthy and well formed, it is likely to be taken up and cared for. Not out of pure compassion, however. The harpies who raise slaves and especially slave girls, for no honest purposes, are prompt to pounce upon any promising looking infant. They will rear it as a speculation; if it is a girl, they will teach it to sing, dance, play. The race of light women in Athens is thus really recruited from among the very best families. The fact is well known, but it is constantly winked at. Aristophanes, the comic poet, speaks of this exposure of children as a common feature of Athenian life. Socrates declares his hearers are vexed when he robs them of pet ideas, "like women who have had their children taken from them." There is little or nothing for men of a later day to say of this custom save condemnation. 1

1 About the only boon gained by this foul usage was the fact that, thanks to it, the number of physically unfit persons in Athens was probably pretty small, for no one would think of bringing up a child which, in its first babyhood, promised to be a cripple.

46. The Celebration of a Birth. — But assuredly in a majority of cases, the coming of a child is more than welcome. If a girl, tufts of wool are hung before the door of the happy home; if a boy, there is set out an olive branch. Five days after the birth, the nurse takes the baby, wrapped almost to suffocation in swaddling bands, to the family hearth in the andron, around which she runs several times, followed doubtless, in merry, frolicking procession, by most of the rest of the family. The child is now under the care of the family gods. There is considerable eating and drinking. Exposure now is no longer possible. A great load is off the mind of the mother. But on the "tenth day" comes the real celebration and the feast. This is the " name day." All the kinsmen are present. The house is full of incense and garlands. The cook is in action in the kitchen. Everybody brings simple gifts, along with abundant wishes of good luck. There is a sacrifice, and during the ensuing feast comes the naming of the child. Athenian names are very short and simple. 1 A boy has often his father's name, but more usually his grandfather's, as, e.g., Themistocles, the son of Neocles, the son of Themistocles: the father's name being usually added in place of a surname. In this way certain names will become a kind of family property, and sorrowful is the day when there is no eligible son to bear them!

The child is now a recognized member of the community. His father has accepted him as a legitimate son, one of his prospective heirs, entitled in due time to all the rights of an Athenian citizen.

47. Life and Games of Young Children. — The first seven years of a Greek boy's life are spent with his nurses and his mother. Up to that time his father takes only un-

1 Owing to this simplicity and the relatively small number of Athenian names, a directory of the city would have been a perplexing affair.

A Day in Old Athens

official interest in his welfare. Once past the first perilous "five days," an Athenian baby has no grounds to complain of his treatment. Great pains are taken to keep him warm and well nourished. A wealthy family will go to some trouble to get him a skilful nurse, those from Sparta being in special demand, as knowing the best how to rear healthy infants. He has all manner of toys, and Aristotle the philosopher commends their frequent donation; otherwise,

he says, children will be always "breaking things in the house." Babies have rattles. As they grow older they have dolls of painted clay or wax, sometimes with movable hands and feet, and also toy dishes, tables, wagons, and animals. Lively boys have whipping toys, balls, hoops, and swings. There is no lack of pet dogs, nor of all sorts of games on the THE MATERNAL SLIPPER. blind man's buff and

"tag" order. 1 Athenian

children are, as a class, very active and noisy. Plato speaks feelingly of their perpetual "roaring." As they grow larger, they begin to escape more and more from the narrow quarters of the courts of the house, and play in the streets.

48. Playing in the Streets. — Narrow, dirty, and dusty as the streets seem, children, even of good families, are allowed to play in them. After a rain one can see boys floating

1 It is not always easy to get the exact details of such ancient games, for the " rules" have seldom come down to us; but generally speaking, the games of Greek children seem extremely like those of the twentieth century.

toy boats of leather in every mud puddle, or industriously making mud pies. In warm weather the favorite if cruel sport is to catch a beetle, tie a string to its legs, let it fly off, then twitch it back again. Leapfrog, hide-and-seek, etc., are in violent progress down every alley. The streets are not at all ideal playgrounds. Despite genteel ideas of dignity and moderation, there is a great deal of foul talk and brawling among the passers, and Athenian children have receptive eyes and ears. Yet on the other hand, there is a notable regard and reverence for childhood. With all its frequent callousness and inhumanity, Greek sentiment abhors any brutality to young children. Herodotus the historian tells of the falling of a roof, whereby one hundred and twenty school children perished, as being a frightful calamity, 1 although recounting cold-blooded massacres of thousands of adults with never a qualm; and Herodotus is a very good spokesman for average Greek opinion.

49. The First Stories and Lessons.—Athens has no kindergartens. The first teaching which children will receive is in the form of fables and goblin tales from their mothers and nurses, — usually with the object of frightening them into "being good," — tales of the spectral Lamiae, or of the horrid witch Mormo who will catch naughty children; or of Empusa, a similar creature, who lurks in shadows and dark rooms; or of the Kobaloi, wild spirits in the woods. Then come the immortal fables of ^Esop with their obvious application towards right conduct. Athenian mothers and teachers have no two theories as to the wisdom of corporal punishment. The rod is never spared to the spoiling of the child, although during the first years the slipper is sufficient. Greek children soon have a healthy fear of their nurses; but they often learn to love them, and funeral monuments will survive to perpetuate their grateful memory.

i Herodotus, VI. 27.

50. The Training of Athenian Girls. — Until about seven years old brothers and sisters grow up in the Gynceconitis together. Then the boys experience a complete change in their lives,

when they are sent to school. The girls will continue about the house until the time of their marriage. It is only in the rarest of cases that the parents feel it needful to hire any kind of tutor for them. What the average girl knows is simply what her mother can teach her. Perhaps a certain number of Athenian women (of good family, too) are downright illiterate; but this is not very often the case. A normal girl will learn to read and write, with her mother for school mistress. 1 Very probably she will be taught to dance, and sometimes to play on some instrument, although this last is not quite a proper accomplishment for young women of good family. Hardly any one dreams of giving a woman any systematic intellectual training. 2 Much more important it is that she should know how to weave, spin, embroider, dominate the cook, and superintend the details of a dinner party. She will have hardly time to learn these matters thoroughly before she is " given a husband," and her childhood days are forever over (see p. 35).

Meantime her brother has been started upon a course of education which, both in what it contains and in what it omits, is one of the most interesting and significant features of Athenian life.

1 There has come down to us a charming Greek terra-cotta(it is true, not from Athens) showing a girl seated on her mother's knee, and learning from a roll which she holds.

2 Plato suggested in his Republic (V. 451 f.) that women should receive the same educational opportunities as the men. This was a proposition for Utopia and never struck any answering chord.

CHAPTER IX. THE SCHOOLBOYS OF ATHENS.

51. Athenians Generally Literate. — Education is not compulsory by law in Athens, but the father who fails to give his son at least a modicum of education falls under a public contempt, which involves no slight penalty. Practically all Athenians are at least literate. In Aristophanes's famous comedy, The Knights, a boorish " sausage-seller" is introduced, who, for the purposes of the play, must be one of the very scum of society, and he is made to cry, " Only consider now my education! I can but barely read, just in a kind of way." 1 Evidently if illiterates are not very rare in Athens, the fellow should have been made out utterly ignorant. " He can neither swim 2 nor say his letters," is a common phrase for describing an absolute idiot. When a boy has reached the age of seven, the time for feminine rule is over; henceforth his floggings, and they will be many, are to come from firm male hands. .

52. Character Building the Aim of Athenian Education. —
The true education is of course begun long before the age of seven. Character not book-learning, is the main object of Athenian education, i.e. to make the boy self-contained, modest, alert, patriotic, a true friend, a dignified gentleman, able to appreciate and participate in all that is true, harmo-

1 Aristophanes, Knights, 11.188-189.

2 Swimming was an exceedingly common accomplishment among the Greeks, naturally enough, so much of their life being spent upon or near the sea.

nious, and beautiful in life. To that end his body must be trained, not apart from, but along with his mind. Plato makes his character Protagoras remark, " As soon as a child understands what is said to him, the nurse, the mother, the pedagogue, and the father vie in their efforts to make him good, by showing him in all that he does that ' this is right/ and ' that is wrong'; * this is pretty/ and ' that is ugly'; so that he may learn what to follow and what to shun. If he obeys willingly — why, excellent. If not, then try by threats and blows to correct him, as men straighten a warped and crooked sapling." Also after he is fairly in school " the teacher is enjoined to pay more attention to his morals and conduct than to his progress in reading and

53. The Schoolboy's Pedagogue. — It is a great day for an Athenian boy when he is given

a pedagogue. This slave (perhaps purchased especially for the purpose) is not his teacher, but he ought to be more than ordinarily honest, kindly, and well informed. His prime business is to accompany the young master everywhere out-of-doors, especially to the school and to the gymnasium ; to carry his books and writing tablets; to give informal help upon his lessons; to keep him out of every kind of mischief; to teach him social good manners; to answer the thousand questions a healthy boy is sure to ask; and finally, in emergencies, if the schoolmaster or father is not at hand, to administer a needful whipping. A really capable pedagogue can mean everything to a boy; but it is asking too much that a purchased slave should be an ideal companion. 1 Probably many pedagogues are responsible for their charges' idleness or downright depravity. It is a dubious system at the best.

1 No doubt frequently the pedagogue would be an old family servant of good morals, loyalty, and zeal. In that case the relation might be delightful.

The assigning of the pedagogue is simultaneous with the beginning of school days; and the Athenians are not open to the charge of letting their children waste their time during possible study hours. As early as Solon's day (about 5.90 B.C.) a law had to be passed forbidding schools to open before daybreak, or to be kept open after dusk. This was in the interest not of good eyesight, but of good morals. Evidently schools had been keeping even longer than through the daylight. In any case, at gray dawn every yawning schoolboy is off, urged on by his pedagogue, and his tasks will continue with very little interruption through the entire day. It is therefore with reason that the Athenian lads rejoice in the very numerous religious holidays.

54. An Athenian School. — Leaving the worthy citizen's home, where we have lingered long chatting on many of the topics the house and its denizens suggest, we will turn again to the streets to seek the school where one of the young sons of the family has been duly conducted (possibly, one may say, driven) by his pedagogue. We have not far to go. Athenian schools have to be numerous, because they are small. To teach children of the poorer classes it is enough to have a modest room and a few stools; an unrented shop will answer. But we will go to a more pretentious establishment. There is an anteroom by the entrance way where the pedagogues can sit and doze or exchange gossip while their respective charges are kept busy in the larger room within. The latter place, however, is not particularly commodious. On the bare wall hang book-rolls, lyres, drinking vessels, baskets for books, and perhaps some simple geometrical instruments. The pupils sit on rude, low benches, each lad with his boxwood tablet covered with wax l upon his lap,

1 This wax tablet was practically a slate. The letters written could be erased with the blunt upper end of the metallic stylus, and the whole surface of the tablet could be made smooth again by a judicious heating.

and presumably busy, scratching letters with his stylus. The master sits on a high chair, surveying the scene. He cultivates a grim and awful aspect, for he is under no delusion that " his pupils love him." " He sits aloft," we are told, "like a juryman, with an expression of implacable wrath, before which the pupil must tremble and cringe." l

Athenian schoolboys have at least their full share of idleness, as well as of animal spirits. There is soon a loiid whisper from one corner. Instantly the ruling tyrant rises. " Antiphon! I have heard you. Come forward ! " If Antiphon is wise, he will advance promptly and submit as cheerfully as possible to a sound caning; if folly possesses him, he will hesitate. At a nod from the master two older boys, who serve as monitors, will seize him with grim chuckles. He will then be fortunate if he escapes being tied to a post and flogged until his back is one mass of welts, and his very life seems in danger. It will be useless for him to complain to his parents. A good schoolmaster is supposed to flog frequently to earn his pay; if he is sparing with the rod or lash, he is probably lacking in energy. Boys will be boys, and there is only one remedy for juvenile shortcomings.

This diversion, of course, with its attendant howling, interrupts the course of the school, but presently matters again become normal. The scholars are so few that probably there is only one teacher, and instruction is decidedly " individual," although poetry and singing are very likely taught " in concert."

55. The School Curriculum. — As to the subjects studied, the Athenian curriculum is well fixed and limited: letters, music, and gymnastics. Every lad must have a certain amount of all of these. The gymnastics will be taught later

1 The quotation is from the late writer Libanius, but it is perfectly true for classic Athens.

in the day by a special teacher at a "wrestling school." The "music" may also be taught separately. The main effort with a young boy is surely to teach him to read and write. And here must be recalled the relative infrequency of complete books in classic Athens. 1 To read public placards, inscriptions of laws, occasional epistles, commercial documents, etc., is probably, for many Athenians, reading enough. The great poets he will learn by ear rather than by eye; and he may go through a long and respected life and never be compelled to read a really sizable volume from end to end. So the teaching of reading is along very simple lines. It is perhaps simultaneous with the learning of writing. The twenty-four letters are learned by sheer power of memory; then the master sets lines upon the tablets to be copied. As soon as possible the boy is put to learning and writing down passages from the great poets. Progress in mere literacy is very rapid. There is no waste of time on history, geography, or physical science; and between the concentration on a single main subject and the impetus given by the master's rod the Athenian schoolboy soon becomes adept with his letters. Possibly a little arithmetic is taught him, but only a little. In later life, if he does not become a trader or banker, he will not be ashamed to reckon simple sums upon his fingers or by means of pebbles; although if his father is ambitious to have him become a philosopher, he may have him taught something of geometry.

Once more we see the total absence of " vocational studies " in this Athenian education. The whole effort is to develop a fair, noble, free, and lofty character, not to earn a living. To set a boy to study with an eye to learning some profitable trade is counted illiberal to the last degree. It is for

1 One gets the impression that books — in the sense of complete volumes — were much rarer in Athens than in Imperial Rome, or in the later Middle Ages up to the actual period of the invention of printing.

this reason that practical arithmetic is discouraged, yet a little knowledge of the art of outline drawing is allowed; for though no gentleman intends to train his son to be a great artist, the study will enable him to appreciate good sculpture and painting. Above all the schoolmaster, who, despite his brutal austerity, ought to be a clear-sighted and inspiring teacher, must lose no opportunity to instil moral lessons, and develop the best powers of his charges. The-ognis, the old poet of Megara, states the case well: —

To rear a child is easy ; but to teach Morals and manners is beyond our reach. To make the foolish wise, the wicked good, That science never yet was understood.

56. The Study of the Poets. — It is for the developing of the best moral and mental qualities in the lads that they are compelled to memorize long passages of the great poets of Hellas. Theognis, with his pithy admonitions cast in semi-proverb form, the worldly wisdom of Hesiod, and of Phocylides are therefore duly flogged into every Attic schoolboy. 1 But the great text-book, dwarfing all others, is Homer, — " the Bible of the Greeks," as later ages will call it. Even in the small school we visit, several of the pupils can repeat five or six long episodes from

both the Iliad and the Odyssey, and there is one older boy present (an extraordinary, but by no means an unprecedented case) who can repeat both of the long epics word for word. 2 Clearly the absence of many books has then its compensations. The average Athenian lad has what seems to be a simply marvelous memory.

And what an admirable text-book and " second reader "

1 Phocylides, whose gnomic poetry is now preserved to us only in scant fragments, was an Ionian, born about 560 B.C. His verses were in great acceptance in the schools.

2 For auch an attainment see Xenophon's Symposium, 3 :5.

the Homeric poems are! What characters to imitate : the high-minded, passionate, yet withal loyal and lovable Achilles who would rather fight gloriously before Troy (though death in the campaign is certain) than live a long life in ignoble ease at home at Phthia; or Odysseus, the " hero of many devices," who endures a thousand ills and surmounts them all; who lets not even the goddess Calypso seduce him from his love to his " sage Penelope "; who is ever ready with a clever tale, a plausible lie, and, when the need comes, a mighty deed of manly valor. The boys will all go home to-night with firm resolves to suffer all things rather than leave a comrade unavenged, as Achilles was tempted to do and nobly refused, and to fight bravely, four against forty, as Odysseus and his comrades did, when at the call of duty and honor they cleared the house of the dastard suitors. True, philosophers like Plato complain: "Homer gives to lads very undignified and unworthy ideas of the gods " ; and men of a later age will assert: " Homer has altogether too little to say about the cardinal virtues of truthfulness and honesty." 1 But making all allowances the Iliad and the Odyssey are still the two grandest secular text-books the world will ever know. The lads are infinitely the better for them.

Three years, according to Plato, are needed to learn the rudiments of reading and writing before the boys are fairly launched upon this study of the poets. For several years more they will spend most of their mornings standing respectfully before their master, while he from his chair reads to them from the roll of one author or another, — the

1 The virtue of unflinching honesty was undoubtedly the thing least cultivated by the Greek education. Successful prevarication, e.g. in the case of Odysseus, was put at altogether too high a premium. It is to be feared that the average Athenian schoolboy was only partially truthful. The tale of " George Washington and the cherry tree " would never have found favor in Athens. The great Virginian would have been blamed for failing to concoct a clever lie.

pupils repeating the lines, time and again, until they have learned them, while the master interrupts to explain every nice point in mythology, in real or alleged history, or a moot question in ethics.

57. The Greeks do not study Foreign Languages. — As the boys grow older the scope of their study naturally increases; but in one particular their curriculum will seem strangely limited. The study of foreign languages has no place in a Greek course of study. That any gentleman should learn say Persian, or Egyptian (unless he intended to devote himself to distant travel), seems far more unprofitable than, in a later age, the study of say Patagonian or Papuan will appear. 1 Down at the Peirseus there are a few shipmasters, perhaps, who can talk Egyptian, Phoenician, or Babylonish. They need the knowledge for their trade, but even they will disclaim any cultural value for their accomplishment. The euphonious, expressive, marvelously delicate tongue of Hellas sums up for the Athenian almost all that is valuable in the world's intellectual and literary life. What has the outer, the "Barbarian," world to give him? — Nothing, many will say, but some gold darics which will corrupt his statesmen, and some spices, carpets, and similar luxuries which good Hellenes can well do without. The Athenian lad will never need to crucify the flesh upon Latin, French, and German, or an equivalent for his own Greek. Therein perhaps

he may be heavily the loser, save that his own mother tongue is so intricate and full of subtle possibilities that to learn to make the full use thereof is truly a matter for lifelong education.

58. The Study of " Music." — But the Athenian has a substitute for this omission of foreign language study: Music.

1 This fact did not prevent the Greeks from having a considerable respect for the traditions and lore of, e.g., the Egyptians, and from borrowing a good many non-Greek usages and inventions; but all this could take place without feeling the least necessity for studying foreign languages.

This is something more comprehensive than "the art of combining tones in a manner to please the ear" [Webster], It is practically the study of whatever will develop the noble powers of the emotions, as contrasted to the mere intellect. 1 Indeed everything which comes within the ample provinces of the nine Muses, even sober history, might be included in the term. However, for special purposes, the study of " Music" may be considered as centering around playing instruments and singing. The teacher very likely resides in a house apart from the master of the school of letters. Aristophanes gives this picture of the good old customs for the teaching of music. "The boys from the same section of the town have to march thinly clad and draw up in good order — though the snow be thick as meal — to the house of the harp master. There he will teach them [some famous tune] raising a mighty melody. If any one acts silly or turns any quavers, he gets a good hard thrashing for ' banishing the Muses !'" 2

Learning to sing is probably the most important item, for every boy and man ought to be able to bear his part in the great chorals which are a notable element in most religious festivals; besides, a knowledge of singing is a great aid to appreciating lyric poetry, or the choruses in tragedy, and in learning to declaim. To learn to sing elaborate solo pieces is seldom necessary, — it is not quite genteel in grown-up persons, for it savors a little too much of the professional. So it is also with instrumental music. The Greeks lack the piano, the organ, the elaborate bass instruments of a later day. Their flutes and harps, although very sweet, might seem thin to a twentieth-century critic.

1 Aristotle [Politics, V. (or VIII.) 1] says that the literary education is to train the mind; while music, though of no practical use, "provides a noble and liberal employment of leisure."

3 Aristophanes's The Clouds. The whole passage is cited in Da vis's Readings in Ancient History, vol. I, pp. 262-255.

But one can gain considerable volume by the great number of instruments, and nearly everybody in Athens can pick at the lyre after a fashion. The common type of harp is the lyre, and it has enough possibilities for the average boy. The more elaborate cithera is usually reserved for professionals. 1 An Athenian lad is expected to be able to accompany his song upon his own lyre and to play in concert with his fellows.

The other instrument in common use is the flute. At its simplest, this is a mere shepherd's pipe. Anybody can make one with a knife and some rushes. Then come elaborations ; two pipes are fitted together into one wooden mouthpiece. Now, we really have an instrument with possibilities. But it is not in such favor in the schools as the lyre. You cannot blow day after day upon the flute and not distort your cheeks permanently. Again the gentleman's son will avoid " professionalism." There are amateur flute players moving in the best society, but the more fastidious frown upon the instrument, save for hired performers.

59. The Moral Character of Greek Music. — Whether it is singing, harp playing, or flute playing, a most careful watch is kept upon the character of the music taught the lads. The master who lets his pupils learn many soft, dulcet, languishing airs will find his charges' parents extremely angry, even to depriving him of their patronage. Very soft music, in "Lydian modes,"

is counted effeminate, fit only for the women's quarters and likely to do boys no good. The riotous type also, of the " Ionic mode," is fit only for drinking songs and is even more under the ban. 2 What is especially in favor

1 For the details of these harp types of instruments see Dictionary of Antiquities.

2 The "Phrygian mode" from which the "Ionic" was derived was still more demoralizing; it was counted " orgiastic," and proper only in certain excited religious rhapsodies.

is the stern, strenuous Dorian mode. This will make boys hardy, manly, and brave. Very elaborate music with trills and quavers is in any case frowned upon. It simply delights the trained ear, and has no reaction upon the character; and of what value is a musical presentation unless it leaves the hearers and performer better, worthier men? Let the average Athenian possess the opportunity, and he will infallibly stamp with disapproval a great part of both the popular and the classical music of the later ages. 1

60. The Teaching of Gymnastics. — The visits to the reading school and to the harp master have consumed a large part of the day; but towards afternoon the pedagogues will conduct their charges to the third of the schoolboys' tyrants : the gymnastic teacher. Nor do his parents count this the least important of the three. Must not their" sons be as physically " beautiful" (to use the common phrase in Athens) as possible, and must they not some day, as good citizens, play their brave part in war? The palcestras (literally "wrestling grounds") are near the outskirts of the city, where land is cheap and a good-sized open space can be secured. Here the lads are given careful instruction under the constant eye of an expert in running, wrestling, boxing, jumping, discus hurling, and javelin casting. They are not expected to become professional athletes, but their parents will be vexed if they do not develop a healthy tan all over their naked bodies, 2 and if they do not learn at least moderate proficiency in the sports and a certain amount of familiarity with elementary military maneuvers. Of course

1 We have extremely few Greek melodies preserved to us, and these few are not attractive to the modern ear. All that can fairly be said is that the Hellenes were obviously such aesthetic, harmoniously minded people that it is impossible their music should have failed in nobility, beauty, and true melody.

2 To have a pale, untanned skin was " womanish " and unworthy of a free Athenian citizen.

boys of marked physical ability will be encouraged to think of training for the various great " games " which culminate at Olympia, although enlightened opinion is against the promoting of professional athletics; and certain extreme philosophers question the wisdom of any extensive physical culture at all, " for (say they) is not the human mind the real thing worth developing?" 1

Weary at length and ready for a hearty meal and sleep, the boys are conducted homeward by their pedagogues.

As they grow older the lads with ambitious parents will be given a more varied education. Some will be put under such teachers of the new rhetoric and oratory, now in vogue, as the famous Isocrates, and be taught to play the orator as an aid to inducing their fellow citizens to bestow political advancement. Certain will be allowed to become pupils of Plato, who has been teaching his philosophy out at the groves of the Academy, or to join some of his rivals in theoretical wisdom. Into these fields, however, we cannot follow them.

61. The Habits and Ambitions of Schoolboys. — It is a clear fact, that by the age say of thirteen, the Athenian education has had a marked effect upon the average schoolboy. Instead of being " the most ferocious of animals," as Plato, speaking of his untutored state describes him, he is now " the most amiable and divine of living beings." The well-trained lad goes now to school

with his eyes cast upon the ground, his hands and arms wrapped in his chiton, making way dutifully for all his elders. If he is addressed by an older man, he stands modestly, looking downward and blushing in a manner worthy of a girl. He has been taught to avoid the Agora, and if he must pass it, never to

The details of the boys' athletic games, being much of a kind with those followed by adults at the regular public gymnasia, are here omitted See Chap. XVII.

linger. The world is full of evil and ugly things, but he is taught to hear and see as little of them as possible. When men talk of his healthy color, increasing beauty, and admire the graceful curves of his form at the wrestling school, he must not grow proud. He is being taught to learn relatively little from books, but a great deal from hearing the conversation of grave and well-informed men. As he grows older his father will take him to all kinds of public gatherings and teach him the working details of the " Democratic Government" of Athens. He becomes intensely proud of his city. It is at length his chief thought, almost his entire life. A very large part of the loyalty which an educated man of a later age will divide between his home, his church, his college, his town, and his nation, the Athenian lad will sum up in two words, — " my polis " ; i.e. the city of Athens. His home is largely a place for eating and sleeping; his school is not a great institution, it is simply a kind of disagreeable though necessary learning shop; his church is the religion of his ancestors, and this religion is warp and woof of the government, as much a part thereof as the law courts or the fighting fleet; his town and his nation are alike the sovran city-state of Athens. Whether he feels keenly a wider loyalty to Hellas at large, as against the Great King of Persia, for instance, will depend upon circumstances. In a real crisis, as at Salamis, — yes. In ordinary circumstances when there is hot feud with Sparta, — no.

62. The " Ephebi." — The Athenian education then is admirably adapted to make the average lad a useful and worthy citizen, and to make him modest, alert, robust, manly, and a just lover of the beautiful, both in conduct and in art. It does not, however, develop his individual bent very strongly; and it certainly gives him a mean view of the dignity of labor. He will either become a leisurely gentleman, whose only proper self-expression will come in warfare,

politics, or philosophy; or — if he be poor—he will at least envy and try to imitate the leisure class.

By eighteen the young Athenian's days of study will usually come to a close. At that age he will be given a simple festival by his father and be formally enrolled in his paternal deme. 1 His hair, which has hitherto grown down toward his shoulders, will be clipped short. He will allow his beard to grow. At the temple of Aglaurus he will (with the other youths of his age) take solemn oath of loyalty to Athens and her laws. For the next year he will serve as a military guard at the Peirseus, and receive a certain training in soldiering. The next year the state will present him with a new shield and spear, and he will have a taste of rougher garrison duty at one of the frontier forts towards Bceotia or Megara. 2 Then he is mustered out. He is an ephebus no longer, but a full-fledged citizen, and all the vicissitudes of Athenian life are before him.

1 One of the hundred or more petty townships or precincts into which Attica was divided.

8 These two years which the ephebi of Athens had to serve under arms have been aptly likened to the military service now required of young men in European countries.

CHAPTER X. THE PHYSICIANS OF ATHENS.

63. The Beginnings of Greek Medical Science. —As we move about the city we cannot but be impressed by the high average of fine physiques and handsome faces. Your typical Greek is fair in color and has very regular features. The youths do not mature rapidly, but thanks to the gymnasia and the regular lives, they develop not merely admirable, but healthy, bodies. The proportion of hale and hearty old men is great; and probably the number of invalids is considerably smaller than in later times and in more artificially reared communities. 1 Nevertheless, the Athenians are certainly mortal, and subject to bodily ills, and the physician is no unimportant member of society, although his exact status is much less clearly determined than it will be in subsequent ages.

' Greek medicine and surgery, as it appears in Homer, is simply a certain amount of practical knowledge gained by rough experience, largely supplemented by primitive superstition. It was quite as important to know the proper prayers and charms wherewith to approach "Apollo the Healer," as to understand the kind of herb poultice which would keep wounds from festering. Homer speaks of As-clepius; however, in early days he was not a god, but simply a skilful leach. Then as we approach historic times the physician's art becomes more regular. Asclepius is elevated

1 A slight but significant witness to the general healthiness of the Greeks is found in the very rare mention in their literature of such a common ill as toothache.

into a separate and important deity, although it is not till 420 B.C. that his worship is formally introduced into Athens. Long ere that time, however, medicine and surgery had won a real place among the practical sciences. The sick man stands at least a tolerable chance of rational treatment, and of not being murdered by wizards and fanatical exorcists.

64. Healing Shrines and their Methods. — There exist in Athens and in other Greek cities real sanatoria 1 ; these are temples devoted to the healing gods (usually Asclepius, but sometimes Apollo, Aphrodite, and Hera). Here the patient is expected to sleep over night in the temple, and the god visits him in a dream, and reveals a course of treatment which will lead to recovery. Probably there is a good deal of sham and imposture about the process. The canny priests know

more than they care to tell about how the patient is worked into an excitable, imaginative state; and of the very human means employed to produce a satisfactory and informing dream. 2 Nevertheless it is a great deal to convince the patient that he is sure of recovery, and that nobody less than a god has dictated the remedies. The value of mental therapeutics is keenly appreciated. Attached to the temple are skilled physicians to " interpret" the dream, and opportunities for prolonged residence with treatment by baths, purgation, dieting, mineral waters, sea baths, all kinds of mild gymnastics, etc. Entering upon one of these temple treatments is, in short, anything but surrendering oneself to unmitigated quackery. Probably a large proportion of the former patients have recovered; and they have testified their gratitude by hanging around

1 The most famous was at Epidaurus, where the Asclepius cult seems to have been especially localized.

2 The "healing sleep" employed at these temples is described, in a kind of blasphemous parody, in Aristophanes's Plutus. (Significant passages are quoted in Davis's Readings in Ancient History, vol. I, pp.258-261.)

the shrine little votive tablets, 1 usually pictures of the diseased parts now happily healed, or, for internal maladies, a written statement of the nature of the disease. This is naturally very encouraging to later patients : they gain confidence by knowing that many cases similar to their own have been thus cured.

These visits to the healing temples are, however, expensive : not everybody has entire faith in them; for many lesser ills also they are wholly unnecessary. Let us look, then, at the regular physicians.

65. An Athenian Physician's Office. — There are salaried public medical officers in Athens, and something like a public dispensary where free treatment is given citizens in simple cases ; but the average man seems to prefer his own doctor. 2 We may enter the office of Menon, a " regular private practitioner," and look about us. The office itself is a mere open shop in the front of a house near the Agora; and, like a barber's shop, is something of a general lounging place. In the rear one or two young disciples (doctors in embryo) and a couple of slaves are pounding up drugs in mortars. There are numbers of bags of dried herbs and little glass flasks hanging on the walls. Near the entrance is a statue of Asclepius the Healer, and also of the great human founder of the real medical science among the Greeks — Hippocrates.

Menon himself is just preparing to go out on his professional calls. He is a handsome man in the prime of life, and takes great pains with his personal appearance. His himation is carefully draped. His finger rings have excellent cameos. His beard has been neatly trimmed, and he has just bathed and scented himself with delicate Assyrian

1 Somewhat as in the various Catholic pilgrimage shrines (e.g. Lourdes) to-day.

2 We know comparatively little of these public physicians; probably they were mainly concerned with the health of the army and naval force, the prevention of epidemics, etc.

nard. He will gladly tell you that he is in no wise a fop, but that it is absolutely necessary to produce a pleasant personal impression upon his fastidious, irritable patients. Menon himself claims to have been a personal pupil of the great Hippocrates, 1 and about every other reputable Greek physician will make the same claim. He has studied more or less in a temple of Asclepius, and perhaps has been a member of the medical staff thereto attached. He has also become a member of the Hippocratic brotherhood, a semi-secret organization, associated with the Asclepius cult, and carefully cherishing the dignity of the profession and the secret arts of the guild.

66. The Physician's Oath. —The oath which all this brotherhood has sworn is noble and notable. Here are some of the main provisions: —

" I swear by Apollo the Physician, and Asclepius and Hygeia; a [Lady Health] and Panaceia [Lady All-Cure] to honor as my parents the master who taught me this art, and to admit to my own instruction only his sons, my own sons, and those who have been duly inscribed as pupils, and who have taken the medical oath, and no others. I will prescribe such treatment as may be for the benefit of my patients, according to my best power and judgment, and preserve them from anything hurtful or mischievous. I will never, even if asked, administer poison, nor advise its use. I will never give a criminal draught to a woman. I will maintain the purity and integrity of my art. Wherever I go, I will abstain from all mischief or corruption, or any immodest action. If ever I hear any secret I will not divulge it. If I keep this oath, may the gods give me success in life and in my art. If I break this oath, may all the reverse fall upon me." 2

1 Who was still alive, an extremely old man. He died in Thessaly in 357 B.C., at an alleged age of 104 years.

8 For the unabridged translation of this oath, see Smith's Dictionary of Antiquities (revised edition), vol. II, p. 154.

67. The Skill of Greek Physicians. — Menon's skill as a physician and surgeon is considerable. True, he has only a very insufficient conception of anatomy. His theoretical knowledge is warped, but he is a shrewd judge of human nature and his practical knowledge is not contemptible. In his private pharmacy his assistants have compounded a great quantity of drugs which he knows how to administer with much discernment. He has had considerable experience in dealing with wounds and sprains, such as are common in the wars or in the athletic games. He understands that Dame Nature is a great healer, who is to be assisted rather than coerced; and he dislikes resorting to violent remedies, such as bleedings and strong emetics. Ordinary fevers and the like he can attack with success. He has no modern anaesthetics or opium, but has a very insufficient substitute in mandragora. He can treat simple diseases of the eye; and he knows how to put gold filling into teeth. His surgical instruments, however, are altogether too primitive. He is personally cleanly; but he has not the least idea of antiseptics; the result is that obscure internal diseases, calling for grave operations, are likely to baffle him. He will refuse to operate, or if he does operate the chances are against the patient. 1 In other words, his medical skill is far in advance of his surgery.

Menon naturally busies himself among the best families of Athens, and commands a very good income. He counts it part of his equipment to be able to persuade his patients, by all the rules of logic and rhetoric, to submit to disagreeable treatment; and for that end has taken lessons in informal oratory from Isocrates or one of his associates. Some of Menon's competitors (feeling themselves less eloquent) have actually a paid rhetorician whom they can take

1 Seemingly a really serious operation was usually turned over by the local physician to a traveling surgeon, who could promptly disappear from the neighborhood if things went badly.

to the bedside of a stubborn invalid, to induce him by irrefutable arguments to endure an amputation. 1

No such honor of course is paid to the intellects of the poorer fry, who swarm in at Menon's surgery. Those who cannot pay to have him bandage them himself, perforce put up with the secondary skill and wisdom of the " disciples." The drug-mixing slaves are expected to salve and physic the patients of their own class; but there seems to be a law against allowing them to attempt the treatment of free-born men.

68. Quacks and Charlatans. — Unluckily not everybody is wise enough to put up with the presumably honest efforts of Menon's underlings. There appears to be no law against allowing anybody who wishes to pose as a physician, and to sell his inexperience and his quack nostrums. Vendors of every sort of cure-all abound, as well as creatures who work on the superstitious and

pretend to cure by charms and hocus-pocus. In the market there is such a swarm of these charlatans of healing that they bring the whole medical profession into contempt. Certain people go so far as to distrust the efficacy of any part of the lore of Asclepius. Saya one poet tartly: —

The surgeon Menedemos, as men say,

Touched as he passed a Zeus of marble white ; Neither the marble nor his Zeus-ship might

Avail the god — they buried him to-day.

And again even to dream of the quacks is dangerous: —

Diophantes, sleeping, saw

Hermas the physician: Diophantes never woke

From that fatal vision. 2

1 Plato tells how Gorgias, the famous rhetorician, was sometimes thus hired. A truly Greek artifice — this substitution of oratory for chloroform!

2Both of these quotations probably date from later than 360 B.C., but they are perfectly in keeping with the general opinion of Greek quackery.

All in all, despite Menon's good intentions and not despicable skill, it is fortunate the gods have made " Good Health" one of their commonest gifts to the Athenians. Constant exercise in the gymnasia, occasional service in the army, the absence of cramping and unhealthful office work, and a climate which puts out-of-door existence at a premium, secure for them a general good health that compensates for most of the lack of a scientific medicine.

CHAPTER XL THE FUNERALS.

69. An Athenian's Will. — All Menon's patients are to-day set out upon the road to recovery. Hipponax, his rival, has been less fortunate. A wealthy and elderly patient, Lyco-phron, died the day before yesterday. As the latter felt his end approaching, he did what most Athenians may put off until close to the inevitable hour — he made his will, and called in his friends to witness it; and one must hope there can be no doubt about the validity, the signets attached, etc., for otherwise the heirs may find themselves in a pretty lawsuit.

The will begins in this fashion: " The Testament of Lyco-phron the Marathonian. 1 May all be well: — but if I do not recover from this sickness, thus do I bestow my estate." Then in perfectly cold-blooded fashion he proceeds to give his young wife and the guardianship of his infant daughter to Stobiades, a bachelor friend who will probably marry the widow within two months or less of the funeral. Lycophron gives also specific directions about his tomb; he gives legacies of money or jewelry to various old associates; he mentions certain favorite slaves to receive freedom, and as specifically orders certain others (victims of his displeasure) to be kept in bondage. Lastly three reliable friends are named as executors.

70. The Preliminaries of a Funeral. — An elaborate funeral is the last perquisite of every Athenian. Even if Lycophron

'In all Athenian legal documents, it was necessary to give the deme of the interested party or parties.

had been a poor man he would now receive obsequies seemingly far out of proportion to his estate and income. It is even usual in Greek states to have laws restraining the amount which may be spent upon funerals, — otherwise great sums may be literally " burned up " upon the funeral pyres. When now the tidings go out that Lycophron's nearest relative has "closed his mouth," after he has breathed his last, all his male kinsfolk and all other persons who hope to be remembered in the will promptly appear in the Agora in black himatia 1 and hasten to the barber shops to have their heads shaved. The widow might shave her hair likewise, with all her slave maids, did not her husband, just ere his death, positively forbid such disfigurements. The women of the family take the body in charge the minute the physician has declared that all is over. The customary obol is put in the mouth of the corpse, 2 and the body is carefully washed in perfumed water, clothed in festal white; then woolen fillets are wound around the head, and over these a crown of vine leaves. So arrayed, the body is ready to be laid out on a couch in the front courtyard of the house, with the face turned toward the door so as to seem to greet everybody who enters. In front of the house there stands a tall earthen vase of water, wherewith the visitors may give themselves a purifying sprinkling, after quitting the polluting presence of a dead body.

71. Lamenting the Dead. — Around this funeral bed the relatives and friends keep a gloomy vigil. The Athenians after all are southern born, and when excited seem highly emotional people. There are stern laws dating from Solon's

1 In the important city of Argos, however, white was the proper funeral color.

2 This was not originally (as later asserted) a fee to Charon the ferryman to Hades, but simply a "minimum precautionary sum, for the dead man's use" (Dr. Jane Harrison), placed in the mouth, where a Greek usually kept his small change.

day against the worst excesses, but what now occurs seems violent enough. The widow is beating her breast, tearing her hair, gashing her cheeks with her finger nails. Lyco-phron's elderly sister has ashes sprinkled upon her gray head and ever and anon utters piteous wails. The slave women in the background keep up a hideous moaning. The men present do not think it undignified to utter loud lamentation and to shed frequent tears. Least commendable of all (from a modern standpoint) are the hired dirge singers, who maintain a most melancholy chant, all the time beating their breasts, and giving a perfect imitation of frantic grief. This has probably continued day and night, the mourners perhaps taking turns by relays.

All in all it is well that Greek custom enjoins the actual funeral, at least, on the second day following the death. 1 The " shade " of the deceased is not supposed to find rest in the nether world until after the proper obsequies. 2 To let a corpse lie several days without final disposition will bring down on any family severe reproach. In fact, on few points are the Greeks more sensitive than on this subject of prompt burial or cremation. After a land battle the victors are bound never to push their vengeance so far as to refuse a " burial truce " to the vanquished; and it is a doubly unlucky admiral who lets his crews get drowned in a sea fight, without due effort to recover the corpses afterward and to give them proper disposition on land.

72. The Funeral Procession. — The day after the " laying-out " comes the actual funeral. Normally it is held as early as possible in the morning, before the rising of the sun. Perhaps while on the way to the Agora we have passed,

1 It must be remembered that the Greeks had no skilled embalmers at their service, and that they lived in a decidedly warm climate.

2 See the well-known case of the wandering shade of Patroclus demanding the proper obsequies from Achilles (Iliad, XXIII. 71).

well outside the city, such a mournful procession. The youngest and stoutest of the male relatives carry the litter : although if Lycophron's relatives had desired a really extravagant display they might have employed a mule car. Ahead of the bier march the screaming flute players, earning their fees by no melodious din. Then comes the litter itself with the corpse arrayed magnificently for the finalities, a honey cake set in the hands, 1 a flask of oil placed under the head. After this come streaming the relatives in irregular procession : the widow and the chief heir (her prospective second husband !) walking closest, and trying to appear as demonstrative as possible : nor (merely because the company is noisy and not stoical in its manner) need we deny that there is abundant genuine grief. All sorts of male acquaintances of the deceased bring up the rear, since it is good form to proclaim to wide Athens that Lycophron had hosts of friends. 2

73. The Funeral Pyre. — So the procession moves through the still gloomy streets of the city, — doubtless needing torch bearers as well as flute players, — and out through some gate, until the line halts in an open field, or better, in a quiet and convenient garden. Here the great funeral pyre of choice dry fagots, intermixed with aromatic cedar, has been heaped. The bier is laid thereon. There are no strictly religious ceremonies. The company stands in a respectful circle, while the nearest male kinsman tosses a pine link upon the oil-soaked wood. A mighty blaze leaps up to heaven, sending its ruddy brightness against the sky now palely flushed with the bursting dawn. The flutists play in softer measures. As the fire rages a few of the relatives toss

1 The original idea of the honey cake was simply that it was a friendly present to the infernal gods; later came the conceit that it was a sop to fling to the dog Cerberus, who guarded the entrance to Hades.

3 Women, unless they were over sixty years of age, were not allowed to join in funeral processions unless they were first cousins, or closer kin, of the deceased.

A Day in Old Athens

upon it pots of rare unguents; and while the flames die down, thrice the company shout their farewells, calling their departed friend by name — " Lycophron! Lycophron ! Ly-cophron!"

So fierce is the flame it soon sinks into ashes. As soon as these are cool enough for safety (a process hastened by pouring on water or wine) the charred bones of the deceased are tenderly gathered up to be placed in a stately urn. The company, less formally now, returns to Athens, and that night there will probably be a great funeral feast at the house of the nearest relative, everybody eating and drinking to capacity " to do Lycophron full honor "; for it is he who is imagined as being now for the last time the host.

74. Honors to the Memory of the Dead. — Eeligion seems to have very little place in the Athenian funeral: there are no priests present, no prayers, no religious hymns. But the dead man is now conceived as being, in a very humble and intangible way, a deity himself: his good will is worth propitiating ; his memory is not to be forgotten. On the third, ninth, and thirtieth days after the funeral there are simple religious ceremonies with offerings of garlands, fruits, libations and the like, at the new tomb; and later at certain times in the year these will be repeated. The more enlightened will of course consider these merely graceful remembrances of a former friend ; but there is a good deal of primitive ancestor worship even in civilized Athens.

Burning is the usual method for the Greeks to dispose of their dead, but the burial of unburned bodies is not unknown to them. Probably, however, the rocky soil and the limited land space around Athens make regular cemeteries less convenient than elsewhere: still it would have been nothing exceptional if Lycophron had ordered in his will that he be put in a handsome pottery coffin to be placed in a burial ground pertaining to his family.

ATHENIAN FUNERAL MONUMENT.

A lady is gazing upon her casket of jewels before bidding them eternal farewell. Note the admirable restraint yet pathos of the scene.

75. The Beautiful Funeral Monuments. — If the noisy funeral customs permitted to the Athenians may repel a later day observer, there can be only praise for the Athenian tombs, or rather the funeral monuments (stelce) which might be set over the urns of ashes or the actual coffins. Nearly every Athenian family has a private field which it uses for sepulchral purposes: but running outside of the city, near the Itonian Gate along the road to the Peirseus, the space to either side of the highway has been especially appropriated for this purpose. Walking hither along this " Street of the Tombs " we can make a careful survey of some of the most touching memorials of Athenian life.

The period of hot, violent grief seems now over; the mourners have settled down in their dumb sense of loss. This spirit of calm, noble resignation is what is expressed upon these monuments. All is chaste, dignified, simple. There are no labored eulogies of the deceased; no frantic expressions of sorrow; no hint (let it be also said) of any hope of reunions in the Hereafter. Sometimes there is simply a plain marble slab or pillar marked with the name of the deceased; and with even the more elaborate monuments the effort often is to concentrate, into one simple scene, the best and worthiest that was connected with the dear departed. Here is the noble mother seated in quiet dignity extending her hand in farewell to her sad but steadfast husband, while her children linger wonderingly by; here is the athlete, the young man in his pride, depicted not in the moment of weakness and death, but scraping his glorious form with his strigil, after some victorious contest in the games; here is the mounted warrior, slain before Corinth whilst battling for his country, represented in the moment of overthrowing beneath his flying charger some despairing foe. We are made to feel that these Athenians were fair and beautiful in their lives, and that in their deaths they were not unworthy. And we

marvel, and admire these monuments the more when we realize that they are not the work of master sculptors but of ordinary paid craftsmen. We turn away praising the city that could produce such noble sculpture and call it mere handicraft, and praising also the calm poise of soul, uncomforted by revealed religion, which could make these monuments common expressions of the bitterest, deepest, most vital emotions which can ever come to men. 1

1 As Von Falke (Greece and Rome, p. 141) well says of these monuments, " No skeleton,

no scythe, no hour-glass is in them to bring a shudder to the beholder. As they [the departed] were in life, mother and daughter, husband and wife, parents and children, here they are represented together, sitting or standing, clasping each other's hands and looking at one another with love and sympathy as if it were their customary affectionate intercourse. What the stone perpetuates is the love and happiness they enjoyed together, while yet they rejoiced in life and the light of day."

CHAPTER XII. TRADE, MANUFACTURES, AND BANKING.

76. The Commercial Importance of Athens. — While the funeral mourners are wending their slow way homeward we have time to examine certain phases of Athenian life at which we have previously glanced, then ignored. Certain it is, most "noble and good" gentlemen delight to be considered persons of polite uncommercial leisure; equally certain it is that a good income is about as desirable in Athens as anywhere else, and many a stately "Eupatrid," who seems to spend his whole time in dignified walks, discoursing on politics or philosophy, is really keenly interested in trades, factories, or farms, of which his less nobly born stewards have the active management. Indeed one of the prime reasons for Athenian greatness is the fact that Athens is the richest and greatest commercial city of Continental Hellas, with only Corinth as a not formidable rival. 1

To understand the full extent of Athenian commercial prosperity we must visit the Peiraeus, yet in the main city itself will be found almost enough examples of the chief kinds of economic activity.

77. The Manufacturing Activities of Athens. — Attica is the seat of much manufacturing. Go to the suburbs: everywhere is the rank odor of the tanneries; down at the

1 Syracuse in distant Sicily was possibly superior to Athens in commerce and economic prosperity, although incomparably behind her in the empire of the arts and literature.

A Day in Old Athens

harbors are innumerable ship carpenters and sail and tackle makers, busy in the shipyards; from almost every part of the city comes the clang of hammer and anvil where hardware of all kinds is being wrought in the smithies ; and finally the pottery makers are so numerous as to require special mention hereafter. But no list of all the manufacturing activities is here possible; enough that practically every known industry is represented in Athens, and the

AT THE SMITHY.

"industrial" class is large. 1 A very large proportion of the industrial laborers are slaves, but by no means all. A good many are real Athenian citizens; a still larger proportion are " metics" (resident foreigners without political rights). The competition of slave labor, however, tends to keep wages very low. An unskilled laborer will have to be content with his 3 obols (9 cents) per day; but a trained workman will demand a drachma (18 cents) or even more. There are no labor unions or trade guilds. A son usually,

1 For a very suggestive list of the numerous kinds of Greek industries (practically all of which would be represented in Athens) see H. J. Edwards, in Whibley's Companion to Greek Studies, p. 431.

though not invariably, follows his father's profession. Each industry and line of work tends to have its own little street or alley, preferably leading off the Agora. "The Street of the Marble Workers," the "Street of the Box Makers," and notably the " Street of the Potters " contain nearly all the workshops of a given kind. Probably you can find no others in the city. Prices are regulated by custom and competition; in case any master artisan is suspected of " enhancing " the price of a needful commodity, or his shady business methods seem dangerous to the public, there is no hesitation in invoking an old law or passing a new one in the Assembly to bring him to account.

Manufacturers are theoretically under a social ban, and indeed yonder petty shoemaker, who, with his two apprentices, first makes up his cheap sandals, then sells them over the low counter before his own shop, is very far from being a " leisurely " member of the " noble and the good." But he who, like the late Lycophron, owns a furniture factory employing nigh threescore slaves, can be sure of lying down on his couch at a dinner party among the very best; for, as in twentieth century England, even manufacture and " trade," if on a sufficiently large scale, cover a multitude of social sins. 1

78. The Commerce of Athens. — Part of Athenian wealth comes from the busy factories, great and small, which seem everywhere; still more riches come in by the great commerce which will be found centered at the Peiraeus. Here is the spacious Deigma, a kind of exchange-house where ship masters can lay out samples of their wares on display,

1 Plato, probably echoing thoughtful Greek opinion, considered it bad for manufacturers to be either too wealthy or too poor; thus a potter getting too rich will neglect his art, and grow idle; if, however, he cannot afford proper tools, he will manufacture inferior wares, and his sons will be even worse workmen than he. Such comment obviously comes from a society where most industrial life is on a small scale.

and sell to the important wholesalers, who will transmit to the petty shopkeepers and the " ultimate consumer." 1

There are certain articles of which various districts make a specialty, and which Athens is constantly importing: Boeotia sends chariots; Thessaly, easy chairs; Chios and Miletos, bedding; and Miletos, especially, very fine woolens. Greece in general looks to Syria and Arabia for the much-esteemed spices and perfumes; to Egypt for papyri for the book rolls; to Babylonia for carpets. To discuss the whole problem of Athenian commerce would require a book in itself; but certain main facts stand out clearly. One is that Attica herself has extremely few natural products to export — only her olive oil, her Hymettus honey, and her magnificent marbles — dazzling white from Pentelicos, gray from Hymettus, blue or black from Eleusis. Again we soon notice the great part which grain plays in Athenian commerce. Attica raises such a small proportion of the necessary breadstuffs, and so serious is the crisis created by any shortage, that all kinds of measures are employed to compel a steady flow of grain from the Black Sea ports into the Peirseus. Here is a law which Demosthenes quotes to us: —

"It shall not be lawful for any Athenian or any metic in Attica, or any person under their control [i.e. slave or freedman] to lend out money on a ship which is not commissioned to bring grain to Athens."

A second law, even more drastic, forbids any such person to transport grain to any harbor but the Peirseus. The penalties for evading these laws are terrific. At set intervals also the Public Assembly (Ecclesia) is in duty bound

1 Of course a very large proportion of Greek manufactured wares were never exported, but were sold direct by the manufacturer to the consumer himself. This had various disadvantages ; but there was this large gain: only one profit was necessary to be added to the mere cost of production. This aided to make Greece (from a modern standpoint) a paradise of low prices.

to consider the whole state of the grain trade: while the dealers in grain who seem to be cornering the market, and forcing up the price of bread, are liable to prompt and disastrous prosecution.

79. The Adventurous Merchant Skippers. — Foreign trade at Athens is fairly well systematized, but it still partakes of the nature of an adventure. The name for "skipper" (naukleros) is often used interchangeably for " merchant." Nearly all commerce is by sea, for land routes are usually slow, unsafe, and inconvenient 1 ; the average foreign trader is also a shipowner, probably too the actual working captain. He has no special commodity, but will handle everything which promises a profit. A war is breaking out in Paphlagonia. Away he sails thither with a cargo of good Athenian shields, swords, and lances. He loads up in that barbarous but fertile country with grain; but leaves enough room in his hold for some hundred skins of choice wine which he takes aboard at Chios. The grain and wine are disembarked at the Peirseus. Hardly are they ashore ere rumor tells him that salt herring 2 are abundant and especially cheap at Corcyra; and off he goes for a return cargo thereof, just lingering long enough to get on a lading of Athenian olive oil.

80. Athenian Money-changers and Bankers. — An important factor in the commerce of Athens is the " Money-changer." There is no one fixed standard of coinage for Greece, let alone the Barbarian world. Athens strikes its money on a standard which has very wide acceptance, but Corinth has another standard, and a great deal of business is also transacted in Persian gold darics. The result is that at the Peirseus

1 Naturally there was a safe land route from Athens across the Isthmus to Corinth and thence to Sparta or towards Elis; again, there would be fair roads into Bceotia.

and near the Agora are a number of little " tables " where alert individuals, with strong boxes beside them, are ready to sell foreign coins to would-be travelers, or exchange darics for Attic drachmae, against a pretty favorable commission.

This was the beginning of the Athenian banker ; but from being a mere exchanger he has often passed far beyond, to become a real master of credit and capital. There are several of these highly important gentlemen who now have a business and fortune equal to that of the famous Pasion, who died in 370 B.C. While the firm of Pasion and Company was at its height, the proprietor derived a net income of at least 100 minse (over $1800) per year from his banking; and more than half as much extra from a shield factory. 1

81. A Large Banking Establishment.—Enter now the "tables" of Nicanor. The owner is a metic; perhaps he claims to come from Rhodes, but the shrewd cast of his eye and the dark hue of his skin gives a suggestion of the Syrian about him. In his open office a dozen young half-naked clerks are seated on low chairs — each with his tablets spread out upon his knees laboriously computing long sums. 2 The proprietor himself acts as the cashier. He has not neglected the exchange of foreign moneys; but that is a mere incidental. His first visitor this morning presents a kind of letter of credit from a correspondent in Syracuse calling for one hundred drachmae. "Your voucher?" asks Nicanor. The stranger produces the half of a coin broken in two across the

middle. The proprietor draws a similar half

1 These sums seem absurdly small for a great money magnate, but the very high purchasing power of money in Athens must be borne in mind. We know a good deal about Pasion and his business from the speeches which Demosthenes composed in the litigation which arose over his estate.

a Without the Arabic system of numerals, elaborate bookkeeping surely presented a sober face to the Greeks. Their method of numeration was very much like that with the so-called Roman numerals.

coin from a chest. The parts match exactly, and the money is paid on the spot. The next coiner is an old acquaintance, a man of wealth and reputation; he is followed by two slaves bearing a heavy talent of coined silver which he wishes the banker to place for him on an advantageous loan, against a due commission. The third visitor is a well-born but fast and idle young man who is squandering his patrimony on flute girls and chariot horses. He wishes an advance of ten minae, and it is given him—against the mortgage of a house, at the ruinous interest of 36 per cent, for such prodigals are perfectly fair prey. Another visitor is a careful and competent ship merchant who is fitting for a voyage to Crete, and who requires a loan to buy his return cargo. Ordinary interest, well secured, is 18 per cent, but a sea voyage, even at the calmest season, is counted extra hazardous. The skipper must pay 24 per cent at least. A poor tradesman also appears to raise a trifle by pawning two silver cups; and an unlucky farmer, who cannot meet his loan, persuades the banker to extend the time "just until the next moon " x — of course at an unmerciful compounding of interest.

82. Drawbacks to the Banking Business. — Nicanor has no paper money to handle, no stocks, no bonds, — and the line between legitimate interest and scandalous usury is by no means clearly drawn. There is at least one good excuse for demanding high interest. It is notoriously hard to collect bad debts. Many and many a clever debtor has persuaded an Athenian jury that all taking of interest is somewhat immoral, and the banker has lost at least his interest, sometimes too his principal. So long as this is the case, a banker's career has its drawbacks; and Demosthenes in a

1 " Watching the moon," i.e. the end of the month when the debts become due, appears to have been the melancholy recreation of many Athenian debtors. See Aristophanes's Clouds, 1. 18.

recent speech has commended the choice by Pasion's son of a factory worth 60 minae per year, instead of his father's banking business worth nominally 100. The former was so much more secure than an income depending on " other people's money!"

Finally it must be said that while Nicanor and Pasion have been honorable and justly esteemed men, many of their colleagues have been rogues. Many a " table " has been closed very suddenly, when its owner absconded, or collapsed in bankruptcy, and the unlucky depositors and creditors have been left penniless, during the "rearrangement of the tables," as the euphemism goes.

83. The Pottery of Athens. — There is one other form of economic activity in Athens which deserves our especial notice, different as it is from the bankers' tables, — the manufacture of earthen vases. A long time might be spent investigating the subject; here there is room only for a hasty glance. For more than two hundred years Attica has been supplying the world with a pottery which is in some respects superior to any that has gone before, and also (all things considered) to any that will follow, through nigh two and a half millenniums. The articles are primarily tall vases and urns, some for mere ornament or for religious purposes,—some for very humble household utility; however, besides the regular vases there is a great variety of dishes,

plates, pitchers, bowls, and cups all of the same general pattern, — a smooth, black glaze 1 covered with figures in the delicate red of the unglazed clay. At first the figures had been in black and the background in red, but by about 500 B.C. the superiority of the black backgrounds had been fully realized and the process perfected. For a long time Athens had a monopoly of this beautiful earthen ware, but now in 360 B.C. there are creditable manufactories in

1 Sometimes this glaze tended to a rich olive green or deep brown.

other cities, and especially in the Greek towns of Southern Italy. The Athenian industry is, however, still considerable ; in fifty places up and down the city, but particularly in the busy quarter of the Ceramicus, the potters' wheels are whirling, and the glazers are adding the elegant patterns.

84. Athenian Pottery an Expression of the Greek Sense of Beauty. — Athens is proud of her traditions of naval and military glory; of the commerce of the Peirseus; of her free laws and constitution; of her sculptured temples, her poets, her rhetoricians and philosophers. Almost equally well might she be proud of her vases. They are not made — let us bear clearly in mind — by avowed artists, servants of the Muses and of the Beautiful; they are the regular commercial products of work-a-day craftsmen. But what craftsmen! In the first place, they have given to every vase and dish a marvelous individuality. There seems to be absolutely no duplication of patterns. 1 Again, since these vases are made for Greeks, they must — no matter how humble and commonplace their use   be made beautiful — elegantly shaped, well glazed, and well painted: otherwise, no matter how cheap, they will never find a market.

The process of manufacture is simple, yet it needs a masterly touch. After the potter has finished his work at the wheel and while the clay is still soft, the decorator makes his rough design with a blunt-pointed stylus. A line of black glaze is painted around each figure. Then the black background is freely filled in, and the details within the figures are added. A surprisingly small number of deft lines are needed to bring out the whole picture. 2 Sometimes the

1 It is asserted that of the many thousands of extant Greek vases that crowd the shelves of modern museums, there are nowhere two patterns exactly alike.

8 In this respect the Greek vase paintings can compete with the best work in the Japanese prints.

glaze is thinned out to a pale brown, to help in the drawing of the interior contours. When the design is completed, we have an amount of life and expression which with the best potters is little short of startling. The subjects treated are infinite, as many as are the possible phases of Greek life. Scenes in the home and on the farm; the boys and their masters at school; the warriors, the merchants, the priests sacrificing, the young gallants serenading a sweetheart ; all the tales, in short, of poet-lore and mythology, — time would fail to list one tenth of them. Fairly we can assert that were all the books and formal inscriptions about the Athenians to be blotted out, these vase paintings, almost photographs one might say, of Athenian daily life, would give us back a very wide knowledge of the habits of the men in the city of Athena.

The potters are justly proud of their work; often they do not hesitate to add their signatures, and in this way later ages can name the " craftsmen " who have transmitted to them these objects of abiding beauty. The designers also are accommodating enough to add descriptive legends of the scenes which they depict, — Achilles, Hercules, Theseus, and all the other heroes are carefully named, usually with the words written above or beside them.

The pottery of Athens, then, is truly Athenian; that is to say, it is genuinely elegant, ornamental, simple, and distinctive. The best of these great vases and mixing bowls are works of art no less than the sculptures of Phidias upon the Parthenon.

CHAPTER XIII. THE ARMED FORCES OF ATHENS.

85. Military Life at Athens. — Hitherto we have seen almost nothing save the peaceful civic side of Athenian life, but it is a cardinal error to suppose that art, philosophy, farming, manufacturing, commerce, and bloodless home politics sum up the whole of the activities of Attica. Athens is no longer the great imperial state she was in the days of Pericles, but she is still one of the greatest military powers in Greece, 1 and on her present armed strength rests a large share of her prestige and prosperity. Her fleet, which is still her particular boast, must of course be seen at the Peiraeus; but as we go about the streets of the main city we notice many men, who apparently had recently entered their house doors as plain, harmless citizens, now emerging, clad in all the warrior's bravery, and hastening towards one of the gates. Evidently a review is to be held of part of the citizen army of Athens. If we wish, we can follow and learn much of the Greek system of warfare in general and of the Athenian army in particular.

Even at the present day, when there is plenty of complaint that Athenians are not willing to imitate the sturdy campaigning of their fathers, the citizens seem always at war, or getting ready for it. Every citizen, physically fit, is liable to military service from his eighteenth to his sixtieth year. To make efficient soldiers is really the main

1 Of course the greatest military power of Greece had been Sparta until 371 B.C., when the battle of Leuctra made Thebes temporarily " the first land power."

end of the constant physical exercise. If a young man takes pride in his hard and fit body, if he flings spears in the stadium, and learns to race in full armor, if he goes on long marches in the hot sun, if he sleeps on the open hillside, or lies on a bed of rushes watching the moon rise over the sea, — it is all to prepare himself for a worthy part in the " big day " when Athens will confront some old or new enemy on the battlefield. A great deal of the conversation among the younger men is surely not about Platonic ideals, Demosthenes's last political speech, nor the best fighting cocks; it is about spears, shield-straps, camping ground, rations, ambuscades, or the problems of naval warfare.

It is alleged with some show of justice that by this time Athenians are so enamored with the pleasures of peaceful life that they prefer to pay money for mercenary troops rather than serve themselves on distant expeditions; and certain it is that there are plenty of Arcadians, Thracians, and others, from the nations which supply the bulk of the mercenaries, always in Athenian pay in the outlying garrisons. Still the old military tradition and organization for the citizens is kept up, and half a generation later, when the freedom of Athens is blasted before Philip the Macedonian at Chaeroneia, it will be shown that if the Athenian militia does not know how to conquer, it at least knows how to die. So we gladly follow to the review, and gather our information.

86. The Organization of the Athenian Army. — After a young ephebus has finished his two years of service in the garrisons he returns home subject to call at the hour of need. When there is necessity to make up an army, enough men are summoned to meet the required number and no more. Thus for a small force only the eligibles between say twenty and twenty-four years of age would be summoned; but in a crisis all the citizens are levied up to

The Armed Forces of Athens 103

the very gray beards. The levy is conducted by the ten Strategi (at once < generals, "admirals/ and«war ministers'), who control the whole armed power of Athens. The recruits summoned have to come with three days' rations to the rendezvous, usually to the Lyceum wrestling ground just outside the city. In case of a general levy the old men are expected to form merely a home guard for the walls; the young men must be ready for hard service over seas.

The organization of the Athenian army is very simple; each of the ten Attic tribes sends its own special battalion or taxis, which is large or small according to the total size of the levy. 1

These taxeis are subdivided into companies or lochoi, of about an average of 100 men each. The taxeis are each under a tribe-colonel (taxiarch), and each company under its captain (locharch). The ten strategi theoretically command the whole army together, but since bitter experience teaches that ten generals are usually nine too many, a special decree of the people often entrusts the supreme command of a force to one commander, or at most to not over three. The other strategi must conduct other expeditions, or busy themselves with their multifarious home duties.

87. **The Hoplites and the Light Troops.** — The unit of the Athenian citizen army, like practically all Greek armies, is the heavy armed infantry soldier, the hoplite. An army of " three thousand men " is often an army of so many hop-lites, unless there is specific statement to the contrary. But really it is of six thousand men, to be entirely accurate: for along with every hoplite goes an attendant, a " light-armed man," either a poor citizen who cannot afford a regular suit of armor, 2 or possibly a trusted slave. These

1 Thus if 3000 men were called out, the average taxis would be 300 strong; but if 6000, then 600.

2 The hoplite's panoply (see description later) was sufficiently expensive to imply that its owner was at least a man in tolerable circumstances.

" light-armed men" carry the hoplites' shields until the battle, and most of the baggage. They have javelins, and sometimes slings and bows. They act as skirmishers before the actual battle: and while the hoplites are in the real death-grip they harass the foe as they can, and guard the camp. When the fight is done they do their best to cover the retreat, or slaughter the flying foe if their own hoplites are victorious.

88. **The Cavalry and the Peltasts.** — There are certain divisions of the army besides the hoplites and this somewhat ineffective light infantry. There is a cavalry corps of 1000. Wealthy young Athenians are proud to volunteer therein; it is a sign of wealth to be able to provide your war horse. The cavalry too is given the place of honor in the great religious processions; and there is plenty of chance for exciting scouting service on the campaign. Again, the cavalry service has something to commend it in that it is accounted much safer than the infantry! 1 The cavalry is, however, a rather feeble fighting instrument. Greek riders have no saddles and no stirrups. They are merely mounted on thin horse pads, and it is very hard to grip the horse with the knees tightly enough to keep from being upset ignominiously while wielding the spear. The best use for the cavalry perhaps is for the riders to take a sheaf of javelins, ride up and discharge them at the foe as skirmishers, then fall back behind the hoplites; though after the battle the horsemen will have plenty to do in the retreat or the pursuit.

The Athenians have of course the Scythian police archers to send into any battle near Athens; they can also hire

1 Greeks could seldom have been brought to imitate the reckless medieval cavaliers. The example of Leonidas at Thermopylae was more commended than imitated. Outside of Sparta at least, few Greeks would have hesitated to flee from a battlefield, when the day (despite their proper exertions) had been wholly lost.

The Armed Forces of Athens 105

mercenary archers from Crete, but the Greek bows are relatively feeble, only three or four feet long —by no means equal to the terrible yew bows which will win glory for England in the Middle Ages. There has also come into vogue, especially since the Peloponnesian war, an improved kind of light-javelin-men, — the "Peltasts," — with small shields, and light armor, but with extra long lances. In recent warfare this type of soldier, carefully trained and agile, has been known to defeat bodies of the old-style over-encumbered hoplites. 1 Nevertheless, most veteran soldiers still believe that the heavy infantryman is everything, and the backbone of nearly every

Greek army is still surely the hoplite. He will continue to be the regular fighting unit until the improved " phalanx," and the " Companion Cavalry " of Philip and Alexander of Macedon teach the captains of the world new lessons.

89. The Panoply of the Hoplite. — We have passed out one of the gates and are very likely in a convenient open space south and east of the city stretching away toward the ever visible slopes of gray Hymettus. Here is a suitable parade ground. The citizen soldiers are slipping on their helmets and tightening up their cuirasses. Trumpets blow from time to time to give orders to " fall in " among the respective lochoi and taxeis. There is plenty of time to study the arms and armor of the hoplites during these preliminaries.

A very brief glance at the average infantryman's defensive weapons tells us that to be able to march, maneuver, and fight efficiently in this armor implies that the Athenian soldier is a well-trained athlete. The whole panoply weighs many pounds. 2 The prime parts in the armor are the

1 Especially the Athenian general Iphicrates was able to cut to pieces a mora (brigade) of Spartan hoplites, in 392 B.C., by skilful use of a force of peltasts.

2 Possibly fifty or more — we have no correct means for an exact estimate.

helmet, the cuirass, the greaves, and the shield. Every able-bodied citizen of moderate means has this outfit hanging in his andronitis, and can don it at brief notice. The helmet is normally of bronze; it is cut away enough in front to leave the face visible, but sometimes a cautious individual will insist on having movable plates (which can be turned up and down) to protect the cheeks. 1 Across the top there

runs a firm metal ridge to catch any hard downright blow, and set into the ridge is a tall nodding crest either of horsehair or of bright feathers—in either case the joy and glory of the wearer.

Buckled around the soldier's body is the cuirass. It comprises a breastplate and a back piece of bronze, joined by thongs, or by straps with ~ a buckle. The metal

Below it hangs a thick fringe of stout strips of leather strengthened with bright metallic studs, and reaching halfway to the knees. From this point to the knees the legs are bare, but next come the greaves, thin pliable plates of bronze fitted to the shape of the leg, and opening at the back. They have to be slipped on, and then are fastened at knees and ankle with leathern straps.

1 The " Corinthian " type of helmets came more closely over the face, and the cheek protectors were not movable ; these helmets were much like th« closed helms of the medieval knights. The Spartans, in their contempt for danger, wore plain pointed steel caps which gave relatively little protection.

But the warrior's main protection is his shield. With a strong, large shield you can fight passing well without any regular body armor; while with the best outfit of the latter you are highly vulnerable without your shield. To know how to swing your shield so as to catch every possible blow, to know how to push and lunge with it against an enemy, to know how to knock a man down with it, if needs be, that is a good part of the soldier's education. The shield is sometimes round, but more often oval. It is about four feet by the longest diameter. It is made of several layers of heavy bull's hide, firmly corded and riveted together, and has a good metal rim and metal boss in the center. On the inside are two handles so that it can be conveniently wielded on the left arm. 1 These shields are brilliantly painted, and although the Greeks have no heraldic devices, there are all manner of badges and distinguishing marks in vogue. Thus all Theban shields are blazoned with a club; Sicyonian shields are marked with the initial " Sigma " (2), and we note that the Athenian shields are all marked Alpha (A)2

90. The Weapons of a Hoplite. — The hoplites have donned their armor. Now they assume their offensive weapons. Every man has a lance and a sword. The lance is a stout weapon with a solid wooden butt, about six feet long in all. It is really too heavy to use as a javelin. It is most effective as a pike thrust fairly into a foeman's face, or past his shield into a weak spot in his cuirass. The sword is usually kept as a reserve weapon in case the lance gets broken. It is not over 25 inches in length, making rather a huge double-edged vicious knife than a saber; but it is terrible for cut

1 Earlier Greek shields seem to have been very large and correspondingly heavy. These had only a single handle; and to aid in shifting them they were swung on straps passed over the left shoulder.

2 This last is a matter of safe inference rather than of positive information.

and thrust work at very close quarters. Simple as these weapons are, they are fearful instruments of slaughter in well-trained hands, and the average Greek has spent a considerable part of his life in being taught how to use them.

91. Infantry Maneuvers. — The final trumpets have blown, and the troops fall into their places. Each tribal taxis lines up its lochoi. The Greeks have no flags nor standards. There is a great deal of shouting by the subaltern officers, and running up and down the ranks. Presently everything is in formal array. The hoplites stand in close order, each man about two feet from the next, 1 leaving no gaps between each division from end to end of the lines. The men are set in

eight long ranks. This is the normal phalanx 2 order. Only those in front can actually lunge and strike at the enemy. The men in the rear will add to the battering force of the charge, and, crowding in closely, wedge themselves promptly to the front, when any of the first rank goes down.

It is an imposing sight when the strategos in charge of the maneuvers, a stately man in a red chlamys, gives the final word " March! "

Loud pipes begin screaming. The long lines of red, blue, and orange plumes nod fiercely together. The sun strikes fire out of thousands of brandished lance tips. The phalanx goes swinging away over the dusty parade ground, the subalterns up and down the files muttering angrily to each inapt recruit to " Keep your distance: " or " Don't advance your shield." The commandant duly orders the " Half turn:" " Left" or " Right turn:" " Formation by squares," and finally the critical " Change front to rear." If this last

1 The object would be to give each man just enough distance to let him make fair use of his lance, and yet have his shield overlap that of his neighbor.

2 The " phalanx " is sometimes spoken of as a Macedonian innovation, but Philip and Alexander simply improved upon an old Greek military formation.

maneuver is successfully accomplished, the strategos will compliment the drill sergeants; for it is notoriously difficult to turn a ponderous phalanx around and yet make it keep good order. The drilling goes on until the welcome order comes, u Ground arms!" and every perspiring soldier lets his heavy shield slip from his arm upon the ground.

92. The Preliminaries of a Greek Battle.—Later in the day, if these are happy times of peace, the whole phalanx, so bristling and formidable, will have resolved itself into its harmless units of honest citizens all streaming home for dinner.

Our curiosity of course asks how does this army act upon the campaign; what, in other words, is a typical Greek battle ? This is not hard to describe. Greek battles, until lately, have been fought according to set formulae in which there is little room for original generalship, though much for ordinary circumspection and personal valor. A battle consists in the charging together of two phalanxes of hop-lites of about equal numbers. If one army greatly overmatches the other, the weaker side will probably retire without risking a contest. With a common purpose, therefore, the respective generals will select a broad stretch of level ground for the struggle, since stony, hilly, or uneven ground will never do for the maneuvering of hoplites. The two armies, after having duly come in sight of one another, and exchanged defiances by derisive shouts, catcalls, and trumpetings, will probably each pitch its camp (protected by simple fortifications) and perhaps wait over night, that the men may be well rested and have a good dinner and breakfast. The soldiers will be duly heartened up by being told of any lucky omens of late, — how three black crows were seen on the right, and a flash of lightning on the left; and the seers and diviners with the army will, at the general's orders, repeat any hopeful oracles they can re-

member or fabricate, e.g. predicting ruin for Thebes, or victory for Athens. In the morning the soldiers have breakfast, then the lines are carefully arrayed a little beyond bowshot from the enemy, who are preparing themselves in similar fashion. Every man has his arms in order, his spear point and sword just from the whetstone, and every buckle made fast. The general (probably in sight of all the men) will cause the seers to kill a chicken, and examine its entrails. " The omens are good; the color is favorable; the gods are with us!" 1 he announces: and then, since he is a Greek among Greeks, he delivers in loud voice an harangue to as many as can hear him, setting forth the patriotic issues at stake in the battle, the call of the fatherland to its sons, the glory of brave valor, the shame of cowardice, probably ending with some practical directions about " Never edging to the right!" and exhorting his men to raise as loud a war-cry as possible, both to encourage themselves and to demoralize the enemy.

93. Joining the Battle. — The troops answer with a cheer, then join in full chorus in the " Pcean — " a fierce rousing charging-song that makes every faint-heart's blood leap faster. Another paean bellowed from the hostile ranks indicates that similar preliminaries have been disposed of there. The moment the fierce chorus ends, the general (who probably is at the post of danger and honor — the right wing) nods to his corps of pipers. The shrill flutes cut the air. The whole phalanx starts forward like one man, and the enemy seem springing to meet it. The tossing color, the flashing arms and armor, make it a sight for men and gods. If the enemy has a powerful archery force, as had the Persians at Marathon, then the phalanx is allowed to advance on the run, — for at all costs one must get

1 It may be suspected that it was very seldom the omens were allowed to be unfavorable when the general was really resolved on battle.

through the terrible zone of the arrow fire and come to grips; but if their bowmen are weak, the hoplites will be restrained, — it is better not to risk getting the phalanx disorganized. Running or marching the troops will emit a terrible roaring: either the slow deep " A! la! la! la!" or something quicker, " Eleleu I" " Eleleu I" and the flutes will blow all the while to give the time for the marching.

Closer at hand the two armies will fairly spring into unfriendly embrace. The generals have each measured his enemy's line and extended his own to match it. 1 With files of about equal depth, and well-trained men on both sides, the first stage of this death grapple is likely to be a most fearful yet indecisive pushing: the men of the front ranks pressing against each other, shield to shield, glaring out of their helmets like wild beasts against the foemen three feet away, and lunging with their lances at any opening between the hostile shields or above them. The comrades behind wedge in the front ranks closer and closer. Men are crushed to death, probably without a wound, just by this hellish impact. The shouts and yells emitted are deafening. There is an unearthly clashing of steel weapons on bronze armor. Every now and then a shrill, sharp cry tells where a soldier has been stabbed, and has gone down in the press, probably to be trampled to death instantly. In this way the two writhing, thrusting phalanxes continue to push on one another at sheer deadlock, until a cool observer might well wonder whether the battle would not end simply with mutual extermination.

1 Any sudden attempt to extend your line beyond the foe's, so as to outflank him, would probably have produced so much confusion in your own phalanx as to promise certain disaster. Of course for an inferior force to accept battle by thinning its line, to be able by extending to meet the long lines of the enemy, would involve the greatest risk of being broken through at the center. The best remedy for inferior numbers was manifestly to decline a decisive battle.

A Day in Old Athens

94. The Climax and End of the Battle. — But look away now from the center, towards the two wings. What the generals of both contending armies have feared and warned against has come to pass. Every hoplite is admirably covered by his great shield on his left side ; but his right is unprotected. It is almost impossible to resist the impulse to take a step toward the right to get under the cover of a comrade's shield. And he in turn has been edging to the right likewise. The whole army has in fact done so, and likewise the whole phalanx of the enemy. So after a quarter of an hour of brisk fighting, the two hosts, which began by joining with lines exactly facing each other, have each edged along so much that each overlaps the other on the right wing, thus :

What will happen now is easy to predict with assurance up to a certain point. The overlapping right wings will each promptly turn the left flank of their enemies, and falling upon the foe front and rear catch them almost helpless. The hoplite is an admirable soldier when standing shoulder to shoulder with his comrades facing his foe; but once beset in the rear he is so wedged in by the press that it is next to impossible for him to turn and fight effectively. Either he will be massacred as he stands or the panic will spread betimes, and simultaneously both left wings will break formation and hurry off the field in little better than flight.

Now will come the real test of discipline and deliberate valor. Both centers are holding stoutly. Everything rests on the respective victorious right wings. Either they will foolishly forget that there is still fighting elsewhere on the field, and with ill-timed huzzaing pursue the men they have just routed, make for their camp to plunder it. or worse

still, disperse to spoil the slain; or, if they can heed their general's entreaties, keep their ranks, and wheeling around come charging down on the rear of the enemy's center. If one right wing does this, while the hostile right wing has rushed off in heedless pursuit, the battle is infallibly won by the men who have kept their heads; but if both right wings turn back, then the real death grapple conies when these two sets of victors in the first phase of the contest clash together in a decisive grapple.

By this time the original phalanx formations, so orderly, and beautiful, have become utterly shattered. The field is covered by little squares or knots of striking, cursing, raging men — clashing furiously together. If there are any effective reserves, now is the time to fling them into the scale. The hitherto timorous light troops and armor bearers rush up to do what they can. Individual bravery and valor count now to the uttermost. Little by little the contest turns against one side or the other. The crucial moment comes. The losing party begins to fear itself about to be surrounded. Vain are the last exhortations of the officers to rally them. "Everyman for himself!" rings theory; and with one mad impulse the defeated hoplites rush off the field in rout. Since they have been at close grip with their enemies, and now must turn their ill-protected backs to the pursuing spears, the massacre of the defeated side is sometimes great. Yet not so great as might be imagined. Once fairly beaten, you must strip off helmet and cuirass, cast away shield and spear, and run like a hare. You have lightened yourself now decidedly. But your foe must keep his ponderous arms, otherwise he cannot master you, if he overtakes you. Therefore the vanquished can soon distance the victors unless the latter have an unusually efficient cavalry and javelin force. However, the victors are likely to enter the camp of the vanquished, and to celebrate duly that night dividing the plunder.

95. The Burial Truce and the Trophy after the Battle. — A few hours after the battle, while the victors are getting breath and refreshing themselves, a shamefaced herald, bearing his sacred wand of office, presents himself. He is from the defeated army, and comes to ask a burial truce. This is the formal confession of defeat for which the victors have been waiting. It would be gross impiety to refuse the request; and perhaps the first watch of the night is spent by detachments of both sides in burying or burning the dead.

The fates of prisoners may be various. They may be sold as slaves. If the captors are pitiless and vindictive, it is not contrary to the laws of war to put the prisoners to death in cold blood; but by the fourth century B.C. Greeks are becoming relatively humane. Most prisoners will presently be released against a reasonable ransom paid by their relatives.

The final stage of the battle is the trophy: the visible sign on the battlefield that here such-and-such a side was victorious. The limbs are lopped off a tree, and some armor captured from the foe is hung upon it. After indecisive battles sometimes both sides set up trophies; in that case a second battle is likely to settle the question. Then when the victors have recovered from their own happy demoralization, they march into the enemy's country; by burning all the farmsteads, driving off the cattle, filling up the wells, girdling the olive and fruit trees, they reduce the defeated side (that has fled to its fortified town) to desperation. If they have any prisoners, they threaten to put them to death. The result, of course, is frequently a treaty of peace in favor of the victors.

96. The Siege of Fortified Towns. — If, however, one party cannot be induced to risk an open battle; or if, despite a defeat, it allows the enemy to ravage the fields, and yet

persists in defending the walls of its town,—the war is likely to be tedious and indecisive. It is notorious that Greeks dislike hard sieges. The soldiers are the fellow townsmen of the generals. If the latter order an assault with scaling ladders and it is repulsed with bloody loss, the generals risk a prosecution when they get home for " casting away the lives of their fellow citizens." * In short, fifty men behind a stout wall and " able to throw anything " are in a position to defy an army.

The one really sure means of taking a town is to build a counter wall around it and starve it out, —a slow and very expensive, though not bloody process. Only when something very great is at stake will a Greek city-state attempt this. 2 There is always another chance, however. Almost every Greek town has a discontented faction within its walls, and many a time there will be a traitor who will betray a gate to the enemy; and then the siege will be suddenly ended in one murderous night.

97. The Introduction of New Tactics. — Greek battles are thus very simple things as a rule. It is the general who, accepting the typical conditions as he finds them, and avoiding any gross and obvious blunders, can put his men in a state of perfect fitness, physical and moral, that is likely to win the day. Of late there has come indeed a spirit of innovation. At Leuctra (371 B.C.) Epaminondas the Theban defeated the Spartans by the unheard-of device of massing a part of his hoplites fifty deep (instead of the orthodox eight or twelve) and crushing the Spartan right wing by

1 In siege warfare Oriental kings had a great advantage over Greek commanders. The former could sacrifice as many of their "slaves" as they pleased, in desperate assaults. The latter had always to bear in mind their accountability at home for any desperate and costly attack.

2 As in the siege of Potidaea (432-429 B.C.), when if Athens had failed to take the place, her hold upon her whole empire would have been jeopardized.

the sheer weight of his charge, before the rest of the line came into action at all. If the experiment had not succeeded, Epaminondas would probably have been denounced by his own countrymen as a traitor, and by the enemy as a fool, for varying from the time-honored long, " even line " phalanx; and the average general will still prefer to keep to the old methods ; then if anything happens, he at least will not be blamed for any undue rashness. Only in Macedon, King Philip II (who is just about to come to the throne) will not hesitate to study the new battle tactics of Epaminondas, and to improve upon them.

The Athenians will tell us that their citizen hoplites are a match for any soldiers in Greece, except until lately the Spartans, and now (since Leuctra) possibly the Thebans. But Corinthians, Argives, Sicyonians, they can confront most readily. They will also add, quite properly, that the army of Athens is in the main for home defense. She does not claim to be a preeminently military state. The glory of Athens has been the mastery of the sea. Our next excursion must surely be to the Peiraeus.

CHAPTER XIV. THE PEIR^US AND THE SHIPPING.

98. The "Long Walls" down to the Harbor Town. —It is some five miles from the city to the Peiraeus, and the most direct route this time lies down the long avenue laid between the Long Walls, and running almost directly southwest. 1 The ground is quite level. If we could catch glimpses beyond the walls, we would see fields, seared brown perhaps by the summer sun, and

here and there a bright-kerchiefed woman gleaning among the wheat stubble. The two walls start from Athens close together and run parallel for some distance, then they gradually diverge so as to embrace within their open angle a large part of the circumference of the Peirseus. This open space is built up with all kinds of shops, factories, and houses, usually of the less aristocratic kind. In fact, all the noxious sights and odors to be found in Athens seem tenfold multiplied as we approach the Peiraeus.

The straight highroad is swarming with traffic: clumsy wagons are bringing down marble from the mountains; other wains are headed toward Athens with lumber and bales of foreign wares. Countless donkeys laden with panniers are

1 These were the walls whereof a considerable section was thrown down by Lysander after the surrender of Athens [404 B.C.]. The demolition was done to the " music of flute girls," and was fondly thought by the victors to mean the permanent crippling of Athens, and therefore " the first day of the liberty of Greece." In 393 B c., by one of the ironies of history, Conon, an Athenian admiral, but in the service of the king of Persia, who was then at war with Sparta, appeared in the Peiraeus, and with Persian men and money rebuilt the walls amid the rejoicings of the Athenians.

being flogged along. A great deal of the carrying is done by half-naked sweating porters; for, after all, slave-flesh is almost as cheap as beast-flesh. So by degrees the two walls open away from us: before us now expands the humming port town; we catch the sniff of the salt brine, and see the tangle of spars of the multifarious shipping. Right ahead, however, dominating the whole scene, is a craggy height,—

THE TOWN OF PEIRAEUS
AND THE HARBORS OF ATHENS

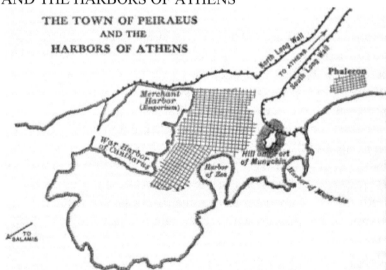

the hill of Munychia, crowned with strong fortifications, and with houses rising terrace above terrace upon its slopes. At the very summit glitters in its white marble and color work the temple of Artemis Munychia, the guardian goddess of the port town and its citadel. 1

99. Munychia and the Havens of Athens. — Making our way up a steep lane upon the northwestern slope, we pass

1 This fortress of Munychia, rather than the Acropolis in Athens, was the real citadel of Attica. It dominated the all-important harbors on which the very life of the state depended.

The Peiraeus and the Shipping 119

within the fortifications, the most formidable near Athens. A band of young ephebi of the garrison eye us as we enter; but we seem neither Spartans nor Thebans and are not molested. From a convenient crag near the temple, the whole scheme of the harbors of Athens is spread out before us, two hundred and eighty odd feet below. Behind us is the familiar plain of Athens with the city, the Acropolis, and the guardian mountains. Directly west lies the expanse of roof of the main harbor town, and then beyond is the smooth blue expanse of the " Port of the Peiraeus," the main mercantile harbor of Athens. Running straight down from Munychia, southwest, the land tapers off into a rocky promontory, entirely girt with strong fortifications. In this stretch of land are two deep round indentations. Cups of bright water they seem, communicating with the outer sea only by narrow entrances which are dominated by stout castles. Zea is the name of the more remote; the " haven" of Munychia is that which seems opening almost at our feet. These both are full of the naval shipping, whereof more hereafter. To the eastward, and stretching down the coast, is a long sandy beach whereon the blue ripples are crumbling between the black fishing boats drawn up upon the strand. This is Phaleron, the old harbor of Athens before Themis-tocles fortified the Peirceus — merely an open roadstead in fact, but still very handy for small craft, which can be hauled up promptly to escape the tempest.

100. The Glorious View from the Hill of Munychia. — These are the chief points in the harbors; but the view from Munychia is most extensive. Almost everything in sight has its legend or its story in sober history. Ten miles away to the southward rise the red rocky hills of Ægina, Athens' old island enemy; and the tawny headlands of the Argolic coast are visible yet farther across the horizon. Again, as we follow the purplish ridge of Mount Ægaleos as it runs

down the Attic coast to westward, we come to a headland, then to a belt of azure water, about a mile wide, then the reddish hills of an irregular island. Every idler on the citadel can tell us all the story. On that headland on a certain fateful morning sat Xerxes, lord of the Persians, with his sword-hands and mighty men about him and his ships before him, to look down on the naval spectacle and see how his slaves would fight. The island beyond is " holy Salamis," and in this narrow strip of water has been the battle which saved the life of Hellas. Every position in the contest seems clearly in sight, even the insignificant islet of Psyttaleia, where Aristeides had landed his men after the battle, and massacred the Persians stationed there " to cut off the Greeks who tried to escape."

The water is indescribably blue, matching the azure of the sky. Ships of all kinds under sails or oars are moving lightly over the havens and the open Saronic bay. It is a matchless spectacle — albeit very peaceful. We now descend to the Peiraeus proper and examine the merchant shipping and wharves, leaving the navy yards and the fighting triremes till later.

101. The Town of Peiraeus. — The Peiraeus has all the life of the Athenian Agora many times multiplied. Everywhere there is work and bustle. Aristophanes has long since described the impression it makes on strangers, 1 —sailors clamoring for pay, rations being served out, figureheads being burnished, men trafficking for corn, for onions, for leeks, for figs, — " wreaths, anchovies, flute girls, blackened eyes, the hammering of oars from the dock yards, the fitting of rowlocks, boatswains' pipes, fifes, and whistling." There is such confusion one can hardly analyze one's surroundings. However, we soon discover the Peiraeus has certain advantages over Athens itself. The streets are

i Acharn. 54 ff.

much wider and are quite straight, 1 crossing at right angles, unlike the crooked alleys of old Athens which seem nothing but built-up cow trails. Down at the water front of the main harbor (the "Peiraeus " harbor to distinguish it from Zea and Munychia) we find about one third, nearest the entrance passage and called the Cantharus, reserved for the use of the war navy. The remainder is turned over to the merchantmen. This section is the famous Emporium, which is such a repository of foreign wares that Isocrates boasts that

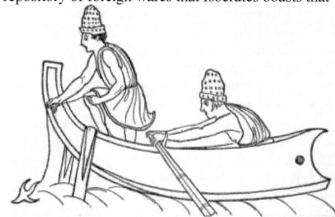

FISHERMEN.

here one can easily buy all those things which it is extremely hard to purchase anywhere else in Hellas. Along the shore run five great stoas or colonnades, all used by the traders for different purposes; — among them are the Long Stoa (Makra! Stoa'), the Deigma (see p. 93) used as a sample house by the wholesalers, and the great Corn Exchange built by Pericles. Close down near the wharves stands also a handsome and frequented temple, that of Athena Euploia (Athena, Giver of good Voyages), to whom many a shipman

1 Pericles employed the famous architect Hippodamus to lay out the Peirseus. It seems to have been arranged much like many of the newer American cities.

offers prayer ere hoisting sail, and many another comes to pay grateful vows after surviving a storm. 1 Time fails us for mentioning all the considerable temples farther back in the town. The Peirseus in short is a semi-independent community; with its shrines, its agoras, its theaters, its court rooms, and other public buildings. The population contains a very high percentage of metics, and downright Barbarians, — indeed, long-bearded Babylonians, clean bronze Egyptians, grinning Ethiopians, never awaken the least comment, they are so familiar.

102. The Merchant Shipping.—We can now cast more particular eyes upon the shipping. Every possible type is represented. The fishing craft just now pulling in with loads of shining tunnies caught near ^Egina are of course merely broad open boats, with only a single dirty orange sail swinging in the lagging breeze. Such vessels indeed depend most of the time upon their long oars. Also just now there goes across the glassy surface of the harbor a slim graceful rowing craft, pulling eight swiftly plying oars to a side. She is a Lembus: probably the private cutter of the commandant of the port. Generally speaking, however, we soon find that all the larger Greek ships are divided into two categories, the "long ships" and the "round ships." The former depend mainly on oars and are for war; the latter trust chiefly to sail power and are for cargo. The craft in the merchant haven are of course nearly all of this last description.

Greeks are clever sailors. They never feel really happy at a great distance from the sea which so penetrates their little country; nevertheless, they have not made all the progress in navigation which, considering the natural ingenuity of the race, might well be expected. The prime difficulty is that Greek ships very seldom have comfortable cabins.

1 There seems to have been still another precinct, sacred to "Zeus and Athena the Preservers," where it was very proper to offer thanksgivings after a safe voyage.

The Peirseus and the Shipping 123

The men expect to sleep on shore every night possible. Only in a great emergency, or when crossing an exceptionally wide gnlf or channel, 1 can a captain expect the average crew to forego the privilege of a warm supper and bivouac upon the strand. This means (since safe anchorages are by no means everywhere) the ships must be so shallow and light they can often be hauled up upon the beach. Even with a pretty large crew, therefore, the limit to a manageable ship is soon reached; and during the whole of the winter season all long-distance voyaging has to be suspended ; while, even in summer, nine sailors out of ten hug close to the land, despite the fact that often the distance of a voyage is thereby doubled.

However, the ships at Peirseus, if not large in size, are numerous enough. Some are simply big open boats with details elaborated. They have a small forecastle and poop built over, but the cargo in the hold is exposed to all wind and weather. The propulsion comes from a single unwieldy square sail swinging on a long yard the whole length of the vessel. Other ships are more completely decked, and depend on two square sails in the place of one. A few, however, are real "deep sea" vessels — completely decked, with two or even three masts ; with cabins of tolerable size, and forward and aft curious projections, like turrets, — the use whereof is by no means obvious, but we soon gather that pirates still abound on the distant seas, and that these turrets are useful when it comes to repelling boarders. The very biggest of these craft run up to 250 gross tons (later day register), 2 although with these ponderous defense-works they seem considerably larger. The average of the ships, however, will reckon only 30 to 40 tons or even smaller. It is really a mistake, any garrulous sailor will tell us, to build merchant ships much

1 For example, the trip from Crete to Cyrene—which would be demanded first, before coasting along to Egypt.

2 The Greeks reckoned their ships by their capacity in talents (= about 60 IDS.), e.g. a ship of 500 talents, of 2000, or (among the largest) 10,000.

bigger. It is impossible to make sailing vessels of the Greek model and rig sail very close to the wind; and in every contrary breeze or calm, recourse must be had to the huge oars piled up along the gunwales. Obviously it is weary work propelling a large ship with oars unless you have a huge and expensive crew, — far better then to keep to the smaller

103. The Three War Harbors and the Ship Houses. — Many other points about these " round ships " interest us; but such matters they share with the men-of-war, and our inspection has now brought us to the navy yard. There are strictly three separate navy yards, one at each of the harbors of Munychia, Zea, and Cantharus, for the naval strength of Athens is so great that it is impossible to concentrate the entire fleet at one harbor. Each of these establishments is protected by having two strong battlements or breakwaters built out, nearly closing the respective harbor entrances. At the end of each breakwater is a tower with parapets for archers, and capstans for dragging a huge chain across the harbor mouth, thus effectively sealing the entrance to any foe. 1 The Zea haven has really the greatest warship capacity, but the Cantharus is a good type for the three. 2 As we approach it from the merchant haven, we see the shelving shore closely lined with curious structures which do not easily explain themselves. There are a vast number of dirty, shelving roofs, slightly tilted upward towards the land side, and set at right angles to the water's edge. They are each about 150 feet long, some 25 feet wide, about 20 feet high, and are set up side by side with no passage between.

1 Ancient harbors were much harder to defend than modern ones, because there was no long-range artillery to prevent an enemy from thrusting into an open haven among defenseless shipping.

2 Zea had accommodation for 196 triremes, Munychia, 82, and the Cantharus, 94.

On close inspection we discover these are ship houses. Under each of the roofs is accommodated the long slim hull of a trireme, kept safe from sea and weather until the time of need, when a few minutes' work at a tackle and capstan will send it down into harbor, ready to tow beside a wharf for outfitting.

104. The Great Naval Arsenal. — The ship houses are not the only large structures at the navy yard. Here is also the great naval arsenal, a huge roofed structure open at the sides and entirely exposed to public inspection. Here between the lines of supporting columns can be seen stacked up the staple requisites for the ships,—great ropes, sail boxes, anchors, oars, etc. Everybody in Athens is welcome to enter and assure himself that the fleet can be outfitted at a minute's notice 1 ; and at ail times crews of half-naked, weather-beaten sailors are rushing hither and yon, carrying or removing supplies to and from the wharves where their ships are lying.

105. An Athenian Trier arch. —Among this unaristocratic crowd we observe a dignified old gentleman with an immaculate himation and a long polished cane. Obsequious clerks and sailing masters are hanging about him for his orders; it is easy to see that he is a trierarch —one of the wealthiest citizens on whom it fell, in turn, at set intervals, to provide the less essential parts of a trireme's outfit, and at least part of the pay for the crew for one year, and to be generally responsible for the efficiency and upkeep of the vessel. 2 This is a year of peace, and the patriotic pressure

1 This arsenal was replaced a little later than the hypothetical time of this narrative by one designed by the famous architect, Philo. It was extremely elegant as well as commodious, with handsome columns, tiled roofs, etc. In 360 B.C., however, the arsenal seems to have been a strictly utilitarian structure.

2 Just how much of the rigging and what fraction of the pay of the crew the government provided is by no means clear from our evidence.

to spend as much on your warship as possible is not so great as sometimes; still Eustathius, the magnate in question, knows that he will be bitterly criticised (nay, perhaps prosecuted in the courts) if he does not do " the generous thing." He is therefore ordering an extra handsome figurehead; promising a bonus to the rowing master if he can get his hands to row in better rhythm than the ordinary crew; and directing that wine of superior quality be sent aboard for the men. 1 It will be an anxious year in any case for Eustathius. He has ill wishers who will watch carefully to see if the vessel fails to make a creditable record for herself during the year, and whether she is returned to the ship house or to the next trierarch in a state of good repair. If the craft does not then appear seaworthy, her last outfitter may be called upon to rebuild her completely, a matter which will eat up something like a talent. Public service therefore does not provide beds of roses for the rich men of Athens.

Eustathius goes away towards one of the wharves, where his trireme, the Invincible, is moored with her crew aboard her. Let us examine a typical Athenian warship.

106. The Evolution of the Trireme.—The genesis of the trireme was the old pentaconter ("fifty-oar ship") which, in its prime features, was simply a long, narrow, open hull, with slightly raised prow and stern cabins, pulling twenty-five oars to a side. There are a few pentaconters still in existence, though the great naval powers have long since scorned them. It was a good while before the battle of Salamis that the Greek sea warriors began to feel the need

It is certain that a public-spirited and lavish trierarch could almost ruin himself (unless very wealthy) during the year he was responsible for the

1 According to various passages in Demosthenes, the cost of a trierarchy for a year varied between 40 minae (say $540) and a talent (about $1000), very large sums for Athenians. The question of the amount of time spent in active service in foreign waters would of course do much to determine the outlay.

of larger warships. It was impossible to continue the simple scheme of the penteconter. To get more oars all on one tier you must make a longer boat, but you could not increase the beam, for, if you did, the whole craft would get so heavy that it would not row rapidly; and the penteconter was already so long in relation to its beam as to be somewhat unsafe. A device was needed to get more oars into the water without increasing the length over much. The

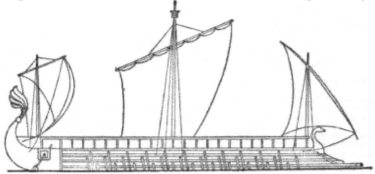

AN ATHENIAN TRIREME.

The scheme for the sails is conjectural, and no attempt is made to show the exact number of oars.

result was the bireme (two-banker) which was speedily replaced by the still more efficient trireme (three-banker), the standard battleship of all the Greek navies. 1

107. The Hull of a Trireme. —The Invincible has a hull of fir strengthened by a solid oak keel, very essential if she is to be hauled up frequently. Her hull is painted black, but there is abundance of scarlet, bright blue, and gilding upon her prow, stern, and upper works. The slim hull itself is about 140 feet long, 14 feet wide, and rides the harbor so

1 By the end of the fourth century B.C. vessels with four and five banks of oars (quadriremes and quinqueremes) had become the regular fighting ships, but they differed probably only in size, not in principle, from the trireme.

lightly as to show that it draws very little water; for the warship, even more perhaps than the merchantman, is built on the theory that her crew must drag her up upon the beach almost every night.

While we study the vessel we are soon told that, although triremes have been in general use since, say, 500 B.C., nevertheless the ships that fought at Salamis were decidedly simpler affairs than those of three generations later. In those old "aphract" vessels the upper tier of rowers had to sit exposed on their benches with no real protection from the enemy's darts ; but in the new " cataphract" ships like the Invincible there is a stout solid bulwark built up to shield the oarsmen from hostile sight and missiles alike. All this makes the ships of Demosthenes's day much handsomer, taller affairs than their predecessors which Themis-tocles commanded; nevertheless the old and the new triremes have most essentials in common. The day is far off when a battleship twenty years old will be called " hopelessly obsolete " by the naval critics. 1

The upper deck of the trireme is about eleven feet above the harbor waves, but the lowest oar holes are raised barely three feet. Into the intervening space the whole complicated rowing apparatus has to be crammed with a good deal of ingenuity. Running along two thirds of the length of thfe hull nearly the whole interior of the vessel is filled with a series of seats and foot rests rising in sets of three. Each man has a bench and a kind of stool beneath him, and sits close to a porthole. The feet of the lowest rower are near the level of the water line; swinging two feet above him and only a little behind him is his comrade of the second tier; higher and behind in turn is he of the third. 2 Run-

1 There is some reason for believing that an Athenian trireme was kept in service for many years, with only incidental repairs, and then could still be counted as fit to take her place in the line of battle.

a The exact system by which these oar benches were arranged, the crew taught to swing together (despite the inequalities in the length of their

ning down the center of the ship on either side of these complicated benches is a broad, central gangway, just under the upper deck. Here the supernumeraries will take refuge from the darts in battle, and here the regular rowers will have to do most of their eating, resting, and sleeping when they are not actually on the benches or on shore.

108. The Rowers' Benches of a Trireme.—With her full complement of rowers the benches of the Invincible fairly swarm with life. There are 62 rowers to the upper tier \'7bthranites), 58 for the middle tier (zygites), and 54 for the lower (thalamites), each man with his own individual oar. The thranites with the longest oars (full 13 feet 6 inches) have the hardest pull and the largest pay, but not one of the 174 oarsmen holds a sinecure. In ordinary cruising, to be sure, the trireme will make use of her sails, to help out a single bank of oars which must be kept going almost all the time. Even then it is weary work to break your back for a couple of hours taking your turn on the benches. But in battle the trireme almost never uses sails. She becomes a vast, many-footed monster, flying over the foam ; and the pace of the three oar banks, swinging together, becomes maddening. Behind their bulwarks the rowers can see little of what is passing. Everything is dependent upon their rowing together in absolute rhythm come what may, and giving instant obedience to orders. The trireme is in one sense like a latter-day steamer in her methods of propulsion; but the driving force is 174 straining, panting humans, not insensate water vapor and steel.

109 . The Cabins, Rigging, and Ram of a Trireme. — Forward and aft of the rowers' benches and the great central gangway are the fore and stern cabins. They furnish something akin to tolerable accommodations for the officers and a favored

oars), and several other like problems connected with the trireme, have received no satisfactory solution by modern investigators.

fraction of the crew. Above the forecastle rises a carved proudly curving prow, and just abaft it are high bulwarks to guard the javelin men when at close quarters with the foe. There is also on either side of the prow a huge red or orange "eye" painted around the hawse holes for the anchors. Above the stern cabin is the narrow deck reserved for the pilot, the " governor " of the ship, who will control the whole trireme with a touch now on one, now on the other, of the huge steering paddles which swing at the sides near the stern. Within the stern cabin itself is the little altar, sacred to the god or goddess to whom the vessel is dedicated, and on which incense will be burned before starting on a long cruise and before going into battle. Two masts rise above the deck, a tall mainmast nearly amidships, and a much smaller mast well forward. On each of these a square sail (red, orange, blue, or even, with gala ships, purple) will be swung from a long yard, while the vessel is cruising; but it is useless to set sails in battle. One could never turn the ship quickly enough to complete the maneuvers. The sails and yards will ordinarily be sent ashore as the first measure when the admiral signals " clear ship for action." We have now examined all of the Invincible except her main weapon, — her beak; for the trireme is really herself one tremendous missile to be flung by the well-trained rowers at the ill-starred foe. Projecting well in front of the prow and close to the water line are three heavy metal spurs serrated one above the other, somewhat thus 1 :

1 Probably at Salamis and in the earlier Athenian navy the ram had been composed of a single long, tapering beak.

Let this fang once crash against a foeman's broadside, and his timbers are crushed in like eggshells.

110. The Officers and Crew of a Trireme. — So much for the Invincible herself, but obviously she is a helpless thing without an efficient crew. The life of an oarsman is far from luxurious, but the pay seems to be enough to induce a goodly number of thetes (the poorest class of the Athenian citizens) to accept service, and the rest can be supplied by hired metics or any kind of foreign nondescript who can be brought into discipline. The rowers are of course the real heart and soul of the trireme; but they are useless without proper training. Indeed it was the superior discipline of the Athenian crews which in the days of Themistocles and Pericles gave Athens the supremacy of the seas. The nominal, and sometimes actual, commander of the trireme is her trierarch; but obviously a cultivated old gentleman like Eustathius is no man to manage the ship in a sea fight. He will name some deputy, perhaps a stout young friend or a son, for the real naval work. Even he may not possess great experience. The real commander of the Invincible is the "governor" (kybernates), a gnarled old seaman, who has spent all his life upon the water. Nominally his main duty is to act as pilot, but actually he is in charge of the whole ship; and in battle the trierarch (if aboard) will be very glad to obey all his " suggestions." Next to the " governor " there is the proireus, another experienced sailor who will have especial charge of the forecastle in battle. Next in turn are two " oar-masters" (toixarchoi), who are each responsible for the discipline and working of one of the long rowers' benches; and following in grade, though highly important, are the Meustes, and the trieraules, who, by voice and by flute respectively, will give the time and if needs be encouragement to the rowers. These are all the regular officers, but naturally for handling the sails and anchors some common

sailors are desirable. The Invincible carries 17 of these. She also has 10 marines (epibatce), men trained to tight in hop-lites* armor and to repel boarders. The Persian ships at Sal-amis carried 30 such warriors, and often various Greek admirals have crowded their decks with these heavy marines; but the true Athenian sea warrior disdains them. Given a good helmsman and well-trained rowers, and you can sink your opponent with your ram, while he is clumsily trying to board you. Expert opinion considers the epibatce somewhat superfluous, and their use in most naval battles as disgracefully unscientific.

111. A Trireme at Sea.—A trireme, then, is an heroic fighting instrument. She goes into battle prepared literally to do or die. If her side is once crushed, she fills with water instantly, and the enemy will be too busy and too inhumane to do anything but cheer lustily when they see the water covered with struggling wretches. But the trireme is also a most disagreeable craft before and after the battle. Her light draft sets her tossing on a very mild sea. In the hot southern climate, with very little ventilation beneath the upper deck, with nigh two hundred panting, naked human beings wedged in together below so closely that there is scarce room for one more, the heat, the smells, the drudgery, are dreadful. No wonder the crew demand that the trierarch and governor " make shore for the night," or that they weary of the incessant grating of the heavy oars upon the thole-pins.

Thus the Invincible will seem to any squeamish voyager, but not so to a distant spectator. For him a trireme is a most marvelous and magnificent sight. A sister ship, the .Dcmae, 1 is just entering the Peiraeus from Lemnos (an isle still under the Athenian sovranty). Her upper works have

a The Greek ships seem to have been named either for mythological characters, or for desirable qualities and virtues.

been all brightened for the home-coming. Long, brilliant streamers trail from her sail yards and poop. The flute player is blowing his loudest. The marines stand on the forecastle in glittering armor. A great column of foam is spouting from her bow. 1 Her oars, eighty-seven to the side, pumiced white and hurling out the spray, are leaping back and forth in perfect unison. The whole vessel seems a thing of springing, ardent life. It is, indeed, a sight to stir the blood. No later sailing ship in her panoply of canvas, no steam battleship with her grim turrets and smoking funnels can ever match the spectacle of a trireme moving in her rhythm and glory.

112. The Tactics of a Naval Battle. — Imagination can now picture a Greek naval battle, fifty, a hundred, two hundred, or more of these splendid battleships flying in two hostile lines to the charge. 2 Round and round they will sail, each pilot watching the moment when an unlucky maneuver by the foe will leave a chance for an attack; and then will come the sudden swinging of the helm, the frantic "Pull hard!" to the oarsmen, the rending crash and shock as the ram tears open the opponent's side, to be followed by almost instant tragedy. If the direct attack on the foe's broadside fails, there is another maneuver. Run down upon your enemy as if striking bow to bow; the instant before contact let your aim swerve — a little. Then call to your men to draw in their oars like lightning while the enemy are still working theirs. If your oarsmen can do the trick in time, you can now ride down the whole of the foemen's exposed oar bank, while saving your own. He is left crippled and helpless, like a huge centipede with all the legs on one side

1 At her best a trireme seems to have been capable of making 8 to 9 knots per hour.

2 A more detailed picture of an ancient naval battle and its tactics can be found in the author's historical novel, A Victor of Salamis (Chap. XXIX).

stripped away. You can now back off deliberately, run out your oars, and in cold blood charge his exposed flank. If he does not now surrender, his people are dead men. Excellent to describe! Not always so excellent in performance. Everything depends on the perfect discipline and handiness of your crew.

113. The Naval Strength of Athens. — The strength of Athens is still upon the sea. Despite her defeats in the Peloponnesian War she has again the first navy in Hellas. All in all she can send out 400 triremes and since each trireme represents a crew of over 200 men, this means that Athens can dispose of over 80,000 souls in her navy, whereof, however, only a minor fraction are Athenian citizens. Athens is quite right in thus laying stress upon her sea power. Her long walls and the Peiraeus make her practically an island. Even after Chaeroneia, Philip of Macedon will be obliged to give her honorable terms, — she has still her great navy. Only after the defeat of her fleet at Amorgos in 322 B.C. will she have to know all the pangs of vassalage to Macedon.

CHAPTER XV. AN ATHENIAN COURT TRIAL.

114. The Frequency of Litigation in Athens. — The visit to the Peiraeus and the study of the shipping have not been too long to prevent a brief visit to one of the most characteristic scenes of Athenian life — a law court. Athens is notorious for the fondness which her citizens display for litigation. In fact it is a somewhat rare and exceptionally peaceable, harmless, and insignificant citizen who is not plaintiff or defendant in some kind of action every few years or

so. Says Aristophanes, " The cicada [grasshopper] sings for only a month, but the people of Athens are buzzing with lawsuits and trials their whole life long. " In the jury courts the contentious, tonguey man can spread himself and defame his enemies to his heart's content; and it must be admitted that in a city like Athens, where everybody seems to know everybody else's business almost every citizen is likely to have a number both of warm friends and of bitter enemies. Athenians do not have merely " cold acquaintances," or " business rivals, " as will men of the twentieth century. They make no pretenses to " Christian charity." They freely call an obnoxious individual their "personal foe" (echthros), and if they can defeat, humiliate, and ruin him, they bless the gods. The usual outlet for such ill-feeling is a fierce and perhaps mutually destructive lawsuit.

Then too, despite Athenian notions of what constitutes a gentleman, many citizens are people of utterly penurious, niggardly habits. Frequently enough the fellow who can 136 discuss all Socrates's theories with you is quarreling with his neighbor over the loan of salt or a lamp wick or some meal for sacrifice. 1 If one of the customary "club-dinners" 2 is held at his house, he will be caught secreting some of the vinegar, lamp oil, or lentils. If he has borrowed something, say some barley, take care; when he returns it, he will measure it out in a vessel with the bottom dented inward. A little ill feeling, a petty grievance carefully cultivated,— the end in due time will be a lawsuit, costly far out of proportion to the originating cause.

115. Prosecutions in Athens. — Athens does not draw a sharp line between public and private litigation. There is no " state " or " district attorney " to prosecute for offenses against public order. Any full citizen can prosecute anybody else upon such a criminal charge as murder, no less than for a civil matter like breach of contract. All this leads to the growth of a mischievous clan — the sycophants. These harpies are professional accusers who will prosecute almost any rich individual upon whom they think they can fasten some technical offense. Their gains are from two quarters. If they convict the defendant, about half of the fine or property taken will go to the informer. But very likely there will be no trial. The victim (either consciously guilty, or innocent but anxious to avoid the risk) will pay a huge blackmail at the first threat of prosecution, and the case is hushed up.

It is true there are very heavy penalties for trumped-up cases, for unwarranted threat of legal proceedings, for perjured evidence; still the abuse of the sycophants exists, and a great many of the lawsuits originate with this uncanny-tribe.

1 Persons of this kidney are delineated to us as typical characters by Theophrastus.

2 The nearest modern equivalent is a " basket lunch."

116. The Preliminaries to a Trial. — There are official arbitrators to settle petty cases, but it is too often that one or both parties declare " the dicasts must settle it," and the lawsuit has to take its way. Athenian legal methods are simple. Theoretically there are no professional lawyers, and every man must look out for himself. The first business is to file your complaint with one of the magistrates (usually one of nine archons), and then with two witnesses give formal summons to your opponent, the defendant, to appear on a set day in court. If he has defaulted, the case is usually ended then in your favor. This hearing before the magistrate is in any event an important part of the trial. Here each side proffers the laws it cites to sustain its claims, and brings its witnesses, who can be more or less cross-examined. All the pertinent testimony is now written down, and the tablets sealed up by the magistrate. At the final trial this evidence will be merely read to the jury, the witness in each instance standing up before the court and admitting, when duly asked, " This is my testimony on the case."

Free men testify under oath, but a slave's oath is counted worthless. The slaves may be the only important witnesses to a given act, but under only one condition can they testify. With the consent of their master they may testify under torture. It is a critical moment at this hearing when a litigant who is confident of his case proudly announces, " I challenge my enemy to put my slaves under torture"; or the other, attacking first, cries out, "I demand that my enemy submit his slaves to torture." Theoretically the challenged party may refuse, practically a refusal is highly dangerous. "If his slaves didn't know something bad, why were they kept silent ? " the jury will ask. So the rack is brought forth. The wretched menials are stretched upon it. One must hope that often the whole process involves more show of cruelty than actual brutality. What now the slavey

gasp out between their twists and howls is duly taken down as " important evidence," and goes into the record. 1

117. The Athenian Jury Courts. — A convenient interval has elapsed since one of these preliminary hearings. To-day has been set for the actual trial before a member of the archons in the " Green " court. Ariston, a wealthy olive farmer, is suing Lamachus, an exporter of the Peirseus, for failing to account for the proceeds of a cargo of olives lately shipped to Naxos. To follow the trial in entirety we should have been at the courthouse at first dawn. Then we would have seen the jurymen come grumbling in, some from the suburbs, attended by link boys. These jurors represent a large fraction of the whole Athenian people. There are about six thousand in all. Pretty nearly every citizen above thirty years of age can give in his name as desiring jury duty; but naturally it is the elderly and the indolent who most prefer the service. One thousand of the six act as mere substitutes; the rest serve as often as the working of a complicated system of drawing by lot assigns them to sit as jurors on a particular case. It is well there are five thousand always thus available, for Athenian juries are very large ; 201, 401, 501, 1001 are numbers heard of, and sometimes even greater. 2 The more important the case, the larger the jury; but Ariston v. Lamachus is only a commonplace affair; 401 jurors are quite enough. Even with that " small court," the audience which the pleaders now have to address will seem huge to any latter-day lawyer who is accustomed

1 Athenian opinion was on the whole in favor of receiving as valid testimony the evidence extorted thus from slaves by mere animal fear. Antiphon the orator speaks of how truth may be wrung from slaves by torture; " by which they are compelled to speak the truth though they must die for it afterward [at the hands of the master they have incriminated], for the present necessity is to each stronger than the future." This has been well called one of the few cases of extreme stupidity on the part of the Athenians.

a The odd unit was no doubt added to prevent a tie.

to his " twelve men in a box "; and needless to say, quite different methods must be used in dealing with such a company. Each " dicast" (to use the proper name) has a boxwood tablet to show at the entrance as his voucher to the Scythian police-archers on duty; he has also a special staff of the color of the paint on the door of the court room. 1 The chamber itself is not especially elegant; a long line of hard benches rising in tiers for the dicasts, and facing these a kind of pulpit for the presiding magistrates, with a little platform for the orators, a small altar for the preliminary sacrifice, and a few stools for attendants and witnesses complete the simple furnishings. There are open spaces for spectators, though no seats; but there will be no lack of an audience today, for the rumor has gone around, " Hypereides has written Ariston's argument." The chance to hear a speech prepared by that famous oration-monger is enough to bring every dicast out early, and to summon a swarm of loiterers up from the not distant Agora.

118. The Juryman's Oath. — The dicasts are assumed to approach their duty with all due solemnity. They have sworn to vote according to the laws of Athens, never to vote for a repudiation of debts, nor to restore political exiles, nor to receive bribes for their votes, nor take bribes in another's behalf, nor let anybody even tempt them with such proffers. They are to hear

both sides impartially and vote strictly according to the merits of the case : and the oath winds up awfully — " Thus do I invoke Zeus, Poseidon, and Demeter to smite with destruction me and my house if I violate any of these obligations, but if I keep them I pray for many blessings." 2

1 Each court room had its distinguishing color. There were about ten regular court rooms, besides some for special tribunals; e.g. the Areopagus for the trial of homicides.

2 We have not the exact text of all the dicasts' oath, but we can reproduce it fairly completely from Demosthenes's Oration against Timocrates.

119. Opening the Trial. The Plaintiff's Speech. — The oath is admirable, but the dicasts are not in a wholly juridical state of mind. Just before the short sacrifice needful to commence proceedings, takes place, old Zenosthenes on the second row nudges his neighbor: " I don't like the looks of that Lamachus. He can't be honest, and gird his chiton that way. I shall vote against him." "And I — my wife knows his wife, and — " The archon rises. The crier bids " silence! " The proceedings begin: but all through the hearing there is whispering and nudging along the jurors' benches. The litigants are quite aware of the situation and are trying their best to win some advantage therefrom.

Ariston is the first to speak. He has taken great pains with the folds of his himation and the trim of his beard this morning. He must be thoroughly genteel, but avoid all appearance of being a dandy. In theory every man has to plead his own case in Athens, but not every man is an equally good orator. If a litigant is very inept, he can simply say a few words, then step aside with "My friend so-and-so will continue my argument", and a readier talker will take his place. 1 Ariston, however, is a fairly clever speaker. Having what he conceives a good case, he has obtained the indirect services of Hypereides, one of the first of the younger orators of Athens. Hypereides has written a speech which he thinks is suitable to the occasion, Ariston has memorized it, and delivers it with considerable gusto. He has solid evidence, as is proved from time to time when he stops to call, " Let the clerk read the testimony of this or that." There often is a certain hum of approbation from the dicasts when he makes his points. He continues bravely, therefore, ever and anon casting an eye upon the clepsydra near at hand, a huge water-clock which, something

1 These " friends," however, were never regular professional advocates; it would have been ruinous to let the jury get the impression that an orator was being directly hired to speak to them.

like an hour glass, marks off the time allotted him. Some of his arguments seem to have nothing to do with the alleged embezzlement. He vilifies his opponent: calls Lamachus's mother coarse names, intimates that as a boy he had no decent schooling, charges him with cowardice in the recent Mantinea campaign in which he served, hints that he has quarreled with his relatives. On the other hand, Ariston grandiloquently praises himself as well born, well educated, an honorable soldier and citizen, a man any Athenian would be glad to consider a friend. It is very plain all these personalia delight the jury. 1 When Ariston's " water has run out" and he concludes his speech, there is a loud murmur of applause running along the benches of the dicasts.

120. The Defendant's Speech. Demonstrations by the Jury. — It is now Lamachus's turn. He also has employed a professional speech-writer (logograplios) of fame, Isaeus, to prepare his defense. But almost at the outset he is in difficulties. Very likely he has a bad case to begin with. He makes it worse by a shrill, unpleasant voice and ungainly gestures. Very soon many dicasts are tittering and whispering jibes to their companions. The evidence does not seem to prove his contentions. As his harangue proceeds, the presiding archon (who has really very little control of the dicasts) is obliged "to remind the gentlemen of the jury that they have taken solemn oath to hear both sides of the question."

Lamachus fights doggedly on. Having put in all his real arguments, he takes refuge also in blackguarding his opponent. Did Ariston get his wealth honestly ? was not his father a rascally grain dealer who starved the people? Yet there is still more impatience among the dicasts.

1 For the depths of personal insult into which Greek litigants could descend there is no better instance than Demosthenes's (otherwise magnificent) Oration on the Crown, wherein he castigates his foe ^schine*.

Lamachus now uses his last weapon. Upon the pleader's stand clamber his five young children clad in black mourning garments. They all weep together, and when not wiping their eyes, hold out their hands like religious suppliants, toward the dicasts. 1

"Ah! Gentlemen of the jury," whines their father, "if you are moved by the voices of your lambs at home, pity these here. Acquit me for their sakes. Do not find against me and plunge these innocent darlings into want and misery, by impoverishing their father."

Appeals like this have swayed more than one jury during the last year, but the fates are all against Lamachus. From a back bench comes a dreaded shout that is instantly caught up by the front tiers also:

"Katdba! Katdba! — Go down! Go down!"

Lamachus hesitates. If he obeys, he loses all the rest of his defense. If he continues now, he enrages many of the dicasts, who will be absolutely sure to find against him. The presiding archon vainly rises, and tries to say something about " fair play." Useless. The uproar continues. Like a flock of scared doves Lamachus and all his five children flee incontinently from the tribune, amid ironical cheers and laughter.

121. The First Verdict—There is silence at length. " The dicasts will proceed to vote," announces the court crier. The huge urns (one of bronze, one of wood) with narrow mouths are passed among the benches. Each juror has two round bronze disks, one solid, one with a hole bored in the middle. The solid acquit, the pierced ones convict. A juror drops the ballot he wishes to count into the bronze urn; the other goes into the wooden urn. The bronze

1 For such an appeal to an Athenian dicastery, see Aristophanes's Wasps. The pertinent passages are quoted in Readings in Ancient History, vol. I, p. 238-40.

urn is carried to the archon, and there is an uneasy hush while the 401 ballots are counted by the court officers. As expected, more than 300 dicasts vote that Ariston is entitled to damages against Lamachus as an embezzler.

122. The Second and Final Verdict. — Ariston is smiling; his friends are congratulating him, but the trial is by no means over. If Lamachus had been found guilty of something for which the law provided an absolute fixed penalty, this second part of the proceedings could be omitted. But here, although the jury has said some damage or penalties are due, it has still to fix the amount. Ariston has now to propose to the dicasts a sum which he thinks is adequate to avenge his wrongs and losses; Lamachus can propose a smaller sum and try to persuade the court that it is entirely proper. Each side must act warily. Athenian jurors are fickle folk. The very men who have just howled down Lamachus may, in a spasm of repentance, vote for absurdly low damages. Again, Lamachus must not propose anything obviously inadequate, otherwise the jurors who have just voted against him may feel insulted, and accept Ariston's estimate. 1 Ariston therefore says that he deserves at least a talent. Lamachus rejoins that half a talent is more than ample, even conceding Ariston's alleged wrongs. The arguments this time are shorter and more to the point. Then comes the second balloting. A second time a majority (smaller this time, but enough) is in favor of Ariston. The better cause has conquered; and there is at least this advantage to the Athenian legal system, there will be no appeal nor tedious technicalities before a " higher court." The verdict of the dicastery is final.

1 Undoubtedly Socrates would have escaped with his life, if (after his original condemnation) he had proposed a real penalty to the jury, instead of an absurdly small fine. The only alternative for the dicasts was to accept the proposition of his opponents, — in his case, death.

123. The Merits and Defects of the Athenian Courts.—

No doubt injustice is sometimes done. Sometimes it is the honest man who hears the dreaded " Kataba!" Sometimes the weeping children have their intended effect. Sometimes it is the arguments about " My opponent's scoundrelly ancestry " which win the verdict. At the same time, your Athenian dicast is a remarkably shrewd and acute individual. He can distinguish between specious rhetoric and a real argument. He is probably honestly anxious to do justice. In the ordinary case where his personal interests or prejudices do not come into play, the decision is likely to match with justice quite as often perhaps as in the intricate court system of a great republic many centuries after the passing of Athens.

Certain features of some Athenian trials have not explained themselves in the example just witnessed. To prevent frivolous or blackmailing litigation it is provided that, if the plaintiff in a suit gets less than one fifth of the ballots in his favor (thus clearly showing he had no respectable case), he is liable to a heavy fine or, in default thereof, exile. Again, we have not waited for the actual closing scene — the dicasts each giving up his colored staff as a kind of voucher to the court officers, and in return getting his three obols (9 cents) daily jury fee, which each man claps promptly in his cheek, and then goes off home to try the case afresh at the family supper.

124. The Usual Punishments in Athens. —Trials involving murder or manslaughter come before the special court of Areopagus, and cannot well be discussed here, but most other criminal cases are tried before the dicasts in much the same way as a civil trial. When the law does not have a set penalty, the jury virtually has to sentence the defendant after convicting him, choosing between one of two proposed penalties. Greek courts can inflict death, exile,

fines, but almost never imprisonment. There is no "penitentiary" or "workhouse" in Athens; and the only use for a jail is to confine accused persons whom it is impossible to release on bail before their trial. The Athens city jail (" The House," as it is familiarly called — Oikema) is a very simple affair, an open building, carelessly guarded and free to visitors all through the daylight. The inmates have to be kept in heavy fetters, otherwise they would be sure to take flight; and indeed escapes from custody are somewhat common.

125. The Heavy Penalty of Exile. — An Athenian will regard locking a criminal up for a term of years as a very foolish and expensive proceeding. If he has nothing wherewith to pay a round fine, why, simply send him into exile. This penalty is direful indeed to a Greek. The exile has often no protector, no standing in the courts of the foreign city, no government to avenge any outrage upon him. He can be insulted, starved, stripped, nay, murdered, often with impunity. Worse still, he is cut off from his friends with whom all his life is tied up; he is severed from the guardian gods of his childhood, — " the City," the city of his birth, hopes, longings, exists no more for him. If he dies abroad, he is not sure of a decent funeral pyre; and meanwhile his children may be hungering at home. So long as the Athenians have this tremendous penalty of exile at their disposal, they do not feel the need of penitentiaries.

126. The Death Penalty at Athens. — There are also the stocks and whipping posts for meting out summary justice to irresponsible offenders. When the death penalty is imposed (and the matter often lies in the discretion of the dicasts), the criminal, if of servile or Barbarian blood, may be put to death in some hideous manner and his corpse tossed into the Barathron, a vile pit on the northwest side of Athens, there to be dishonored by the kites and crows.

The execution of Athenian citizens, however, is extremely humane. The condemned is given a cup of poisonous hemlock juice and allowed to drink it while sitting comfortably among his friends in the prison. Little by little his body grows numb; presently he becomes senseless, and all is over without any pain. 1 The friends of the victim are then at liberty to give his body a suitable burial.

An Athenian trial usually lasts all day, and perhaps we have been able to witness only the end of it. It may well happen, however, that we cannot attend a dicastery at all. This day may be one which is devoted to a meeting of the public assembly, and duty summons the jurors, not to the court room, but to the Pnyx. This is no loss to us, however. We welcome a chance to behold the Athenian Ecclesia in action.

1 No one can read the story of the death of Socrates in the prison, as told by Plato in the Phsedo, without feeling (aside from the noble philosophical setting) how much more humane were such executions by hemlock than is the modern gallows or electric chair.

CHAPTER XVI. THE ECCLESIA OF ATHENS.

127. The Rule of Democracy in Athens. — The Ecclesia, or Public Assembly, of Athens is something more than the chief governmental organ in the state. It is the great leveling engine which makes Athens a true democracy, despite the great differences in wealth between her inhabitants, and the marked social pretentions of " the noble and the good" — the educated classes. At this time Athens is profoundly wedded to her democratic constitution. Founded by Solon and Clisthenes, developed by Themisto-cles and Pericles, it was temporarily overthrown at the end of the Peloponnesian War; but the evil rule then of the " Thirty Tyrants " has proved a better lesson on the evils of oligarchic rule than a thousand rhetoricians' declamations upon the advantages of the " rule of the many" as against the " rule of the few." Attica now acknowledges only one Lord— King Demos —"King Everybody" — and until the coming of bondage to Macedon there will be no serious danger of an aristocratic reaction.

128. Aristocracy and Wealth. Their Status and Burdens. —

True, there are old noble families in Athens, — like the Alcmseonidae whereof Pericles sprang, and the Eumolpidse who supply the priests to Demeter, the Earth Mother. But these great houses have long since ceased to claim anything but social preeminence. Even then one must take pains not to assume airs, or the next time one is litigant before the dicastery, the insinuation of " an undemocratic, 147

oligarchic manner of life " will win very many adverse votes among the jury. Nobility and wealth are only allowed to assert themselves in Athens when justified by an extraordinary amount of public service and public generosity.

Xenophon in his Memorabilia makes Socrates tell Critobu-lus, a wealthy and self-important individual, that he is really so hampered by his high position as to be decidedly poor. " You are obliged," says Socrates, " to offer numerous and magnificent sacrifices; you have to receive and entertain sumptuously a great many strangers, and to feast [your fellow] citizens. You have to pay heavy contributions towards the public service, keeping horses and furnishing choruses in peace times and in war bearing the expense of maintaining triremes and paying the special war taxes; and if you fail to do all this, they will punish you with as much severity as if you were caught stealing their money."

129. Athenian Society Truly Democratic up to a Certain Point. — Wealth, then, means one perpetual round of public services and obligations, sweetened perhaps with a little empty praise, an inscription, an honorary crown, or best of all, an honorary statue "to the public benefactor" as the chief reward. On the other hand -one may be poor and be a thoroughly self-respecting, nay, prominent citizen. Socrates had an absurdly small invested fortune and the gods

knew that he did little enough in the way of profitable labor. 1 He had to support his wife and three children upon this income. He wore no chiton. His himation was always an old one, unchanged from summer to winter. He seems to have possessed only one pair of good sandals all his life. His rations were bread and water, save when he was invited out. Yet this man was welcome in the " very best society."

1 Socrates's regular income from invested property seems to have been only about $12 per year. It is to be hoped his wife, Xanthippe, had a little property of her own!

Alcibiades, leader of the fast, rich set, and many more of the gilded youth of Athens dogged his heels. One meets not the slightest evidence that his poverty ever prevented him from carrying his philosophic message home to the wealthy and the noble. There is no snobbishness, then, in this Athenian society. Provided a man is not pursuing a base mechanic art or an ignoble trade, provided he has a real message to convey, — whether in literature, philosophy, or statecraft,—there are no questions " who was your father?" or "what is your income?" 1 Athens will hear him and accept his best. For this open-mindedness — almost unique in ancient communities — one must thank King Demos and his mouthpiece, the Ecclesia.

Athenians are intensely proud of their democracy. In ^Eschylus's Persians, Atossa, the Barbarian queen, asks concerning the Athenians: —

" Who is the lord and shepherd of their flock ? " Very prompt is the answer: —

"They are not slaves, they bow to no man's rule."

Again in Euripides's Suppliants there is this boast touching Athens:—

"No will of one

Holdeth this land: it is a city and free. The whole folk year by year, in parity of service is our king."

130. The Voting Population of Athens. — Nevertheless when we ask about this " whole folk," and who the voters are, we soon discover that Athens is very far from being a pure democracy. The multitudes of slaves are of course without votes, and so is the numerous class of the important, cultivated, and often wealthy metics. To get Athenian citizenship is notoriously hard. For a stranger (say a metic who

1 Possibly the son of a man whose parents notoriously had been slaves in Athens would have found many doors closed to him.

had done some conspicuous public service) to be given the franchise, a special vote must be passed by the Ecclesia itself; even then the new citizen may be prosecuted as undeserving before a dicastery, and disfranchised. Again, only children both of whose parents are free Athenian citizens can themselves be enrolled on the carefully guarded lists in the deme books. The status of a child, one of whose parents is a metic, is little better than a bastard. 1

Under these circumstances the whole number of voters is very much less than at a later day will appear in American communities of like population. Before the Peloponnesian War, when the power of Athens was at its highest point, there were not less than 30,000 full citizens and possibly as many as 40,000. But those days of imperial power are now ended. At present Athens has about 21,000 citizens, or a few more. It is impossible, however, to gather all these in any single meeting. A great number are farmers living in the remote villages of Attica; many city dwellers also will be too busy to think the 3-obol (9-cent) fee for attendance worth their while. 2 Six thousand seems to be a good number for ordinary occasions and no doubt much business can be despatched with less, although this is the legal quorum set for most really vital matters. Of course a great crisis, e.g. a declaration of war, will bring out nearly every voter whose farm is not too distant.

131. Meeting Times of the Ecclesia. — Four times in

1 Of course women were entirely excluded from the Ecclesia, as from all other forms of public life. The question of "woman's rights" had been agitated just enough to produce comedies like Aristophanes's Parliament of Women, and philosophical theories such as appear in Plato's Republic.

2 Payment for attendance at the Pnyx seems to have been introduced about 390 B.C. The original payment was probably only one obol, and then from time to time increased. It was a sign of the relative decay of political interest in Athens when it became needful thus to reward the commonalty for attendance at the Assembly.

«very prytany 1 the Ecclesia must be convened for ordinary business, and oftener if public occasion requires. Five days' notice has to be given of each regular meeting, and along with the notice a placard announcing the proposals which are to come up has to be posted in the Agora. But if there is a sudden crisis, formalities can be thrown to the winds; a sudden bawling of the heralds in the streets, a great smoky column caused by burning the traders' flimsy booths in the Agora,— these are valid notices of an extraordinary meeting to confront an immediate danger.

If this has been a morning when the Ecclesia has been in session, nothing unusual has occurred at first in the busy Agora, except that the jury courts are hardly in action, and a bright flag is whipping the air from the tall flagpole by the Pnyx (the Assembly Place). Then suddenly there is a shouting through the Agora. The clamor of traffic around the popular flower stalls ceases; everybody who is not a slave or metic (and these would form a large fraction of the crowd of marketers) begins to edge down toward one end of the Agora. Presently a gang of Scythian police-archers comes in sight. They have a long rope sprinkled with red chalk wherewith they are "netting" the Agora. The chalk will leave an infallible mark on the mantle of every tardy citizen, and he who is thus marked as late at the meeting will lose his fee for attendance, if not subject himself to a fine. So there is a general rush away from the Agora and down one of the various avenues leading to the Pnyx.

132. The Pnyx (Assembly Place) at Athens. — The Pnyx is an open space of ground due west from the Acropolis.

1<(A prytany" was one tenth of a year, say 35 or 36 days, during which time the 50 representatives of one of the ten Athenian tribes then serving as members of the Council of 500 (each tribe taking its turn) held the presidency of the Council and acted as a special executive committee of the government. There were thus at least 40 meetings of the Ecclesia each year, as well as the extraordinary meetings.

It originally sloped gently away towards the northeast, but a massive retaining wall had been built around it, in an irregular semicircle, and the space within filled with solidly packed earth sloping inwards, making a kind of open air auditorium. It is a huge place, 394 feet long, and 213 feet at the widest. The earthen slope is entirely devoid of seats; everybody casts himself down sprawling or on his haunches, perhaps with an old himation under him. Directly before the sitters runs a long ledge hewn out of the rock, forming, as it were, the " stage" side of the theater. Here the rock has been cut away, so as to leave a sizable stone pulpit standing forth, with a small flight of steps on each side. This is the Bema, the orator's stand, whence speak the " demagogues," 1 the molders of Athenian public opinion. In front of the Bema there is a small portable altar for the indispensable sacrifices. In the rear of the Bema are a few planks laid upon the rock. Here will sit the fifty Prytanes in charge of the meeting. There is a handsome chair for the presiding officer upon the Bema itself. These are all the furnishings of the structure wherein Athens makes peace and war, and orders her whole civil and foreign policy. The Hellenic azure is the only roof above her sovran law makers. To the right, as the orators stand on the Bema, they can point toward the Acropolis and its glittering temples ; to the left towards the Peiraeus, and the blue sea with the inevitable memories of glorious Salamis. Surely it will be easy to fire all hearts with patriotism!

133. The Preliminaries of the Meeting.—Into this space the voters swarm by hundreds — all the citizens of Athens, from twenty years and upward, sufficiently interested to come. At each crude entrance stands a corps of watchful

A " demagogue " (= people-leader) might well be a great statesman, and not necessarily a cheap and noisy politician.

lexiarchs and their clerks, cheeking off those present and turning back interlopers. As the entering crowds begin to thin, the entrance ways are presently closed by wicker hurdles. The flag fluttering on high is struck. The Ecclesia is ready for action.

Much earlier than this, the farmers and fishermen from the hill towns or from Salamis have been in their places, grumbling at the slowness of the officials. People sit down where they can; little groups and clans together, wedged in closely, chattering up to the last minute, watching every proceeding with eyes as keen as cats'. All the gossip left over from the Agora is disposed of ere the prytanes — proverbially late — scramble into their seats of honor. The police-archers move up and down, enforcing a kind of order. Amid a growing hush a sucking pig is solemnly slaughtered by some religious functionary at the altar, and the dead victim carried around the circuit of the Pnyx as a symbolic purification of the audience.

" Come inside the purified circuit," enjoins a loud herald to the little groups upon the edge. l

Then comes a prayer invoking the gods' favor upon the Athenians, their allies, and this present meeting in particular, winding up (the herald counts this among the chief parts of his duty) with a tremendous curse on any wretch who should deceive the folk with evil counsel. After this the real secular business can begin. Nothing can be submitted to the Ecclesia which has not been previously considered and matured by the Council of 500. The question to be proposed is now read by the herald as a " Pro-boitr leuma " — a suggested ordinance by the Council. Vast as is the audience, the acoustic properties of the Pnyx are excel-

1 Aristophanes's Acharnians (11. 50 ff.) gives a valuable picture of this and other proceedings at the Pnyx, but one should never forget the poet's exaggerations for comedy purposes, nor his deliberate omission of matters likely to be mere tedious detail to his audience.

lent, and all public officers and orators are trained to harangue multitudes in the open air, so that the thousands get every word of the proposition.

134. Debating a Proposition. — "Kesolved by the Boule, the tribe Leontis holding the prytany, and Heraclides being clerk, upon the motion of Tim on the son of Tim on the Eleusinian, 1 that" — and then in formal language it is proposed to increase the garrison of the allied city of Byzantium by 500 hired Arcadian mercenaries, since the king of Thrace is threatening that city, and its continued possession is absolutely essential to the free import of grain into Attica.

There is a hush of expectancy ; a craning of necks.

" Who wishes to speak?" calls the herald.

After a decent pause Timon, the mover of the measure, comes forward. He is a fairly well-known character and commands a respectable faction among the Demos. There is some little clapping, mixed with jeering, as he mounts the Benia. The president of the prytanes — as evidence that he has now the right to harangue — hands him a myrtle wreath which he promptly claps on his head, and launches into his argument. Full speedily he has convinced at least a large share of the audience that it was sheer destruction to leave Byzantium without an efficient garrison. Grain would soon be at famine prices if the town were taken, etc., etc. The only marvel is that the merciful gods have averted the disaster so long in the face of such neglect. — Why had the board of strategi, responsible in such matters, neglected this obvious duty? [Cheers intermixed with catcalls.] This was not the way the men who won Marathon had dealt with dangers, nor later worthies like Nicias or Thrasybulus.

1 This seems to have been the regular form for beginning a probouleuma although nearly all our information comes from the texts of proposals after they have been made formal decrees by the sovran Demos.

[More cheers and catcalls.] He winds up with a splendid invocation to Earth, Sky, and Justice to bear witness that all this advice is given solely with a view to the weal of Athens.

" He had Isocrates teach him how to launch that peroration," mutters a crabbed old citizen behind his peak-trimined beard, as Timon descends amid mingled applause and derision.

"Very likely; Iphicrates is ready to answer him," replies a fellow.

" Who wishes to speak ? " the herald demands again. From a place directly before the Bema a well-known figure, the elderly general, Iphicrates, is rising. At a nod from the president, he mounts the Bema and assumes the myrtle. He has not Timon's smooth tones nor oratorical manner. He is a man of action and war, and no tool of the Agora coteries. A salvo of applause greets him. Very pithily he observes that Byzantium will be safe enough if the city will only be loyal to the Athenian alliance. Athens needs all her garrisons nearer home. Timon surely knows the state of the treasury. Is he going to propose a special tax upon his fellow countrymen to pay for those 500 mercenaries ? [Loud laughter and derisive howls directed at Timon.] Athens needs to keep her strength for real dangers; and those are serious enough, but not at Byzantium. At the next meeting he and the other strategi will recommend — etc., etc. When Iphicrates quits the Bema there is little left of Timon's fine " Earth, Sky, and Justice."

135. Voting at the Pnyx.—But other orators follow on both sides. Once Timon, egged on by many supporters, tries to gain the Bema a second time, but is told by the president that one cannot speak twice on the same subject. Once the derision and shouting becomes so violent that the president has to announce, "Unless there is silence I must adjourn the meeting." Finally, after an unsuccessful effort to amend the

proposal, by reducing the garrison at Byzantium to 250, the movers of the measure realize that the votes will probably be against them. They try to break up the meeting.

" I hear thunder! " " "I feel rain ! " they begin shouting, and such ill omens, if really in evidence, would be enough to force an adjournment; but the sky is delightfully clear. The president simply shrugs his shoulders; and now the Pnyx is fairly rocking with the yell, " A vote ! A vote!"

The president rises. Taking the vote in the Ecclesia is a very simple matter when it is a plain question of " yes " or " no " on a proposition. 1

" All who favor the probouleuma of Timon will raise the right hand!"

A respectable but very decided minority shows itself.

" Those who oppose."

The adverse majority is large. The morning is quite spent. There is a great tumult. Men are rising, putting on their himatia, ridiculing Timon; while the herald at a nod from the president declares the Ecclesia adjourned.

136. The Ecclesia as an Educational Instrument. — Timon and his friends retire crestfallen to discuss the fortunes of war. They are not utterly discouraged, however. The Ecclesia is a fickle creature. What it withholds to-day it may grant to-morrow. Iphicrates, whose words have carried such weight now, may soon be howled down and driven from the Bema much as was the unfortunate litigant in the jury court. Still, with all its faults, the Ecclesia is the great school for the adults of Athens. All are on terms of perfect equality. King Demos is not the least respecter of wealth and family. Sophistries are usually

1 When an individual had to be voted for, then ballots were used.

penetrated in a twinkling by some coarse expletive from a remote corner of the Pnyx. Every citizen understands the main issues of the public business. He is part of the actual working government, not once per year (or less often) at the ballot box, but at least forty times annually; and dolt he would be, did he not learn at least all the superficialities of statecraft. He may make grievous errors. He may be misled by mob prejudice or mob enthusiasm ; but he is not likely to persist in a policy of crass blundering very long. King Demos may indeed rule a fallible human monarchy, but it is thanks to him, and to his high court held at the Pnyx, that Athens owes at least half of that sharpness of wit and intelligence which is her boast.

CHAPTER XVII. THE AFTERNOON AT THE GYMNASIA.

137. The Gymnasia. Places of General Resort.—The

market is thinning after a busy day ; the swarms of farmer-hucksters with their weary asses are trudging homeward; the schoolrooms are emptying; the dicasteries or the Eccle-sia, as the case may be, have adjourned. Even the slave artisans in the factories are allowed to slacken work. The sun, a ball of glowing fire, is slowly sinking to westward over the slopes of ^Egaleos; the rock of the Acropolis is glowing as if in flame; intense purple tints are creeping over all the landscape. The day is waning, and all Athenians who can possibly find leisure are heading towards the suburbs for a walk, a talk, and refreshment of soul and body at the several Gymnasia.

Besides various private establishments and small " wrestling schools" for the boys, there are three great public Gymnasia at Athens, — the Lyceum to the east of the town; the Cynosarges l to the southward; and last, but not at all least, the Academy. This is the handsomest, the most famous, the most characteristic. We shall do well to visit it.

138. The Road to the Academy. — We go out toward the northwest of the city, plunging soon into a labyrinth of garden walls, fragrant with the fruit and blossoms within, wander amid dark olive groves where the solemn leaves of

1 The Cynosarges was the only one of these freely opened to such Athenians as had non-

Athenian mothers. The other two were reserved for the strictly "full citizens."

the sacred trees are talking sweetly; and presently mount a knoll by some suburban farm buildings, then look back to find that slight as is the elevation, here is a view of marvelous beauty across the city, the Acropolis, and the guardian mountains. From the rustling ivy coverts come the melodious notes of birds. We are glad to learn that this is the suburb of Colonus, the home of Sophocles the tragedian, and here is the very spot made famous in the renowned chorus of his (Edipous at Colonus. It is too early, of course, to enjoy the nightingale which the poet asserts sings often amid the branches, but the scene is one of marvelous charm. We are not come, however, to admire Colonus. The numerous strollers indicate our direction. Turning a little to the south, we see, embowered amid the olive groves which line the unseen stream of the Cephissos, a wall, and once beyond it find ourselves in a kind of spacious park combined with an athletic establishment. This is the Academy, — founded by Hipparchus, son of Peisistratus the tyrant, but given its real embellishments and beauty by Cimon, the son of Miltiades the victor of Marathon.

139. The Academy. — The Academy is worthy of the visit. The park itself is covered with olive trees and more graceful plane trees. The grass beneath us is soft and delightful to the bare foot (and nearly everybody, we observe, has taken off his sandals). There are marble and bronze statues skilfully distributed amid the shrubbery — shy nymphs, peeping fauns, bold satyrs. Yonder is a spouting fountain surmounted by a noble Poseidon with his trident; above the next fountain rides the ocean car of Amphitrite. Presently we come to a series of low buildings. Entering, we find them laid out in a quadrangle with porticoes on every side, somewhat like the promenades around the Agora. Inside the promenades open a series of ample rooms for the use of professional athletes during

stormy weather, and for the inevitable bathing and anointing with oil which will follow all exercise. This great square court formed by the "gymnasium" proper is swarming with interesting humanity, but we pass it hastily in order to depart by an exit on the inner side and discover a second more conventionally laid out park. Here to right and to left are short stretches of soft sand divided into convenient sections for wrestling, for quoit hurling, for javelin casting, and for jumping; but a loud shout and cheering soon draw us onward. At the end of this park we find the stadium ; a great oval track, 600 feet (a stadium) for the half circuit, with benches and all the paraphernalia for a foot race. The first contests have just ended. The racers are standing, panting after their exertions, but their friends are talking vehemently. Out in the sand, near the statue of Hermes (the patron god of gymnasia) is a dignified and self-conscious looking man in a purple-edged chiton — the gymnasiarch, the official manager of the Academy. While he waits to organize a second race we can study the visitors and habitues of the gymnasium.

140. The Social Atmosphere and Human Types at the Academy.—What the Pnyx is to the political life of Athens, this the Academy and the other great gymnasia are to its social and intellectual as well as its physical life. Here in daily intercourse, whether in friendly contest of speed or brawn, or in the more valuable contest of wits, the youth of Athens complete their education after escaping from the rod of the schoolmaster. Here they have daily lessons on the mottoes, which (did such a thing exist) should be blazoned on the coat of arms of Greece, as the summing up of all Hellenic wisdom: —

" Know thyself," and again: —

u Be moderate."

Precept, example, and experience teach these truths at the gymnasia of Athens. Indeed, on days when the Ecclesia is not in session, when no war is raging, and they are not busy with a lawsuit, many Athenians will spend almost the whole day at the Academy. For whatever are your interests, here you are likely to find something to engross you.

It must be confessed that not everybody at the Academy comes here for physical or mental improvement. We see a little group squatting and gesticulating earnestly under an old olive tree — they are obviously busy, not with philosophic theory, but with dice. Again, two young men pass us presenting a curious spectacle. They are handsomely dressed and over handsomely scented, but each carries carefully under each arm a small cock; and from time to time they are halted by friends who admire the birds. Clearly these worthies' main interests are in cockfighting; and they are giving their favorites " air and exercise" before the deadly battle, on which there is much betting, at the supper party that night. Also the shouting and rumbling from a distance tells of the chariot course, where the sons of the more wealthy or pretentious families are lessening their patrimonies by training a " two " or a " four " to contend at the Isthmian games or at Olympia.

141. Philosophers and Cultivated Men at the Gymnasia.— All these things are true, and Athens makes full display here of the usual crop of knaves or fools. Nevertheless this element is in the minority. Here a little earlier or a little later than our visit (for just now he is in Sicily) one could see Plato himself — walking under the shade trees and expounding to a little trailing host of eager-eyed disciples the fundamental theories of his ideal Commonwealth. Here are scores of serious bearded faces, and heads sprinkled with gray, moving to and fro in small groups, discussing in mc-

/odious Attic the philosophy, the poetry, the oration, which has been partly considered in the Agora this morning, and which will be further discussed at the symposium tonight. Everything is entirely informal. Even white-haired gentlemen do not hesitate to cast off chiton and himation and spring around nimbly upon the sands, to " try their distance " with the quoits, or show the young men that they have not forgotten accuracy with the javelin, or even, against men of their own age, to test their sinews in a mild wrestling bout. It is undignified for an old man to attempt hard feats beyond his advanced years. No one expects any great proficiency from most of those present. It is enough to attempt gracefully, and to laugh merrily if you do not succeed. Everywhere there is the greatest good nature, and even frolicking, but very little of the really boisterous.

142. The Beautiful Youths at the Academy. — Yet the majority of the visitors to the Academy have an interest that is not entirely summed up in proper athletics, or in the baser sports, or in philosophy. Every now and then a little whisper runs among the groups of strollers or athletes: " There he goes! — a new one ! How beautiful!" — and there is a general turning of heads.

A youth goes by, his body quite stripped, and delicately bronzed by constant exposure to the sun. His limbs are graceful, but vigorous and straight, his chest is magnificently curved. He lifts his head modestly, yet with a proud and easy carriage. His hair is dark blonde; his profile very "Greek" — nose and forehead joining in unbroken straight line. A little crowd is following him; a more favored comrade, a stalwart, bearded man, walks at his side. No need of questioning now whence the sculptors of Athens get their inspiration. This happy youth, just out of the schoolroom, and now to be enrolled as an armed ephebus, will be the model soon for some immortal bronze or marble.

The Afternoon at the Gymnasia 163

Fortunate is he, if his humility is not ruined by all the admiration and flattery; if he can remember the injunctions touching "modesty," which master and father have repeated so long; if he can remember the precept that true beauty of body can go only with true beauty of soul. Now at least is his day of hidden or conscious pride. All Athens is commending him. He is the reigning toast, like the " belle " of a later age. Not the groundlings only, but the poets, rhetoricians, philosophers, will gaze after him, seek an introduction, compliment him delicately, give themselves the pleasure of making him blush deliciously, and go back to their august problems unconsciously stimulated and refreshed by this vision of "the godlike." 1

143. The Greek Worship of Manly Beauty. — The Greek worship of the beautiful masculine form is something which the later world will never understand. In this worship there is too often a coarseness, a sensual dross, over which a veil is wisely cast. But the great fact of this worship remains : to the vast majority of Greeks " beauty " does not imply a delicate maid clad in snowy drapery; it implies a perfectly shaped, bronzed, and developed youth, standing forth in his undraped manhood for some hard athletic battle. This ideal possesses the national life, and affects the entire Greek civilization. Not beauty in innocent weakness, but beauty in resourceful strength—before this beauty men bow down. 2

i For pertinent commentary on the effect of meeting a beautiful youth upon very grave men, see, e.g., Plato's Charmides (esp. 158 a) and Lysis (esp. 206 d). Or better still in Xenophon's Symposium (I. 9), where we hear of the beautiful youth Autolycus, " even as a bright light at night draws every eye, so by his beauty drew on him the gaze of all the company [at the banquet]. Not a man was present who did not feel his emotions stirred by the sight of him,"

* Plato (Republic, p. 402) gives the view of enlightened Greek opinion when he states, "There can be no fairer spectacle than that of a man who

It is this masculine type of beauty, whether summed up in a physical form or translated by imagery into the realm of the spirit, that Isocrates (a very good mouthpiece for average enlightened opinion) praises in language which strains even his facile rhetoric. " [Beauty] is the first of all things in majesty, honor, and divineness. Nothing devoid of beauty is prized; the admiration of virtue itself comes to this, that of all manifestations of life, virtue is the most beautiful. The supremacy of beauty over all things can be seen in our own disposition toward it, and toward them. Other things we merely seek to attain as we need them, but beautiful things inspire us with love, love which is as much stronger than wish as its object is better. To the beautiful alone, as to the gods, we are never tired of doing homage; delighting to be their slaves rather than to be the rulers of others."

Could we put to all the heterogeneous crowd in the wide gymnasium the question, " What things do you desire most ?" the answer " To be physically beautiful" (not " handsome " merely, but " beautiful") would come among the first wishes. There is a little song, very popular and very Greek. It tells most of the story.

The best of gifts to mortal man is health ;

The next the bloom of beauty's matchless flower; The third is blameless and unfraudful wealth;

The fourth with friends to speed youths' joyous hour. 1

Health and physical beauty thus go before wealth and the passions of friendship, — a true Greek estimate!

combines the possession of moral beauty in his soul, with outward beauty of body, corresponding and harmonizing with the former, because the same great pattern enters into both."

1 Translation by Milman. The exact date of this Greek poem is uncertain, but its spirit is entirely true to that of Athens at the time of this sketch.

The Afternoon at the Gymnasia 165

144. The Detestation of Old Age. — Again, we are quick to learn that this "beauty" is the beauty of youth. It is useless to talk to an Athenian of a "beautiful old age." Old age is an evil to

be borne with dignity, with resignation if needs be, to be fought against by every kind of bodily exercise; but to take satisfaction in it ? — impossible. It means a diminishing of those keen powers of physical and intellectual enjoyment which are so much to every normal Athenian. It means becoming feeble, and worse than feeble, ridiculous. The physician's art has not advanced so far as to prevent the frequent loss of sight and hearing in even moderate age. No hope of a future renewal of noble youth in a happier world gilds the just man's sunset. Old age must, like the untimely passing of loved ones, be endured in becoming silence, as one of the fixed inevitables; but it is gloomy work to pretend to find it cheerful. Only the young can find life truly happy. Euripides in The, Mad Heracles speaks for all his race: —

Tell me not of the Asian tyrant,

Or of palaces plenished with gold; For such bliss I am not an aspirant,

If youth I might only behold: — Youth that maketh prosperity higher, And ever adversity lighter. 1

145. The Greeks unite Moral and Physical Beauty. — But

here at the Academy, this spirit of beautiful youth, and the "joy of life," is everywhere dominant. All around us are the beautiful bodies of young men engaged in every kind of graceful exercise. When we question, we are told that current belief is that in a great majority of instances there is a development and symmetry of mind corresponding to the glory of the body. It is contrary to all the prevalent

iMahaffy, translator. Another very characteristic lament for the passing of youth is left us by the early elegiac poet Mimnermus.

notions of the reign of " divine harmony " to have it other-wise. The gods abhor all gross contradictions! Even now men will argue over a strange breach of this rule; — why did heaven suffer Socrates to have so beautiful a soul set in so ugly a body ? — Inscrutable are the ways of Zeus!

However, we have generalized and wandered enough. The Academy is a place of superabounding activities. Let us try to comprehend some of them.

146. The Usual Gymnastic Sports and their Objects.—

Despite all the training in polite conversation which young men are supposed to receive at the gymnasium, the object of the latter is after all to form places of athletic exercise. The Athenians are without most of those elaborate field games such as later ages will call "baseball" and "football"; although, once learned, they could surely excel in these prodigiously. They have a simple "catch" with balls, but it hardly rises above the level of a children's pastime. The reasons for these omissions are probably, first, because so much time is devoted to the "palaestra" exercises ; secondly, because military training eats up about all the time not needed for pure gymnastics.

The " palaestra " exercises, taught first at the boys' training establishments and later continued at the great gymnasia, are nearly all of the nature of latter-day "field sports." They do not depend on the costly apparatus of twentieth century athletic halls; and they accomplish their ends with extremely simple means. The aim of the instructor is really twofold — to give his pupils a body fit and apt for war (and we have seen that to be a citizen usually implies being a hoplite), and to develop a body beautiful to the eye and efficient for civil life. The naturally beautiful youth can be made more beautiful; the naturally homely youth can be made at least passable under the care of a skilful gymnastic teacher.

The Afternoon at the Gymnasia 167

147. Professional Athletes: the Pancration. — Athletics, then, are a means to an end and should not be tainted with professionalism. True, as we wander about the Academy we see heavy

and over brawny individuals whose " beauty " consists in flattened noses, mutilated ears, and mouths lacking many teeth, and who are taking their way to the remote quarter where boxing is permitted. Here they will wind hard bull's hide thongs around their hands and wrists, and pummel one another brutally, often indeed (if in a set contest) to the very risk of life. These men are obviously professional athletes who, after appearing with some success at the " Nemea," are in training for the impending " Pythia " at Delphi. A large crowd of youths of the less select kind follows and cheers them; but the better public opinion frowns on them. They are denounced by the philosophers. Their lives no less than their bodies "are not beautiful" — i.e. they offend against the spirit of harmony inherent in every Greek. Still less are they in genteel favor when, the preliminary boxing round being finished, they put off their boxing thongs and join in the fierce Pancration, a not unskilful combination of boxing with wrestling, in which it is not suffered to strike with the knotted fist, but in which, nevertheless, a terrible blow can be given with the bent fingers. Kicking, hitting, catching, tripping, they strive together mid the " Euge ! Euge ! — Bravo! Bravo! " of their admirers until one is beaten down hopelessly upon the sand, and the contest ends without harm. Had it been a real Pancration, however, it would have been desperate business, for it is quite permissible to twist an opponent's wrist, and even to break his fingers, to make him give up the contest. Therefore it is not surprising that the Pancration, even more than boxing, is usually reserved for professional athletes.

148. Leaping Contests. — But near at hand is a more pleasing contest. Youths of the ephebus age are practicing leap

ing. They have no springboard, no leaping pole, but only a pair of curved metal dumb-bells to aid them. One after another their lithe brown bodies, shining with the fresh olive oil, come forward on a lightning run up the little mound of earth, then fly gracefully out across the soft sands. There is much shouting and good-natured rivalry. As each lad leaps, an eager attendant marks his distance with a line drawn by the pickaxe. The lines gradually extend ever farther from the mound. The rivalry is keen. Finally, there is one leap that far exceeds the rest. 1 A merry crowd swarms around the blushing victor. A grave middle-aged man takes the ivy crown from his head, and puts it upon the happy youth. " Your father will take joy in you," he says as the knot breaks up.

149. Quoit Hurling. — Close by the leapers is another stretch of yellow sand reserved for the quoit throwers. The contestants here are slightly older, — stalwart young men, who seem, as they fling the heavy bronze discus, to be reaching out eagerly into the fulness of life and fortune before them. Very graceful are the attitudes. Here it was the sculptor Miron saw his " Discobolus " which he immortalized and gave to all the later world ; "stooping down to take aim, his body turned in the direction of the hand which holds the quoit, one knee slightly bent as though he meant to vary the posture and to rise with the throw." 2 The caster, however, does not make his attempt standing. He takes a short run, and then the whole of his splendid body seems to spring together with the cast.

150. Casting the Javelin. — The range of the quoit hurlers in turn seems very great, but we cannot delay to await the

1 If the data of the ancients are to be believed, the Greeks achieved records in leaping far beyond those of any modern athletes, but it is impossible to rely on data of this kind.

2 The quotation is from Lucian (Roman Imperial period).

issue. Still elsewhere in the Academy they are hurling the javelin. Here is a real martial exercise, and patriotism as well as the natural athletic spirit urges young men to excel. The long light lances are being whirled at a distant target with remarkable accuracy; and well they may, for every contestant has the vision of some hour when he may stand on the poop of a trireme and hear the dread call, "All hands repel boarders," or need all his darts to break up the rush of a pursuing band of hoplites.

151. Wrestling.—The real crowds, however, are around the wrestlers and the racers. Wrestling in its less brutal form is in great favor. It brings into play all the muscles of a man; it tests his resources both of mind and body finely. It is excellent for a youth and it fights away old age. The Greek language is full of words and allusions taken from the wrestler's art. The palaestras for the boys are called " the wrestling school " par excellence. It is no wonder that now the ring on the sands is a dense one and constantly growing. Two skilful amateurs will wrestle. One — a speedy rumor tells us — is, earlier and later in the day, a rising comic poet ; the other is not infrequently heard on the Bema. Just at present, however, they have forgotten anapests and oratory. A crowd of cheering, jesting friends thrusts them on. Forth they stand, two handsome, powerful men, well oiled for suppleness, but also sprinkled with fine sand to make it possible to get a fair grip in the contest.

For a moment they wag their sharp black beards at each other defiantly, and poise and edge around. Then the poet, more daring, rushes in, and instantly the two have grappled — each clutching the other's left wrist with his right hand. The struggle that follows is hot and even, until a lucky thrust from the orator's foot lands the poet in a sprawling heap; whence he rises with a ferocious grin and renews the

contest. The second time they both fall together. "A tie!" calls the long-gowned friend who acts as umpire, with an officious flourish of his cane.

The third time the poet catches the orator trickily under the thigh, and fairly tears him off the ground; but at the fourth meeting the orator slips his arm in decisive grip about his opponent's waist and with a mighty wrench upsets him.

" Two casts out of three, and victory!"

Everybody laughs good-naturedly. The poet and the orator go away arm in arm to the bathing house, there to have another good oiling and rubbing down by their slaves, after removing the heavily caked sand from their skin with the strigils. Of course, had it been a real contest in the " greater games," the outcome might have been more serious; for the rules allow one to twist a wrist, to thrust an arm or foot into the foeman's belly, or (when things are desperate) to dash your forehead — bull fashion — against your opponent's brow, in the hope that his skull will prove weaker than yours.

152. Foot Races. — The continued noise from the stadium indicates that the races are still running; and we find time to go thither. The simple running match, a straightaway dash of 600 feet, seems to have been the original contest at the Olympic games ere these were developed into a famous and complicated festival; and the runner still is counted among the favorites of Greek athletics. As we sit upon the convenient benches around the academy stadium we see at once that the track is far from being a hard, well-rolled " cinder path "; on the contrary, it is of soft sand into which the naked foot sinks if planted too firmly, and upon it the most adept " hard-track " runner would at first pant and flounder helplessly. The Greeks have several kinds of foot races, but none that are very short. The

shortest is the simple stadium (600 feet), a straight hard dash down one side of the long oval; then there is the "double course" (diaulos) down one side and back; the "horse race"—twice clear around (2400 feet) ; and lastly the hard-testing "long course" (dolichos) which may vary in length according to arrangement, — seven, twelve, twenty,

THE RACE IN ARMOR.

or even twenty-four stadia, we are told; and it is the last (about three miles) that is one of the most difficult contests at Olympia.

At this moment a party of four hale and hearty men still in the young prime are about to compete in the "double race." They come forward all rubbed with the glistening oil, and crouch at the starting point behind the red cord held by two attendants. The gymnasiarch stands watchfully by, swinging his cane to smite painfully whoever, in over eagerness, breaks away before the signal. All is ready; at his nod the rope falls. The four fly away together, pressing their elbows close to their sides, and going over the soft sands with long rhythmic leaps, rather than with the usual rapid running motion. A fierce race it is, amid much exhortation from friends and shouting. At length, as so often,—when speeding back towards the

stretched cord, — the rearmost runner suddenly gathers amazing speed, and, flying with prodigious leaps ahead of his rivals, is easily the victor. His friends are at once about him, and we hear the busy tongues advising, "You must surely race at the Pythia; the Olympia; etc."

This simple race over, a second quickly follows: five heavy, powerful men this time, but they are to run in full hoplite's armor — the ponderous shield, helmet, cuirass, and greaves. This is the exacting "Armor Race" (Hoplito-dromos), and safe only for experienced soldiers or professional athletes. 1 Indeed, the Greeks take all their foot races very seriously, and there are plenty of instances when the victor has sped up to the goal, and then dropped dead before the applauding stadium. There are no stop watches in the Academy; we do not know the records of the present or of more famous runners; yet one may be certain that the "time" made, considering the very soft sand, has been exceedingly fast.

153. The Pentathlon: the Honors paid to Great Athletes. — We have now seen average specimens of all the usual athletic sports of the Greeks. Any good authority will tell us, however, that a truly capable athlete will not try to specialize so much in any one kind of contest that he cannot do justice to the others. As an all around well-trained man he will try to excel in the Pentathlon, the " five contests." Herein he will successfully join in running, javelin casting, quoit throwing, leaping, and wrestling. 2 As the contest proceeds the weaker athletes will be

1 It was training in races like these which enabled the Athenians at Marathon to "charge the Persians on the run" (Miltiades* orders), all armored though they were, and so get quickly through the terrible zone of the Persian arrow fire.

2 The exact order of these contests, and the rules of elimination as the games proceeded, are uncertain — perhaps they varied with time and place.

eliminated; only the two fittest will be left for the final trial of strength and skill. Fortunate indeed is "he who overcometh " in the Pentathlon. It is the crown of athletic victories, involving, as it does, no scanty prowess both of body and mind. The victor in the Pentathlon at one of the great Pan-Hellenic games (Olympian, Pythian, Isthmian, or Nemean) or even in the local Attic contest at the Pan-athenaea is a marked man around Athens or any other Greek city. Poets celebrate him; youths dog his heels and try to imitate him; his kinsfolk take on airs; very likely he is rewarded as a public benefactor by the government. But there is abundant honor for one who has triumphed in any of the great contests; and even as we go out we see people pointing to a bent old man and saying, " Yes; he won the quoit hurling at the Nernea when Ithycles was archon." 1 . . . The Academy is already thinning. The beautiful youths and their admiring " lovers " have gone homeward. The last race has been run. We must hasten if we would not be late to some select symposium. The birds are more melodious than ever around Colonus; the red and golden glow upon the Acropolis is beginning to fade; the night is sowing the stars; and through the light air of a glorious evening we speed back to the city.

iThis would make it 398 B.C. The Athenians dated their year by the name of their " first Archon " (Archon eponymos).

CHAPTER XVIII. ATHENIAN COOKERY AND THE SYMPOSIUM.

154. Greek Meal Times. — The streets are becoming empty. The Agora has been deserted for hours. As the warm balmy night closes over the city the house doors are shut fast, to open only for the returning master or his guests, bidden to dinner. Soon the ways will be almost silent, to be disturbed, after a proper interval, by the dinner guests returning homeward. Save for these, the streets will seem those of a city of the dead: patrolled at rare intervals by the Scythian archers, and also ranged now and then by cutpurses watching for an unwary stroller, or miscreant roisterers trolling lewd songs, and pounding on honest men's doors as they wander from tavern to tavern in search of the lowest possible pleasures.

We have said very little of eating or drinking during our visit in Athens, for, truth to tell, the citizens try to get through the day with about as little interruption for food and drink as possible. But now, when warehouse and gymnasium alike are left to darkness, all Athens will break its day of comparative fasting.

Roughly speaking, the Greeks anticipate the latter-day " Continental" habits in their meal hours. The custom of Germans and of many Americans in having the heartiest meal at noonday would never appeal to them. The hearty meal is at night, and no one dreams of doing any serious work after it. When it is finished, there may be pleasant discourse or varied amusements, but never real business; 174

and even if there are guests, the average dinner party breaks up early. Early to bed and early to rise, would be a maxim indorsed by the Athenians.

Promptly upon rising, our good citizen has devoured a few morsels of bread sopped in undiluted wine; that has been to him what " coffee and rolls " will be to the Frenchman, — enough to carry him through the morning business, until near to noon he will demand something more satisfying. He then visits home long enough to partake of a substantial dejeuner (ariston, first breakfast = akratismd). He has one or two hot dishes — one may suspect usually warmed over from last night's dinner—and partakes of some more wine. This ariston will be about all he will require until the chief meal of the day—the regular dinner (delpnori) which would follow sunset.

155. Society desired at Meals. —The Athenians are a gregarious sociable folk. Often enough the citizen must dine alone at home with " only " his wife and children for company, but if possible he will invite friends (or get himself invited out). Any sort of an occasion is enough to excuse a dinner-party, — a birthday of some friend, some kind of family happiness, a victory in the games, the return from, or the departure upon, a journey:—all these will answer; or indeed a

mere love of good fellowship. There are innumerable little eating clubs; the members go by rotation to their respective houses. Each member contributes either some money or has his slave bring a hamper of provisions. In the fine weather picnic parties down upon the shore are common. 1 "Anything to bring friends together" — in the morning the Agora, in the afternoon the gymnasium, in the evening the symposium — that seems to be the rule of Athenian life.

1 Such excursions were so usual that the literal expression " Let us banquet at the shore " (o"/i/*epov dKTdoru/jxv) came often to mean simply "Let us have a good time."

However, the Athenians seldom gather to eat for the mere sake of animal gorging. They have progressed since the Greeks of the Homeric Age. Odysseus* is made to say to Alcinotis that there is nothing more delightful than sitting at a table covered with bread, meat, and wine, and listening to a bard's song; and both Homeric poems show plenty of gross devouring and guzzling. There is not much of this in Athens, although Boeotians are still reproached with being voracious, swinish "flesh eaters," and the Greeks of South Italy and Sicily are considered as devoted to their fare, though of more refined table habits. Athenians of the better class pride themselves on their light diet and moderation of appetite, and their neighbors make considerable fun of them for their failure to serve satisfying meals. Certain it is that the typical Athenian would regard a twentieth century table d'hdte course dinner as heavy and unrefined, if ever it dragged its slow length before him.

156. The Staple Articles of Food.—However, the Athenians have honest appetites, and due means of silencing them. The diet of a poor man is indeed simple in the extreme. According to Aristophanes his meal consists of a cake, bristling with bran for the sake of economy, along with an onion and a dish of sow thistles, or of mushrooms, or some other such wretched vegetables; and probably, in fact, that is about all three fourths of the population of Attica will get on ordinary working days, always with the addition of a certain indispensable supply of oil and wine.

Bread, oil, and wine, in short, are the three fundamentals of Greek diet. With them alone man can live very healthfully and happily; without them elaborate vegetable and meat dishes are poor substitutes. Like latter-day Frenchmen or Italians with their huge loaves or macaroni, bread in one form or another is literally the staff of life to the

1 Odyssey, IX. 5-10.

Athenian Cookery and the Symposium 177

Greek. He makes it of wheat, barley, rye, millet, or spelt, but preferably of the two named first. As a rule the wheat flour alone is baked up into loaves. The barley meal is kneaded (not baked) and eaten raw or half raw as a sort of porridge. Of wheat loaves there are innumerable shapes on sale in the Agora, — slender rolls, convenient loaves, and also huge loaves needing two or three bushels of flour, exceeding even those made in a later day in Normandy. At every meal the amount of bread or porridge consumed is enormous; there is really little else at all substantial. Persian visitors to the Greeks complain that they are in danger of rising from the table hungry.

But along with the inevitable bread goes the inevitable olive oil. No latter-day article will exactly correspond to it. First of all it takes the place of butter as the proper condiment to prevent the bread from being tasteless. 1 It enters into every dish. The most versatile cook will be lost without it. Again, at the gymnasium we have seen its great importance to the athletes and bathers. It is therefore the Hellenic substitute for soap. Lastly, it fills the lamps which swing over every dining board. It takes the place of electricity, gas, or petroleum. No wonder Athens is proud of her olive trees. If she has to import her grain, she has a surplus for export of one of the three great essentials of Grecian life.

The third inevitable article of diet is wine. No one has dreamed of questioning its vast desirability under almost all circumstances. Even drunkenness is not always improper. It may be highly fitting, as putting one in a " divine frenzy," partaking of the nature of the gods. Musseus the semi-mythical poet is made out to teach that the reward of virtue will be something like perpetual intoxication in the next

i There was extremely little cow's butter in Greece. Herodotus (iv. 2) found it necessary to explain the process of " cow-cheese-making " among the Scythians.

world. ^Eschines the orator will, ere long, taunt his opponent Demosthenes in public with being a " watcr drinker "; and Socrates on many occasions has given proof that he possessed a very hard head. Yet naturally the Athenian has too acute a sense of things fit and dignified, too noble a perception of the natural harmony, to commend drunkenness on any but rare occasions. Wine is rather valued as imparting a happy moderate glow, making the thoughts come faster, and the tongue more witty. Wine raises the spirits of youth, and makes old age forget its gray hairs. It chases away thoughts of the dread hereafter, when one will lose consciousness of the beautiful sun, and perhaps wander a "strengthless shade" through the dreary underworld.

There is a song attributed to Anacreon, and nearly everybody in Athens approves the sentiment: —

Thirsty earth drinks up the rain, Trees from earth drink that again ; Ocean drinks the air, the sun Drinks the sea, and him, the moon. Any reason, canst thou think, I should thirst while all these drink? 1

157. Greek Vintages. — All Greeks, however, drink their wine so diluted with water that it takes a decided quantity to produce a " reaction." The average drinker takes three parts water to two of wine; if he is a little reckless the ratio is four of water to three of wine; equal parts " make men mad" as the poet says, and are probably reserved for very wild dinner parties. As for drinking pure wine no one dreams of the thing — it is a practice fit for Barbarians. There is good reason, however, for this plentiful use of water. In their original state Greek wines were very strong, perhaps almost as alcoholic as whisky, and the

1 Translation from Von Falke's Greece and Rome.

Athenians have no Scotch climate to excuse the use of such stimulants. 1

No wine served in Athens, however, will appeal to a later-day connoisseur. It is all mixed with resin, which perhaps makes it more wholesome, but to enjoy it then becomes an acquired taste. There are any number of choice vintages, and you will be told that the local Attic wine is not very desirable, although of course it is the cheapest. Black wine is the strongest and sweetest; white wine is the weakest; rich golden is the driest and most wholesome. The rocky isles and headlands of the ^gean seem to produce the best vintage—Thasos, Cos, Lesbos, Rhodes, all boast their grapes; but the best wine beyond a doubt is from Chios. 2 It will fetch a inina ($18) the "metreta," i.e. nearly 50 cents per quart. At this same time you can buy a "metreta" of common Attic wine for four drachmae (72 cents), or say two cents per quart. The latter — when one considers the dilution — is surely cheap enough for the most humble.

158. Vegetable Dishes.—Provided with bread, oil, and wine, no Athenian will long go hungry; but naturally these are not a whole feast. As season and purse may afford they will be supplanted by such vegetables as beans (a staple article), peas, garlic, onions, radishes, turnips, and asparagus ; also with an abundance of fruits,—besides figs (almost a fourth indispensable at most meals), apples, quinces, peaches,

1 There was a wide difference of opinion as to the proper amount of dilution. Odysseus (Odyssey, IX. 209) mixed his fabulously strong wine from Maron in Thrace with twenty times its

bulk of water. Hesiod abstemiously commended three parts of water to one of wine. Zaleucus, the lawgiver of Italian Locri, established the death penalty for drinking unmixed wine save by physicians' orders (Athenseus, X. 33).

2 Naturally certain foreign vintages had a demand, just because they were foreign. Wine was imported from Egypt and from various parts of Italy. It was sometimes mixed with sea water for export, or was made aromatic with various herbs and berries. It was ordinarily preserved in great earthern jars sealed with pitch.

pears, plums, cherries, blackberries, the various familiar nuts, and of course a plenty of grapes and olives. The range of selection is in fact decidedly wide: only the twentieth century visitor will miss the potato, the lemon, and the orange; and when he pries into the mysteries of the kitchen a great fact at once stares him in the face. The Greek must dress his dishes without the aid of sugar. As a substitute there is an abundant use of the delicious Hy-mettus honey, — "fragrant with the bees,"—but it is by no means so full of possibilities as the white powder of later days. Also the Greek cook is usually without fresh cow's milk, and most goat's milk probably takes its way to cheese. No morning milk carts rattle over the stones of Athens.

159. Meat and Fish Dishes. — Turning to the meat dishes, we at once learn that while there is a fair amount of farm poultry, geese, hares, doves, partridges, etc., on sale in the market, there is extremely little fresh beef or even mutton, pork, and goat's flesh. It is quite expensive, and counted too hearty for refined diners. The average poor man in fact hardly tastes flesh except after one of the great public festivals; then after the sacrifice of the "hecatomb" of oxen, there will probably be a distribution of roast meat to all the worshipers, and the honest citizen will take home to his wife an uncommon luxury — a piece of roast beef. But the place of beef and pork is largely usurped by most excellent fish. The waters of the JSgean abound with fish. The import of salt fish (for the use of the poor) from the Propontis and Euxine is a great part of Attic commerce. A large part of the business at the Agora centers around the fresh fish stalls, and we have seen how extortionate and insolent were the fishmongers. Sole, tunny, mackerel, young shark, mullet, turbot, carp, halibut, are to be had, but the choicest regular delicacies are the great Copaic eels from Boeotia; these, " roasted on the coals and wrapped in beet leaves,"

Athenian Cookery and the Symposium 181

are a dish fit for the Great King. Lucky is the host who has them for his dinner party. Oysters and mussels too are in demand, and there is a considerable sale of snails, " the poor man's salad," even as in present-day France.

Clearly, then, if one is not captious or gluttonous, there should be no lack of good eating in Athens, despite the reputation of the city for abstemiousness. Let us pry therefore into the symposium of some good citizen who is dispensing hospitality to-night.

160. Inviting Guests to a Dinner Party. —

Who loves thee, him summon to thy board; Far off be he who hates.

This familiar sentiment of Hesiod, one Prodicus, a well-to-do gentleman, had in mind when he went to the Agora this morning to arrange for a dinner party in honor of his friend Hermogenes, who was just departing on a diplomatic mission to the satrap of Mysia. While walking along the Painted Porch and the other colonnades he had no difficulty in seeing most of the group he intended to invite, and if they did not turn to greet him, he would halt them by sending his slave boy to run and twitch at their mantles, after which the invitation was given verbally. Prodicus, however, deliberately makes arrangements for one or two more than those he has bidden. It will be entirely proper for his guests to bring friends of their own if they wish; and very likely some intimate whom he has been unable to find will invite himself without any bidding.

At the Agora Prodicus has had much to do. His house is a fairly large and well-furnished one, his slaves numerous and handy, but he has not the cook or the equipment for a really elaborate symposium. At a certain quarter on the great square he finds a contractor who will supply all the extra appointments for a handsome dinner party — tables, extra lamps, etc. Then he puts his slave boy to bawling out:

"Who wants an engagement to cook a dinner?" This promptly brings forward a sleek, well-dressed fellow whose dialect declares that he is from Sicily, and who asserts he is an expert professional cook. Prodicus engages him and has a conference with him on the profound question of " whether the tunnies or the mullets are better to-day, or will there be fresh eels ? " This point and similar minor matters settled, Prodicus makes liberal purchases at the fish and vegetable stalls, and his slaves bear his trophies homeward.

161. Preparing for the Dinner. The Sicilian Cook. — All

that afternoon the home of Prodicus is in an uproar. The score of slaves show a frantic energy. The aula is cleaned and scrubbed: the serving girls are busy hanging festoons of leaves and weaving chaplets. The master's wife — who does not dream of actually sharing in the banquet — is nevertheless as active and helpful as possible; but especially she is busy trying to keep the peace between the old house servants and the imported cook. This Sicilian is a notable character. To him cookery is not a handicraft : it is the triumph, the quintessence of all science and philosophy. He talks a strange professional jargon, and asserts that he is himself learned in astronomy   for that teaches the best seasons, e.g. for mackerel and haddock; in geometry, — that he might know how a boiler or gridiron should be set to the best advantage; in medicine, that he might prepare the most wholesome dishes. In any case he is a perfect tyrant around the kitchen, grumbling about the utensils, cuffing the spit-boy, and ever bidding him bring more charcoal for the fire and to blow the bellows faster. 1 By the time evening is at hand Prodicus and his house

1 The Greeks seem to have cooked over a rather simple open fireplace with a wood or charcoal fire. They had an array of cooking utensils, however, according to all our evidence, elaborate enough to gladden a very exacting modern chef.

Athenian Cookery and the Symposium 183

are in perfect readiness. The bustle is ended; and the master stands by the entrance way, clad in his best and with a fresh myrtle wreath, ready to greet his guests. No ladies will be among these. Had there been any women invited to the banquet, they would surely be creatures of no very honest sort; and hardly fit, under any circumstances, to darken the door of a respectable citizen. The mistress and her maids are " behind the scenes." There may be a woman among the hired entertainers provided, but for a refined Athenian lady to appear at an ordinary symposium is almost unthinkable. 1

162. The Coming of the Guests. — As each guest comes, he is seen to be elegantly dressed, and to wear now, if at no other time, a handsome pair of sandals. 2 He has also taken pains to bathe and to perfume himself. As soon as each person arrives his sandals are removed in the vestibule by the slaves and his feet are bathed. No guest comes alone, however: every one has his own body servant with him, who will look after his footgear and himation during the dinner, and give a certain help with the serving. The house therefore becomes full of people, and will be the scene of remarkable animation during the next few hours.

Prodicus is not disappointed in expecting some extra visitors. His guest of honor, Hermogenes, has brought along two, whom the host greets with the polite lie: " Just in time for dinner. Put off your other business. I was looking for you in the Agora and could not find you." 3 Also there thrusts in a half genteel, half rascally fellow, one Palladas, iln marriage parties and other strictly family affairs women were allowed to take part; and we have an amusing fragment of Menander as to how, on such rare occasions, they monopolized the conversation.

2 Socrates, by way of exception to his custom, put on some fine sandals •when he was invited to a banquet.

«It is with such a white fib that the host Agathon salutes Aristodemus, Socrates's companion, in Plato's Symposium.

who spends all his evenings at dinner parties, being willing to be the common butt and jest of the company (having indeed something of the ability of a comic actor about him) in return for a share of the good things on the table. These " Parasites " are regular characters in Athens, and no symposium is really complete without them, although often their fooleries cease to be amusing. 1

163. The Dinner Proper. — The Greeks have not anticipated the Romans in their custom of making the standard dinner party nine persons on three couches, — three guests on each. Prodicus has about a dozen guests, two on a couch. They " lie down" more or less side by side upon the cushioned divans, with their right arms resting on brightly striped pillows and the left arms free for eating. The slaves bring basins of water to wash their hands, and then beside each couch is set a small table, already garnished with the first course, and after the casting of a few bits of food upon the family hearth fire, — the conventional " sacrifice " to the house gods, — the dinner begins.

Despite the elaborate preparations of the Sicilian cook, Prodicus offers his guests only two courses. The first consists of the substantial dishes — the fish, the vegetables, the meat (if there is any). Soups are not unknown, and had they been served might have been eaten with spoons; but Athens like all the world is innocent of forks, and fingers take their place. Each guest has a large piece of soft bread on which he wipes his fingers from time to time and presently

1 Ol these " Parasites" or "Flies" (as owing to their migratory habits they were sometimes called), countless stories were told, whereof the following is a sample: There was once a law in Athens that not over thirty guests were to be admitted to a marriage feast, and an officer was obliged to count all the guests and exclude the superfluous. A "fly" thrust in on one occasion, and the officer said : " Friend, you must retire. I find one more here than the law allows." " Dear fellow," quoth the " fly," " you are utterly mistaken, as you will find, if you will kindly count again — only beginning with me."

Athenian Cookery and the Symposium 185

casts it upon the floor. 1 When this first course is finished, the tables are all taken out to be reset, water is again poured over the hands of the guests, and garlands of flowers are passed. The use of garlands is universal, and among the guests, old white headed and bearded Sosthenes will find nothing more undignified in putting himself beneath a huge wreath of lilies than an elderly gentleman of a later day will find in donning the "conventional" dress suit. The conversation, — which was very scattering at first, — becomes more animated. A little wine is now passed about. Then back come the tables with the second course — fruits, and various sweetmeats and confectionery with honey as the staple flavoring. Before this disappears a goblet of unmixed wine is passed about, and everybody takes a sip: " To the Good Genius," they say as the cup goes round.

164. Beginning the Symposium. — Prodicus at length gives a nod to the chief of his corps of servers.

" Bring in the wine!" he orders. The slaves promptly whisk out the tables and replace them with others still smaller, on which they set all kinds of gracefully shaped beakers and drinking bowls. More wreaths are distributed, also little bottles of delicate ointment. While the guests are praising Prodicus's nard, the servants have brought in three huge " mixing bowls " (craters) for the wines which are to furnish the main potation.

So far we have witnessed not a symposium, but merely a dinner; and many a proper party has broken up when the last of the dessert has disappeared; but, after all, the drinking bout is the real crown of the feast. It is not so much the wine as the things that go with the wine that are so delightful. As to what these desirable condiments are, opinions differ. Plato (who is by no means too much of a philosopher to be a real man of the world) says in his

Protagoras that mere conversation is the thing at a sym. posium. " When the company are real gentlemen and men of education, you will see no flute girls nor dancing girls nor harp girls; they will have no nonsense nor games, but will be content with one another's conversation." 1 But this ideal, though commended, is not always followed in decidedly intellectual circles. Xenophon 2 shows us a select party wherein Socrates participated, in which the host has been fain to hire in a professional Syracusian entertainer with two assistants, a boy and a girl, who bring their performance to a climax by a very suggestive dumb-show play of the story of Bacchus and Ariadne. Prodicus's friends, being solid, somewhat pragmatic men — neither young sports nor philosophers — steer a middle course. There is a flute girl present, because to have a good symposium without some music is almost unimaginable; but she is discreetly kept in the background.

165. The Symposiarch and his Duties. — "Let's cast for our Symposiarch!" is Prodicus's next order, and each guest in turn rattles the dice box. Tyche (Lady Fortune) gives the presidency of the feast to Eunapius, a bright-eyed, middle-aged man with a keen humor, but a correct sense of good breeding. He assumes command of the symposium; takes the ordering of the servants out of Prodicus's hands, and orders the wine to be mixed in the craters with proper dilution. He then rises and pours out a libation from each bowl "to the Olympian Gods," "to the Heroes," and "to Zeus the Saviour," and casts a little incense upon the altar. The guests all sing a Pcean, not a warrior's charging song this time, but a short hymn in praise of the Wine-God, some lilting catch like Alceeus's

1 Plato again says (Politicals, 277 6), " To intelligent persons, a living being is mor« truly delineated by language and discourse than by any painting or work of art."

2 In his Symposium — which is far less perfect as literature than Plato's, but probably corresponds more to the average instance.

Athenian Cookery and the Symposium 187

In mighty flagons hither bring The deep red blood of many a vine,

That we may largely quaff and sing The praises of the God of wine.

166. Conversation at the Symposium. — After this the symposium will proceed according to certain general rules which it is Eunapius's duty to enforce; but in the main a "program" is something to be avoided. Everybody must feel himself acting spontaneously and freely. He must try to take his part in the conversation and neither speak too seldom nor too little. It is not " good form " for two guests to converse privately among themselves, nor for anybody to dwell on unpleasant or controversial topics. Aristophanes has laid down after his way the proper kind of things to talk about. 1 " [Such as] < how Ephudion fought a fine pancratium with Ascondas though old and gray headed, but showing great form 'and muscle.' This is the talk usual among refined people [or again] * some manly act of your youth; for example, how you chased a boar or a hare, or won a torch race by some bold device.' [Then when fairly settled at the feast] straighten your knees and throw yourself in a graceful and easy manner upon the couch. Then make some observations upon the beauty of the appointments, look up at the ceiling and praise the tapestry of

the room."

As the wine goes around, tongues loosen more and more. Everybody gesticulates in delightful southern gestures, but does not lose his inherent courtesy. The anecdotes told are often very egoistic. The first personal pronoun is used extremely often, and " I" becomes the hero of a great many exploits. The Athenian, in short, is an adept at praising himself with affected modesty, and his companions listen good-humoredly, and retaliate by praising themselves.

167. Games and Entertainments. — By the time the craters are one third emptied the general conversation is beginning to be broken up. It is time for various standard diversions. Eunapius therefore begins by enjoining on each guest in turn to sing a verse in which a certain letter must not appear, and in event of failure to pay some ludicrous forfeit. Thus the bald man is ordered to begin to comb his hair; the lame man (halt since the Mantinea campaign), to stand up and dance to the flute player, etc. There are all kinds of guessing of riddles — often very ingenious as become the possessors of " Attic salt." Another diversion is to compare every guest present to some mythical monster, a process which infallibly ends by getting the "Parasite" likened to Cerberus, the Hydra, or some such dragon, amid the laughter of all the rest. At some point in the amusement the company is sure to get to singing songs: — " Scolia " — drinking songs indeed, but often of a serious moral or patriotic character, whereof the oft-quoted song in praise of Har-modius and Aristogeiton the tyrant-slayers is a good example. 1 No "gentleman" will profess to be a public singer, but to have a deep, well-trained voice, and to be able to take one's part in the symposium choruses is highly desirable, and some of the singing at Prodicus's banquet is worth hearing.

Before the evening is over various games will be ordered in, especially the cottabus, which is in great vogue. On the top of a high stand, something like a candelabrum, is balanced rather delicately a little saucer of brass. The players stand at a considerable distance with cups of wine. The game is to toss a small quantity of wine into the balanced saucer so smartly as to make the brass give out a clear ringing sound, and to tilt over upon its side. 2 Much shouting,

1 Given in Readings in Ancient History, Vol. I, p. 117, and in many other volumes.

2 This was the simplest form of the cottabus game; there were numerous elaborations, but our accounts of them are by no means clear.

merriment, and a little wagering ensues. While most of the company prefer the cottabus, two, who profess to be experts, call for a gaming board and soon are deep in the " game of towns " — very like to latter-day " checkers," played with a board divided into numerous squares. Each contestant has thirty colored stones, and the effort is to surround your opponent's stones and capture them. Some of the company, however, regard this as too profound, and after trying their skill at the cottabus betake themselves to the never failing chances of dice. Yet these games are never suffered (in refined dinner parties) to banish the conversation. That after all is the center, although it is not good form to talk over learnedly of statecraft, military tactics, or philosophy. If such are discussed, it must be with playful abandon, and a disclaimer of being serious; and even very grave and gray men remember Anacreon's preference for the praise of " the glorious gifts of the Muses and of Aphrodite " rather than solid discussions of "conquest and war."

168. Going Home from the Feast: Midnight Revellers. —At length the oil lamps have begun to burn dim. The tired slaves are yawning. Their masters, despite Prodicus's intentions of having a very proper symposium, have all drunk enough to get unstable and silly. Eunapius gives the signal. All rise, and join in the final libation to Hermes. "Shoes and himation, boy," each says to his slave, and with thanks to their host they all fare homeward.

Such will be the ending to an extremely decorous feast. With gay young bloods present, however, it might have degenerated into an orgy; the flute girl (or several of them) would have contributed over much to the "freedom "; and when the last deep crater had been emptied, the whole company would have rushed madly into the street, and gone whirling away through the darkness, — harps and

flutes sounding, boisterous songs pealing, red torches tossing. Eevellers in this mood would be ready for anything. Perhaps they would end in some low tavern at the Peiraeus to sleep off their liquor; perhaps their leader would find some other Symposium in progress, and after loud knoekings, force his way into the house, even as did the mad Alcibiades, who (once more to recall Plato) thrust his way into Agathon's feast, staggering, leaning on a flute girl, and shouting " Where's Agathon!" Such an inroad would be of course the signal for more and ever more hard drinking. The wild invaders might make themselves completely at home, and dictate all the proceedings: the end would be even as at Agathon's banquet, where everybody but Socrates became completely drunken, and lay prone on the couches or the floor. One hopes that the honest Prodicus has no such climax to his symposium.

... At length the streets grow quiet. Citizens sober or drunken are asleep: only the vigilant Scythian archers patrol the ways till the cocks proclaim the first gray of dawn.

CHAPTER XIX COUNTRY LIFE AROUND ATHENS

169. Importance of his Farm to an Athenian. — We have followed the doings of a typical Athenian during his ordinary activities around the city, but for the average gentleman an excursion outside the town is indispensable at least every two or three days, and perhaps every day. He must visit his farm; for his wealth and income are probably tied up there, rather than in any unaristocratic commercial and manufacturing enterprises. Homer's " royal" heroes are not ashamed to be skilful at following the plow 1 : and no Athenian feels that he is contaminating himself by " trade " when he supervises the breeding of sheep or the raising of onions. We will therefore follow in the tracks of certain well-to-do citizens, when we turn toward the Itonian gate sometime during the morning, while the Agora is still in a busy hum, even if thus we are curtailing our hypothetical visits to the Peirseus or to the bankers.

170. The Country by the Ilissus; the Greeks and Natural Beauty. — Our companions are on horseback (a token of tolerable wealth in Athens), but the beasts amble along not too rapidly for nimble grooms to run behind, each ready to aid his respective master. Once outside the gate the regular road swings down to the south towards Phalerum ; we, however, are in no great haste and desire to see as much as possible. The farms we are seeking lie well north of the

i See Odysseus's boasts, Odyssey, XVIII. 360 et passim. The gentility of farming is emphasized by a hundred precepts from Hesiod. 101

city, but we can make a delightful circuit by skirting the city walls with the eastern shadow of the Acropolis behind us, and going at first northeast, along the groves and leafy avenues which line the thin stream of the Ilissus, 1 the second " river " of Athens.

Before us through the trees came tantalizing glimpses of the open country running away towards shaggy gray Hymettus. Left to itself the land would be mostly arid and seared brown by the summer sun; but everywhere the friendly work of man is visible. One can count the little green oblong patches, stretching even up the mountain side, marked with gleaming \white farm buildings or sometimes with little temples and chapels sacred to the rural gods. Once or twice also we notice a plot of land which seems one tangled waste of trees and shrubbery. This is a sacred temenos, an inviolate grove, set apart to some god; and within the fences of the compound no mortal dare set foot under pain of direful sacrilege and pollution.

Following a kind of bridle path, however, we are soon amid the groves of olive and other trees, while the horses plod their slow way beside the brook. Not a few citizens going or coming from Athens meet us, for this is really one of the parks and breathing spaces of the closely built city. The Athenians and Greeks in general live in a land of such natural beauty that they take this loveliness as a matter of course. Very seldom do their poets indulge in deliberate descriptions of " beautiful landscapes "; but none the less the fair things of nature have penetrated deeply into their souls. The constant allusions in Homer and the other masters of song to the great storm waves, the deep shades of the forest, the crystal brooks, the pleasant rest for wanderers under the shade trees, the plains bright with spring

J The Ilissus, unlike its sturdier rival, the Cephisus, ran dry during the summer heats; but there was enough water along its bed to create a dense vegetation.

flowers, the ivy twining above- a grave, the lamenting nightingale, the chirping cicada, tell their own story; men seldom describe at length what is become warp and woof of their inmost lives. The mere fact that the Greeks dwell constantly in such a beautiful land, and have learned to love it so intensely, makes frequent and set descriptions thereto seem trivial.

171. Plato's Description of the Walk by the Ilissus.— Nevertheless occasionally this inborn love of the glorious outer world must find its expression, and it is of these very groves along the Ilissus that we have one of the few " nature pieces" in Athenian literature. As the plodding steeds take their way let us recall our Plato — his Phcedrus, written probably not many years before this our visit.

Socrates is walking with Phaedrus outside the walls, and urges the latter : " Let us go to the Ilissus and sit down in some quiet spot." " I am fortunate," answers Phaedrus, " in not having my sandals on, and, as you never have any, we may go along the brook and cool our feet. This is the easiest way, and at midday is anything but unpleasant." He adds that they will go on to the tallest plane tree in the distance, "where are shade and gentle breezes, and grass whereon we may either sit or lie. . . . The little stream is delightfully clear and bright. I can fancy there might well be maidens playing near [according to the local myth of Boreas's rape of Orithyia]." And so at last they come to the place, when Socrates says: " Yes indeed, a fair and shady resting place it is, full of summer sounds and scents. There is the lofty and spreading plane tree, and the agnus castus, high and clustering in the fullest blossom and the greatest fragrance, and the stream which flows beneath the plane tree is deliciously cool to the feet. Judging by the ornaments and images [set] about, this must be a spot sacred to Achelous and the Nymphs; moreover there is a sweet breeze

and the grasshoppers are chirruping; and the greatest charm of all is the grass like a pillow, gently sloping to the head." l

172. The Athenian Love of Country Life. — So the two friends had sat them down to delve in delightful profundities ; but following the bridle path, the little brook and its groves end for us all too soon. We are in the open country around Athens, and the fierce rays of Helios beat strongly on our heads. We are outside the city, but by no means far from human life. Farm succeeds farm, for the land around Athens has a goodly population to maintain, and there is a round price for vegetables in the Agora. Truth to tell, the average Athenian, though he pretends to love the market, the Pnyx, the Dicasteries, and the Gymnasia, has a shrewd hankering for the soil, and does not care to spend more time in Athens than necessary. Aristophanes is full of the contrasts between " country life " and " city life " and almost always with the advantage given the former. Says his Strepsiades (in The Clouds), " A country life for me — dirty, untrimmed, lolling around at ease, and just abounding in bees and sheep and oil cake." His Diceaeopolis (Acharnians) voices clearly the independence of the farmer: "How I long for peace. 2 I'm disgusted with the city ; and yearn for my own farm which never bawled out [as in the markets]

'buy my coals' or 'buy my vinegar' or 'oil,' or knew the word 'buy,' but just of itself produced everything." And his Trygaeus (in The Peace) states the case better yet: " Ah ! how eager I am to get back into the fields, and break up my little farm with the mattock again . . . [for I remember] what kind of a life we had there; and those cakes of dried fruits, and the figs, and the myrtles, and the sweet

1 Jewett, translator; slightly altered.

3 I.e. the end of the Peloponnesian War, which compelled the farming population to remove inside the walls.

new wine, and the violet bed next to the well, and the olives we so long for!"

There is another reason why the Athenians rejoice in the country. The dusty streets are at best a poor playground for the children, the inner court of the house is only a respectable prison for the wife. In the country the lads can enjoy themselves; the wife and the daughters can roam about freely with delightful absence of convention. There will be no happier day in the year than when the master says, " Let us set out for the farm."

173. Some Features of the Attic Country.—Postponing our examination of Athenian farmsteads and farming methods until we reach some friendly estate, various things strike us as we go along the road. One is the skilful system of irrigation, — the numerous watercourses drawn especially from the Cephisus, whereby the agriculturists make use of every possible scrap of moisture for the fields, groves, and vineyards. Another is the occasional olive tree we see standing, gnarled and venerable, but carefully fenced about; or even (not infrequently) we see fences only with but a dead and utterly worthless stump within. Do not speak lightly of these "stumps," however. They are none the less "moriai" — sacred olive trees of Athena, and carefully tended by public wardens. 1 Contractors are allowed to take the fruit

1 Athenians loved to dwell on the "divine gift" of the olive. Thus Euripides sang (Troades, 799) : —

In Salamis, filled with the foaming
Of billows and murmur of bees, Old Telamon stayed from his roaming
Long ago, on a throne of the seas, Looking out on the hills olive laden,
Enchanted, where first from the earth The gray-gleaming fruit of the Maiden
Athena had birth. —MURRAY, translator.
The hero Telamon was reputed an uncle of Achilles and one of the early kings of Salamis.

A Day in Old Athens

of the live trees under carefully regulated conditions ; but no one is allowed to remove the stumps, much less hew down a living tree. An offender is tried for " impiety " before the high court of the Areopagus, and his fate is pretty surely

death, for the country people, at least, regard their sacred trees with a fanatical devotion which it would take long to explain to a stranger.

Also upon the way one is pretty sure to meet a wandering beggar — a shrewd-eyed, bewhiskered fellow. He carries, not a barrel organ and monkey, but a blinking tame crow

perched on his shoulder, and at every farmstead he halts to whine his nasal ditty and ask his dole.

Good people, a handful of barley bestow On the child of Apollo, the sleek sable crow ; Or a trifle of wheat, 0 kind friends, give ; — Or a wee loaf of bread that the crow may live.

It is counted good luck by the housewife to have a chance to feed a "holy crow," and the owner's pickings are goodly. By the time we have left the beggar behind us we are at the farm whither our excursion has been tending.

174. An Attic Farmstead. — We are to inspect the landed estate of Hybrias, the son of

Xanthippus. It lies north of Athens on the slopes of Anchesmus, one of the lesser hills

ITINERANT PIPER WITH HIS Doc.

which roll away toward the marble-crowned summits of Pentelicus. Part of the farm lands lie on the level ground watered by the irrigation ditches; part upon the hillsides, and here the slopes have been terraced in a most skilful fashion, in order to make the most of every possible inch of ground, and also to prevent any of the precious soil from being washed down by the torrents of February and March. The owner is a wealthy man, and has an extensive establishment ; the farm buildings — once whitewashed, but now for the most part somewhat dirty — wander away over a large area. There are wide courts, deep in manure, surrounded by barns; there are sties, haymows, carefully closed granaries, an olive press, a grain mill, all kinds of stables and folds, likewise a huge irregularly shaped house wherein are lodged the numerous slaves and the hired help. The general design of this house is the same as of a city house

— the rooms opening upon an inner court, but naturally its dimensions are ampler, with the ampler land space.

Just now the courtyard is a noisy and animated sight. The master has this moment ridden in, upon one of his periodic visits from Athens ; the farm overseer has run out to meet him and report, and half a dozen long, lean hunting dogs — Darter, Eoarer, Tracker, Active, and more 1 — are dancing and yelping, in the hope that their owner will order a hare hunt. The overseer is pouring forth his usual burden of woe about the inefficient help and the lack of rain, and Hybrias is complaining of the small spring crop

— " Zeus send us something better this summer !" While these worthies are adjusting their troubles we may look around the farm.

175. Plowing, Reaping, and Threshing. — Thrice a year the Athenian farmer plows, unless he wisely determines

1 For an exhaustive list of names for Greek dogs, see Xenophon'g curious Ussay on Hunting, ch. VII, § 5.

A Day in Old Athens

to let his field lie fallow for the nonce; and the summer plowing on Hybrias's estate is now in progress. Up and down a wide field the ox team is going. 1 The plow is an extremely primitive affair— mainly of wood, although over the sharpened point which forms the plowshare a plate of iron has been fitted. Such a plow requires very skilful

handling to cut a good furrow, and the driver of the team has no sinecure.

In a field near by, the hinds are reaping a crop of wheat which was late in ripening. 2 The workers are bending with semicircular sickles over their hot task ; yet they form a merry, noisy crowd, full of homely "harvest songs," nominally in honor of Demeter, the Earth Mother, but ranging upon every conceivable rustic topic. Some laborers are cutting the grain, others, walking behind, are binding into sheaves and piling into clumsy ox wains. Here and there a sheaf is standing, and we are told that this is left "for luck," as an offering to the rural Field Spirit; for your farm hand is full of superstitions. Also amid the workers a youth is passing with a goodly jar of cheap wine, to which the harvesters make free to run from time to time for refreshment.

Close by the field is the threshing floor. More laborers

1 Mules were sometimes used for drawing the plow, but horses, it would seem, never.

2 The regular time for reaping the October-sown wheat was May or June.

WOMEN POUNDING MEAL.

— not a few bustling country lasses among them — are spreading out the sheaves with wooden forks, a little at a time, in thin layers over this circular space, which is paved with little cobblestones. More oxen and a patient mule are being driven over it — around and around — until every kernel is trodden out by their hoofs. Later will come the tossing and the winnowing; and, when the grain has been thoroughly cleaned, it will be stored in great earthern jars for the purpose of sale or against the winter.

176. Grinding at the Mill.—Nearer the farmhouses there rises a dull grinding noise. It is the mill preparing the flour for the daily baking, for seldom — at least in the country — will a Greek grind flour long in advance of the time of use. There the round upper millstone is being revolved upon an iron pivot against its lower mate and turned by a long wooden handle. Two nearly naked slave boys are turning this wearily — far pleasanter they consider the work of the harvesters, and very likely this task is set them as a punishment. As the mill revolves a slave girl pours the grain into a hole in the center of the upper millstone. As the hot, slow work goes on, the two toilers chant together a snatch from an old mill song, and we catch the monotonous strain: —

Grind, mill, grind,
For Pittacus did grind —
Who was king over great Mytilene.

It will be a long time before there is enough flour for the day. The slaves can at least rejoice that they live on a large farm. If Hybrias owned a smaller estate, they would probably be pounding up the grain with mortar and pestle

— more weary yet.

177. The Olive Orchards.— We, at least, can leave them to their work, and escape to the shade of the orchards and the

vineyards. Like every Athenian farmer, Hybrias has an olive orchard. The olives are sturdy trees. They will grow in any tolerable soil and thrive upon the mountain slopes up to as far as 1800 feet above sea level. They are not large trees, and their trunks are often grotesquely gnarled, but there is always a certain fascination about the wonderful shimmer of their leaves, which flash from gray

GATHERING THE OLIVE HARVEST.

to silver-white in a sunny wind. Hybrias has wisely planted his olives at wide intervals, and in the space between the ground has been plowed up for grain. Olives need little care. Their harvest comes late in the autumn, after all the other crops are out of the way. They are among the most profitable products of the farm, and the owner will not mind the poor wheat harvest " if only the olives do well." 1

1 The great drawback to olive culture was the great length of time required to mature the trees—sixteen years. The destruction of the trees,

178. The Vineyards. — The fig orchard forms another great part of the farm, but more interesting to strangers are the vineyards. Some of the grapes are growing over pointed stakes set all along the upland terraces; a portion of the vineyards, however, is on level ground. Here a most picturesque method has been used for training the vines. Tall and graceful trees have been set out — elm, maple, oak, poplar. The lower limbs of the trees have been cut away and up their trunks and around their upper branches now swing the vines in magnificent festoons. The growing vines have sprung from tree to tree. The warm breeze has set the rich clusters — already turning purple or golden — swaying above our heads. The air is filled with brightness, greenery, and fragrance. The effect of this " vineyard grove " is magical.

179. Cattle, Sheep, and Goats. — There is also room in the orchards for apples, pears, and quinces, but there is nothing distinctive about their culture. If we are interested in cattle, however, we can spend a long time at the barns, or be guided out to the upland pasture where Hybrias's flocks and herds are grazing. Horses are a luxury. They are almost never used in farm work, and for riding and cavalry service it is best to import a good courser from Thessaly; no attempt, therefore, is made to breed them here. But despite the small demand for beef and butter a good many cattle are raised; for oxen are needed for the plowing and carting, oxhides have a steady sale, and there is a regular call for beeves for the hecatombs at the great public sacrifices. Sheep are in greater acceptance. Their wool is of large importance to a land which knows comparatively little of cotton. They can live on scanty pastur-

e.g. in war by a ravaging invader, was an infinitely greater calamity than the burning of the standing grain or even of the farmhouses. Probably it was the ruin of their olive trees which the Athenians mourned most during the ravaging of Attica in the Peloponnesian War.

A Day in Old Athens

age where an ox would starve. Still more in favor are goats. Their coarse hair has a thousand uses. Their flesh and cheese are among the most staple articles in the Agora. Sure-footed and adventurous, they scale the side of the most unpromising crags in search of herbage and can sometimes be seen perching, almost like birds, in what seem utterly

inaccessible eyries. Thanks to them the barren highlands of Attica are turned to good account, — and between goat raising and bee culture an income can sometimes be extracted from the very summits of the mountains. As for the numerous swine, it is

RURAL SACRIFICE TO A WOODEN STATUE OF DIONYSUS.

enough to say that they range under Hybrias's oak forest and fatten

on the acorns, although their swineherd, wrapped in a filthy sheepskin, is a far more loutish and ignoble fellow than the " divine Eumaeus " glorified in the Odyssey.

180. The Gardens and the Shrine. — Did we wish to linger, we could be shown the barnyard with its noisy retinue of hens, pheasants, guinea fowl, and pigeons; and we would be asked to admire the geese, cooped up and being gorged for fattening, or the stately peacocks preening their splendors. We would also hear sage disquisitions from the "oldest inhabitants " on the merits of fertilizers, especially on the uses of mixing seaweed with manure, also we would be told of the almost equally important process of burying a toad in a sealed jar in the midst of a field to save the corn from

the crows and the field mice. Hybrias laughs at such superstitions — "but what can you say to the rustics?" Hybrias himself will display with more refined pride the gardens used by his wife and children when they come out from Athens, — a fountain feeding a delightful rivulet; myrtles, roses, and pomegranate trees shedding their perfumes, which are mingled with the odors from the beds of hyacinths, violets, and asphodel. In the center of the gardens rises a chaste little shrine with a marble image and an altar, always covered with flowers or fruit by the mistress and her women. " To Artemis," reads the inscription, and one is sure that the virgin goddess takes more pleasure in this fragrant temple than in many loftier fanes. 1

We are glad to add here our wreaths ere turning away from this wholesome, verdant country seat, and again taking our road to Athens.

1 For the description of a very beautiful and elaborate country estate, with a temple thereon to Artemis, see Xenophon's Anabasis, bk. V. 3.

CHAPTER XX. THE TEMPLES AND GODS OF ATHENS.

181. Certain Factors in Athenian Religion. — We have seen the Athenians in their business and in their pleasure, at their courts, their assemblies, their military musters, and on their

peaceful farms ; yet one great side of Athenian life has been almost ignored — the religious side. A " Day in Athens " spent without taking account of the gods of the city and their temples would be a day spent with almost half-closed eyes. 1

It is far easier to learn how the Athenians arrange their houses than how the average man among them adjusts his attitude toward the gods. While any searching examination of the fundamentals of Greek cultus and religion is here impossible, two or three facts must, nevertheless, be kept in mind, if we are to understand even the outward side of this Greek religion which is everywhere in evidence about us.

First of all we observe that the Greek religion is a religion of purely natural growth. No prophet has initiated it, or claimed a new revelation to supplement the older views. It has come from primitive times without a visible break even down to the Athens of Plato. This explains at once why so many time-honored stories of the Olympic deities are very gross, and why the gods seem to give countenance

1 No attempt is made in this discussion to enumerate the various gods and demigods of the conventional mythology, their regular attributes, etc. It is assumed the average history or manual of mythology gives sufficient information.

to moral views which the best public opinion has long since called scandalous and criminal. The religion of Athens, in other words, may justly claim to be judged by its best, not by its worst; by the morality of Socrates, not of Homer.

Secondly, this religion is not a church, nor a belief, but is part of the government. Every Athenian is born into accepting the fact that Athena Polias is the divine warder of the city, as much as he is born into accepting the fact that it is his duty to obey the strategi in battle. To repudiate the gods of Athens, e.g. in favor of those of Egypt, is as much iniquity as to join forces against the Athenians if they are at war with Egypt; — the thing is sheer treason, and almost unthinkable. For countless generations the Athenians have worshipped the " Ancestral Gods." They are proud of them, familiar with them ; the gods have participated in all the prosperity of the city. Athena is as much a part of Attica as gray Hymettus or white-crowned Pentelicus ; and the very fact that comedians, like Aristophanes, make good-natured fun of the divinities indicates that " they are members of the family."

Thirdly, notice that this religion is one mainly of outward reverence and ceremony. There is no " Athenian church " ; nobody has drawn up an " Attic creed " — "I believe in Athena, the City Warder, and in Demeter, the Earth Mother, and in Zeus, the King of Heaven, etc." Give outward reverence, participate in the great public sacrifices, be careful in all the minutiae of private worship, refrain from obvious blasphemies — you are then a sufficiently pious man. What you believe is of very little con sequence. Even if you privately believe there are no gods at all, it harms no one, provided your outward conduct is pious and moral.

182. What constitutes "Piety" in Athens. —Of course there have been some famous prosecutions for " impiety." Socrates was the most conspicuous victim; but Socrates

was a notable worshipper of the gods, and certainly all the charges of his being an " atheist" broke down. What he was actually attacked with was "corrupting the youth of Athens," i.e. giving the young men such warped ideas of their private and public duties that they ceased to be moral and useful citizens. But even Socrates was convicted only with difficulty 1 ; a generation has passed since his death. Were he on trial at present, a majority of the jury would probably be with him.

The religion of Athens is something very elastic, and really every man makes his own creed for himself, or — for paganism is almost never dogmatic — accepts the outward cultus with everybody else, and speculates at his leisure on the nature of the deity. The great bulk of the uneducated are naturally content to accept the old stories and superstitions with unthinking credulity. It is enough to know that one must pray to Zeus for rain, and to Hermes for luck in a slippery business bargain. There are a few philosophers who, along with perfectly correct outward observance, teach privately that the old Olympian system is a snare and folly. They pass around the daring word which Xenophanes uttered as early as the sixth century B.C.: —

One God there is, greatest of gods and mortals,
Not like to man is he in mind or in body.
All of him sees, all of him thinks, and all of him hearkens.

This, of course, is obvious pantheism, but it is easy to cover up all kinds of pale monotheism or pantheism under vague references to the omnipotence of " Zeus."

183. The Average Athenian's Idea of the Gods.—The average intelligent citizen probably has views midway be-

1 It might be added that if Socrates had adopted a really worldly wise line of defense, he would probably have been acquitted, or subjected merely to a mild pecuniary penalty.

The Temples and Gods of Athens 207

tvveen the stupid rabble and the daring philosophers. To him the gods of Greece stand out in full divinity, honored and worshipped because they are protectors of the good, avengers of the evil, and guardians of the moral law. They punish crime and reward virtue, though the punishment may tarry long. They demand a pure heart and a holy mind of all that approach them, and woe to him who wantonly defies their eternal laws. This is the morality taught by the master tragedians, ./Eschylus and Sophocles, and accepted by the best public opinion at Athens; for the insidious doubts cast by Euripides upon the reality of any divine scheme of governance have never struck home. The scandalous stories about the domestic broils on Olympus, in which Homer indulges, only awaken good-natured banter. It is no longer proper—as in Homeric days— to pride oneself on one's cleverness in perjury and common falsehood. Athenians do not have twentieth century notions about the wickedness of lying, but certain it is the gods do not approve thereof. In short, most of the better class of Athenians are genuinely "religious"; nevertheless they have too many things in this human world to interest them to spend overmuch time in adjusting their personal concepts of the deity to any system of theology.

184. Most Greeks without belief in Immortality. — Yct one thing we must add. This Greek religious morality is built up without any clear belief in a future life. Never has the average Hellene been able to form a satisfactory conception of the soul's existence, save dwelling within a mortal body and under the glorious light of beloved Helios. To Homer the after life in Hades was merely the perpetuation of the shadows of departed humanity, " strengthless shades " who live on the gloomy plains of asphodel, feeding upon dear memories, and incapable of keen emotions or any real mental or physical progress or action. Only a few great sinners

like Tantalus, doomed to eternal torture, or favored heings like Menelaus, predestined to the " Blessed Isles," are ordained to any real immortality. As the centuries advanced, and the possibilities of this terrestrial world grew ever keener, the hope of any future state became ever more vague. The fear of a gloomy shadow life in Hades for the most part disappeared, but that was only to confirm the belief that death ends all things.

Where'er his course man tends, Inevitable death impends, And for the worst and for the best, Is strewn the same dark couch of rest. 1

So run the lines of a poet whose name is forgotten, but who spoke well the thought of his countrymen.

True there has been a contradiction of this gloomy theory. The " Orphic Mysteries," those secret religious rites which have gained such a hold in many parts of Greece, including Athens, probably hold out an earnest promise to the "initiates " of a blessed state for them hereafter. The doctrine of a real elysium for the good and a realm of torment for the evil has been expounded by many sages. Pindar, the great bard of Thebes, has set forth the doctrine in a glowing ode. 2 Socrates, if we may trust the report Plato gives of him, has spent his last hours ere drinking the hemlock, in adducing cogent, philosophic reasons for the immortality of the soul. All this is true, — and it is also true that these ideas have made no impression upon the general Greek consciousness. They are accepted half-heartedly by a relatively few exceptional thinkers. Men go through life and face death with no real expectation of future reward or punishment, or of reunion with the dear departed. If the gods

iMilman, translator.

5 Quoted in Readings in Ancient History, vol. I, pp. 261-262, and in many works in Greek literature.

The Temples and Gods of Athens 209

are angry, you escape them at the grave; if the gods are friendly, all they can give is wealth, health, honor, a hale old age, and prosperity for your children. The instant after death the righteous man and the robber are equal. This fundamental deduction from the Greek religion must usually, therefore, be made — it is a religion for this world only. Let us see what are its usual outward operations.

185. The Multitude of Images of the Gods.—Gods are everywhere in Athens. You cannot take the briefest walk without being reminded that the world is full of deities. There is a " Herm " l by the main door of every house, as well as a row of them across the Agora. At many of the street crossings are little shrines to Hecate; or statues of Apollo Agyieus, the street guardian; or else a bay tree stands there, a graceful reminder of this same god, to which it is sacred. In every house there is the small altar whereon garlands and fruit offerings are daily laid to Zeus Herkeios, and another altar to Hestia. On one or both of these altars a little food and a little wine are cast at every meal. All public meetings or court sessions open with sacrifice; in short, to attempt any semi-important public or private act without inviting the friendly attention of the deity is unthinkable. To a well-bred Athenian this is second instinct ; he considers it as inevitable as the common courtesies of speech among gentlemen. Plato sums up the current opinion well, "All men who have any decency, in the attempting of matters great or small, always invoke divine aid." 2

»A stone post about shoulder high, surmounted by a bearded head. Contrary to modern impression, the average Greek did not conceive of Hermes as a beautiful youth. He was a grave, bearded man. The youthful aspect came through the manipulation of the Hermes myths by the master sculptors — e.g. Praxiteles.

186. Greek Superstition. — In many cases, naturally, piety runs off into crass superstition. The gods, everybody knows, frequently make known future events by various signs. He who can understand these signs will be able to adjust his life accordingly and enjoy great prosperity. Most educated men take a sensible view of " omens," and do not let them influence their conduct absurdly. Some, however, act otherwise. There is, for instance, Laches, one of the guests at Prodicus's feast. He lives in a realm of mingled hopes and fears, although he is wealthy and well-educated. 1 He is all the time worried about dreams, and paying out money to the sharp and wily "seer" (who counts him his best client) for " interpretations." If a weasel crosses his path, he will not walk onward until somebody else has gone before him, or until he has thrown three stones across the road. He is all the time worrying about the significance of sudden noises, meteors, thunder; especially he is disturbed when he sees birds flying in groups or towards unlucky quarters of the heavens. 2 Laches, however, is not merely religious — although he is always

asking " which god shall I invoke now ? " or " what are the omens for the success of this enterprise ? " His own associates mock him as being superstitious, and say they never trouble themselves about omens save in real emergencies. Still it is " bad luck " for any of them to stumble over a threshold, to meet a hare suddenly, or especially to find a snake (the companion of the dead) hidden in the house.

187. Consulting Omens. — Laches's friends, however, all regularly consult the omens when they have any important enterprise on hand — a voyage, a large business venture, a

1 See Theophratus's character, " The Superstitious Man." a The birds of clearest omen were the great birds of prey — hawks, " Apollo's swift messengers," and eagles, " the birds of Zeus." It was a good omen if the birds flew from left to right, a bad omen if in the reverse direction.

marriage treaty, etc. There are several ready ways, not expensive; the interpreters are not priests, only low-born fellows as a rule, whose fees are trifling. You can find out about the future by casting meal upon the altar fire and noticing how it is burned, by watching how chickens pick up consecrated grain, 1 by observing how the sacrificial smoke curls upward, etc. The best way, however, is to examine the entrails of the victim after a sacrifice. Here everything depends on the shape, size, etc., of the various organs, especially of the liver, bladder, spleen, and lungs, and really expert judgment by an experienced and high-priced seer is desirable. The man who is assured by a reliable seer, " the livers are large and in fine color," will go on his trading voyage with a confident heart.

188. The Great Oracles. — Assuredly there is a better way still to read the future; at least so Greeks of earlier ages have believed. Go to one of the great oracles, whereof that of Apollo at Delphi is the supreme, but not the unique, example. Ask your question in set form from the attendant priests, not failing to offer an elaborate sacrifice and to bestow all the " gifts " (golden tripods, mixing bowls, shields, etc.) your means will allow. Then (at Delphi) wait silent and awe-stricken while the lady Pythia, habited as a young girl, takes her seat on a tripod over a deep cleft in the rock, whence issues an intoxicating vapor. She inhales the gas, sways to and fro in an ecstasy, and now, duly " inspired," answers in a somewhat wild manner the queries which the priest will put in behalf of the suppliants. Her incoherent words are very hard to understand, but the priest duly " interprets " them, i.e. gives them to the suppliant in the form of hexameter verses. Sometimes the

1 A very convenient way, — for it was a good sign if the chickens ate eagerly and one could always get a fair omen by keeping the fowls hungry a few hours ere " putting the question " !

meaning of these verses is perfectly clear. Very often they are truly "Delphic," with a most dubious meaning — as, in that oft-quoted instance, when the Pythia told Croesus if he went to war with Cyrus, "he would destroy a mighty monarchy," and lo, he destroyed his own !

Besides Delphi, there are numerous lesser oracles, each with its distinctive method of "revelation." But there is none, at least of consequence, within Attica, while a journey to Delphi is a serious and highly expensive undertaking. And as a matter of fact Delphi has partially lost credit in Athens. In the great Persian War Delphi un-patriotically " medized " — gave oracles friendly to Xerxes and utterly discouraging to the patriot cause. Then after this conviction of false prophesy, the oracle fell, for most of the time, into the hands of Sparta, and was obviously very willing to " reveal " things only in the Lacedaemonian interest. Hellenes generally and the Spartans in particular have still much esteem for the utterances of the Pythia, but Athenians are not now very partial to her. Soon will come the seizure of Delphi by the Phocians and the still further discrediting of this once great oracle.

189. Greek Sacrifices. — The two chief elements of Greek worship, however, are not consideration of the future, but sacrifice and prayer. Sacrifices in their simple form, as we have seen, take place continually, before every routine act. They become more formal when the proposed action is really important, or when the suppliant wishes to give thanks for some boon, or, at rarer intervals, to desire purification from some offense. There is no need of a priest for the simpler sacrifices. The father of the family can pour out the libation, can burn the food upon the altar, can utter the prayer for all his house; but in the greater sacrifices a priest is desirable, not as a sacred intermediary betwixt god and man, but as an expert to advise the worshipper what are the

competent rites, and to keep him from ignorantly angering heaven by unhappy words and actions. 1

Let us witness a sacrifice of this more formal kind, and while so doing we can tread upon the spot we have seemed in a manner to shun during our wanderings through Athens, the famous and holy Acropolis.

190. The Route to the Acropolis. — Phormion, son of Cresphontes, has been to Arcadia, and won the pentathlon in some athletic contests held at Mantinea. Although not equal to a triumph in the " four great Panhellenic contests," it was a most notable victory. Before setting out he vowed a sheep to Athena the Virgin if he conquered. The goddess was kind, and Phormion is very grateful. While the multitudes are streaming out to the Gymnasia, the young athlete, brawny and handsome, surrounded by an admiring coterie of friends and kinsmen, sets out for the Acropolis.

Phormion's home is in the "Ceramicus," the so-called " potters' quarter." His walk takes him a little to the west of the Agora, and close to the elegant temple of Hephaestos, 2 but past this and many other fanes he hastens. It was not the fire god which gave him fair glory at Mantinea. He goes onward until he is forced to make a detour to the left, at the craggy, rough hill of Areopagus which rises before him. Here, if time did not press, he might have tarried to pay respectful reverence before a deep fissure cleft in the side of the rock. In front of this fissure stands a little altar. All Phormion's company look away as they pass the spot, and they mutter together "Be propitious, 0 Eumen-ides!" (literally, Well-minded Ones). For like true Greeks

1 There were almost no hereditary priesthoods in Attica (outside the Eumolpidae connected with the mystical cult of Eleusis). Almost anybody of good character could qualify as a priest with due training, and there was little of the sacrosanct about the usual priestly office.

2 This temple, now called the Theseum, is the only well preserved ancient temple in modern Athens.

they delight to call foul things with fair and propitious names; and that awful fissure and altar are sacred to the Erinyes (Furies), the horrible maidens, the trackers of guilt, the avengers of murder; and above their cave, on these rude

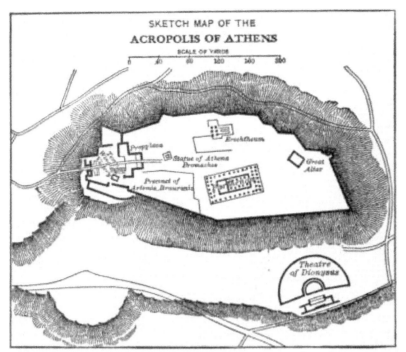

SKETCH MAP OF THE
ACROPOLIS OF ATHENS

rocks, sits the august court of the Areopagus when it meets as a " tribunal of blood " to try cases of homicide.

Phormion's party quicken their steps and quit this spot of ill omen. Then their sight is gladdened. The whole glorious Acropolis stands out before them.

191. The Acropolis of Athens. — Almost every Greek city has its own formidable citadel, its own acropolis, — for " citadel" is really all this word conveys. Corinth boasts of its " Acro-Corinthus," Thebes of its " Cadmeia," — but the Acropolis is in Athens. The later world will care little

for any other, and the later world will be right. The Athenian stronghold has long ceased to be a fortress, though still it rises steep and strong. It is now one vast temple compound, covered with magnificent buildings. Whether considered as merely a natural rock commanding a marvelous view, or as a consecrated museum of sculpture and architecture, it deserves its immortality. We raise our eyes to the Rock as we approach it.

The Acropolis dominates the plain of Athens. All the city seems to adjust itself to the base of its holy citadel. It lifts itself as tawny limestone rock rising about 190 feet above the adjacent level of the town. 1 In form it is an irregular oval with its axis west and east. It is about 950 feet long and 450 feet at its greatest breadth. On every side but the west the precipice falls away sheer and defiant, rendering a feeble garrison able to battle with myriads. 2 To the westward, however, the gradual slope makes a natural pathway always possible, and human art has long since shaped this with convenient steps. Nestling in against the precipice are various sanctuaries and caves; e.g. on the northwestern side, high up the slope beneath the precipice, open the uncanny grottoes of Apollo and of Pan. On the southern side, close under the very shadow of the citadel, is the temple of Asclepius, and, more to the southeast, the great open theater of Dionysus has been scooped out of the rock, a place fit to contain an audience of some 15,000. 3

1 It is nearly 510 feet above the level of the sea.

2 Recall the defense which the Acropolis was able to make against Xerxes's horde, when the garrison was small and probably ill organized, and had only a wooden barricade to eke out the

natural defenses.

*The stone seats of this theater do not seem to have been built till about 340 B.C. Up to that time the surface of the ground sloping back to the Acropolis seems simply to have been smoothed off, and probably covered with temporary wooden seats on the days of the great dramatic festivals.

So much for the bare " bones " of the Acropolis; but now under the dazzling sunshine how it glitters with indescribable splendor! Before us as we ascend a whole succession of buildings seem lifting themselves, not singly, not in hopeless confusion, but grouped admirably together by a kind of wizardry, so that the harmony is perfect, — each visible, brilliant column and pinnacle, not merely flashing its own beauty, but suggesting another greater beauty just behind.

192. The Use of Color upon Athenian Architecture and Sculptures. — While we look upward at this group of temples and their wealth of sculpture, let us state now something we have noticed during all our walks around Athens, but have hitherto left without comment. Every temple and statue in Athens is not left in its bare white marble, as later ages will conceive is demanded by " Greek architecture" and statuary, but is decked in brilliant color — " painted," if you will use an almost unfriendly word. The columns and gables and ceilings of the buildings are all painted. Blue, red, green, and gold blaze on all the members and ornaments. The backgrounds of the pediments, metopes, and frieze are tinted some uniform color on which the sculptured figures in relief stand out clearly. The figures themselves are tinted or painted, at least on the hair, lips, and eyes. Flesh-colored warriors are fighting upon a bright red background. The armor and horse trappings on the sculptures are in actual bronze. The result is an effect indescribably vivid. Blues and reds predominate: the flush of light and color from the still more brilliant heavens above adds to the effect. Shall we call it garish? We have learned to know the taste of Athenians too well to doubt their judgment in matters of pure beauty. And they are right. Under an Athenian sky temples and statues almost demand a wealth of color which in a somber clime

The Temples and Gods of Athens 217

would seem intolerable. The brilliant lines of the Acropolis buildings are the just answer of the Athenian to the brilliancy of Helios.

193. The Chief Buildings on the Acropolis. — And now to

ascend the Acropolis. We leave the discussion of the details of the temples and the sculpture to the architects and archaeologists. The whole plateau of the Rock is covered with religious buildings, altars, statues. We pass through the Propylaea, the worthy rival of the Parthenon behind, a magnificent portal, with six splendid Doric columns facing us; and as we go through them, to right and to left open out equally magnificent columned porticoes. 1 As we emerge from the Propylaea the whole vision of the sacred plateau bursts upon us simultaneously. We can notice only the most important of the buildings. At the southwestern point of the Acropolis on the angle of rock which juts out beyond the Propylaea is the graceful little temple of the " Wingless Victory," built in the Ionic style. The view commanded by its bastion will become famous throughout the world. Behind this, nearer the southern side, stands the less important temple of Artemis Brauronia. Nearer the center and directly before the entrance rises a colossal brazen statue — " monstrous," many might call its twenty-six feet of height, save that a master among masters has cast the spell of his genius over it. This is the famous Athena Promachos, 2 wrought by Phidias out of the spoils of Marathon. The warrior goddess stands in full armor and rests upon her mighty lance. The gilded lance tip gleams so dazzlingly we may well believe the tale that sailors use it for a first landmark as they sail up the coast from Cape Sunium.

1 That to the north was the larger and contained a kind of picture gallery.

Looking again upon the complex of buildings we single out another on the northern side:

an irregularly shaped temple, or rather several temples joined together, the Erech-theum, wherein is the sanctuary of Athena Polias (the revered "City Warden"), the ancient wooden statue, grotesque, beloved, most sacred of all the holy images in Athens. And here on the southern side of this building is the famous Caryatid porch; the "Porch of the Maidens," which will be admired as long as Athens has a name. But our eyes refuse to linger long on any of these things. Behind the statue of the Promachos, a little to the southern side of the plateau, stands the Parthenon — the queen jewel upon the crown of Athens.

194. The Parthenon.—Let others analyze its sculptures and explain the technical reasons why Ictinus and Callicrates, the architects, and Phidias, the sculptor, created here the supreme masterpiece for the artistic world. We can state only the superficialities. It is a noble building by mere size; 228 feet measure its side, 101 feet its front. Forty-six majestic Doric columns surround it; they average thirty-four feet in height, and six feet three inches at the base. All these facts, however, do not give the soul of the Parthenon. Walk around it slowly, tenderly, lovingly. Study the elaborate stories told by the pediments, — on the east front the birth of Athena, on the west the strife of Athena and Poseidon for the possession of Athens. Trace down the innumerable lesser sculptures on the " metopes " under the cornice, — showing the battles of the Giants, Centaurs, Amazons, and of the Greeks before Troy; finally follow around, on the whole inner circuit of the body of the temple, the frieze, 1 showing in bas-relief the Panathenaic procession, with the beauty, nobility, and youth of Athens marching in

1 This, of course, is on the outside wall of the " cella," but inside the surrounding colonnade.

glad festival; comprehend that these sculptures will never be surpassed in the twenty-four succeeding centuries ; that here are supreme examples for the artists of all time, — and then, in the face of this final creation, we can realize that the Parthenon will justify its claim to immortality.

One thing more. There are hardly any straight lines in the Parthenon. To the eye, the members and the steps of the substructure may seem perfectly level; but the measuring rod betrays marvelously subtle curves. As nature abhors right angles in her creations of beauty, so have these Greeks. Rigidity, unnaturalness, have been banished. The Parthenon stands, not merely embellished with inimitable sculptures, but perfectly adjusted to the natural world surrounding. 1

We have seen only the exterior of the Parthenon. We must wait now ere visiting the interior, for Phormion is beginning his sacrifice.

195. A Sacrifice on the Acropolis. — Across the sacred plateau advances the little party. As it goes under the Propylaea a couple of idle temple watchers 2 give its members a friendly nod. The Acropolis rock itself seems deserted, save for a few worshippers and a party of admiring Achaean visitors who are being shown the glories of the Parthenon. 3 There seems to be a perfect labyrinth of statues of gods, heroes, and departed worthies, and almost as many altars, great and small, placed in every direction.

1 It was an inability to discover and execute these concealed curves which give certain of the older modern imitations of the Parthenon their unpleasant impressions of hardness and rigidity.

2 The most important function of these watchers seems to have been to prevent dogs from entering the Acropolis. Probably they were inefficient old men favored with sinecure offices.

8 The Acropolis seems to have become a great " show place " for visitors to Athens soon after the completion of the famous temples.

Phormion leads his friends onward till they come near to the wide stone platform somewhat in the rear of the Parthenon. Here is the " great altar " of Athena, whereon the "hecatombs" will be sacrificed, even a hundred oxen or more, 1 at some of the major public festivals; and close beside it stands also a small and simple altar sacred to Athena Parthenos, Athena the Virgin. Suitable attendants have been in readiness since dawn waiting for worshippers. One of Phormion's party leads behind him a bleating white lamb "without blemish." 2 It is a short matter now to bring the firewood and the other necessaries. The sacrifice takes place without delay.

First a busy "temple sweeper" goes over the ground around the altar with a broom; then the regular priest, a dignified gray-headed man with a long ungirt purple chiton, and a heavy olive garland, comes forward bearing a basin of holy water. This basin is duly passed to the whole company as it stands in a ring, and each in turn dips his hand and sprinkles his face and clothes with the lustral water. Meantime the attendant has placed another wreath around the head of the lamb. The priest raises his hand.

"Let there be silence," he commands (lest any unlucky word be spoken); and in a stillness broken only by the auspicious twittering of the sparrows amid the Parthenon gables, he takes barley corns from a basket, and sprinkles them on the altar and over the lamb. With his sacred knife he cuts a lock of hair from the victim's head and casts it on

1 We know by an inscription of 169 oxen being needed for a single Athenian festival.

2 This was a very proper creature to sacrifice to a great Olympian deity like Athena. Goats were not suitable for her, although desirable for most of the other gods. It was unlawful to sacrifice swine to Aphrodite. When propitiating the gods of the underworld, — Hades, Persephone, etc., —a black victim was in order. Poor people could sacrifice doves, cocks, and other birds.

The Temples and Gods of Athens

the fire. Promptly now the helper comes forward to complete the sacrifice. Phormion and his friends are a little anxious. Will the lamb take fright, hang back, and have to be dragged to its unwilling death ? The clever attendant has cared for that. A sweet truss of dried clover is lying just under the altar. The lamb starts forward, bleating joyously. As it bows its head 1 as if consenting to its fate, the priest stabs it dexterously in the neck with his keen blade. The helper claps a bowl under the neck to catch the spurting blood. A flute player in readiness, but hitherto silent, suddenly strikes up a keen blast to drown the dying moans of the animal. Hardly has the lamb ceased to struggle before the priest and the helper have begun to cut it up then and there. SACRIFICING A PIG.

Certain bits of the

fat and small pieces from each limb are laid upon the altar, and promptly consumed. These are the goddess's peculiar portion, and the credulous at least believe that she, though unseen, is present to eat thereof; certainly the sniff of the burning meat is grateful to her divine nostrils. The priest and the helper are busy taking off the hide and securing the best joint — these are their "fees " for professional services. All the rest will be duly gathered up by Phormion's body

1 If a larger animal — an ox — failed to bow its head auspiciously, the omen could be rectified by suddenly splashing a little water in the ears.

servant and borne home, — for Phormion will give a fine feast on " sacred mutton " that night. 1

Meantime, while the goddess's portion burns, Phormion approaches the altar, bearing a shallow cup of unmixed wine, and flings it upon the flame.

" Be propitious, O Lady," he cries, " and receive this my drink offering." 2

The sacrifice is now completed. The priest assures Phormion that the entrails of the victim foretokened every possible favor in future athletic contests — and this, and his insinuating smile, win him a silver drachma to supplement his share of the lamb. Phormion readjusts the chaplet upon his own head, and turns towards the Parthenon. After the sacrifice will come the prayer.

196. The Interior of the Parthenon and the Great Image of Athena. — The whole Acropolis is the home of Athena. The other gods harbored thereon are only her inferior guests. Upon the Acropolis the dread goddess displays her many aspects. In the Erechtheum we worship her as Athena Polias, the ancient guardian of the hearths and homes of the city. In the giant Promachos, we see her the leader in war, — the awful queen who went with her fosterlings to the deadly grappling at Marathon and at Salamis; in the little temple of " Wingless Victory " 3 we see her as Athena the Victorious, triumphant over Barbarian and Hellenic foe; but in the Parthenon we adore her in her purest conception —

1 As already suggested (page 180) a sacrifice (public, or, if on a large scale, private) was about the only occasion on which Athenians tasted beef, pork, or mutton.

2 The original intention of this libation at the sacrifice was very clearly to provide the gods with wine to " wash down " their meat.

•The term "Wingless Victory" (Nike Apteros) has reference to a special type and aspect of Athena, not to the goddess Nike (Victory) pure and simple.

The Temples and Gods of Athens

the virgin queen, now chaste and calm, her battles over, the
pure, high incarnation of all " the beautiful and the good"
that may possess spirit and
mind, — the sovran intellect,
in short, purged of all carnal,
earthy passion. It is meet
that such a goddess should
inhabit such a dwelling as the
Parthenon. 1

Phormion passes under the eastern porch, and does not forget (despite the purification before the sacrifice) to dip the whisk broom, lying by the door, in the brazen laver of holy water and again to sprinkle himself. He passes out of the dazzling sunlight into a chamber that seems at first to be lost in a vast, impenetrable gloom. He pauses and gazes upward; above him, as little by little his eyes get their adjustment, a faint pearly light seems streaming downward. It is coming through the translucent marble slabs of the roof of the great temple. 2 Then out of the gloom gleam shapes, objects, — a

ATHENA PARTHENOS. "Varvakeion Model" of the great Athena of Phidias.

1 There was still another aspect in which Athena was worshipped on the Acropolis. She had a sacred place (temenos), though without a temple, sacred to her as Athena Ergane — Athena Protectress of the Arts.

2 This seems to be the most reasonable way to assume that the cella of the Parthenon was lighted, in view of the danger, in case of open skylights, of damage to the holy image by wind and rain.

face. He catches the glitter of great jewels and of massy gold, as parts of the rich garments and armor of some vast image. He distinguishes at length a statue, — the form of a woman, nearly forty feet in height. Her left hand rests upon a mighty shield; her right hand holds a winged "Victory," itself of nigh human size. Upon her breast is the awful aegis, the especial breastplate of the high gods. Around the foot of her shield coils a serpent. Upon her head is a mighty helmet. And all the time that these things are becoming manifest, evermore clearly one beholds the majestic face, — sweetness without weakness, intellectuality without coldness, strength mingled justly with compassion. This is the Athena Parthenos, the handiwork of Phidias. 1

We will not heap up description. What boots it to tell that the arms and vesture of this "chryselephantine " statue are of pure gold; that the flesh portions are of gleaming ivory; that Phidias has wrought the whole so nobly together that this material, too sumptuous for common artists, becomes under his assembling the perfect substance for the manifestation of deity ?

. . . Awestruck by the vision, though often he has seen it, Phormion stands long in reverent silence. Then at length, casting a pinch of incense upon the brazier, constantly smoking before the statue, he utters his simple prayer.

197. Greek Prayers. •— Greek prayers are usually very pragmatic. "Who," asks Cicero, who can speak for both Greeks and Romans in this particular, " ever thanked the gods that he was a good man? Men are thankful for riches,

1 Of this statue no doubt there could be said what Dion Chrysostomos said of the equally famous " Zeus " erected by Phidias atOlympia. "The man most depressed with woes, forgot his ills whilst gazing on the statue, so much light and beauty had Phidias infused within it." Besides the descriptions in the ancient writers we get a clear idea of the general type of the Athena Parthenos from recently discovered statuettes, especially the " Varvakeion " model (40$ inches high). This last is cold and lifeless as a work of art, but fairly accurate as to details.

The Temples and Gods of Athens 225

honor, safety. . . . We beg of the sovran God [only] what makes us safe, sound, rich and prosperous."* Phormion is simply a very average, healthy, handsome young Athenian. While he prays he stretches his hands on high, as is fitting to a deity of Olympus. 2 His petition runs much as follows: —

"Athena, Queen of the JSgis, by whatever name thou lovest best, 3 give ear.

" Inasmuch as thou dids't heed my vow, and grant me fair glory at Mantinea, bear witness I have been not ungrateful. I have offered to thee a white sheep, spotless and undefined. And now I have it in my mind to attempt the pentathlon at the next Isthmia at Corinth. Grant me victory even in that; and not one sheep but five, all as good as this to-day, shall srnoke upon thine altar. Grant also unto me, my kinsmen and all my friends, health, riches and fair renown."

A pagan prayer surely; and there is a still more pagan epilogue. Phormion has an enemy, who is not forgotten.

"And oh! gracious, sovran Athena, blast my enemy Xenon, who strove to trip me foully in the foot race. May his wife be childless or bear him only monsters; may his whole house perish ; may all his wealth take flight; may his friends forsake him ; may war soon cut him off, or may he die amid impoverished, dishonored old age. If this my sacrifice has found favor in thy sight, may all these evils come upon him unceasingly. And so will I adore thee and sacrifice unto thee all my life." *

1 Cicero, De Nat. Deor. ii. 36.

2 In praying to a deity of the lower world the hands would be held down. A Greek almost never knelt, even in prayer. He would have counted it degrading.

8 This formula would be put in, lest some favorite epithet of the divinity be omitted.

4 Of ten a curse would become a real substitute for a prayer; e.g. at Athens, against a rascally and traitorous general, a solemn public curse would be pronounced at evening by all the priests and priestesses of the

The curse then is a most proper part of a Greek prayer! Phormion is not conscious of blasphemy. He merely follows invariable custom.

It is useless to expect " Christian sentiments " in the fourth century B.C., yet perhaps an age should be judged, not by its average, but by its best. Athenians can utter nobler prayers than those of the type of Phormion. Xeno-phon makes his model young householder Ischomenus pray nobly " that I may enjoy health and strength of body, the respect of my fellow citizens, honorable safety in times of war, and wealth honestly increased." 1

There is a simple little prayer also which seems to be a favorite with the farmers. Its honest directness carries its own message.

" Rain, rain, dear Zeus, upon the fields of the Athenians and the plains." 2

Higher still ascends the prayer of Socrates, when he begs for " the good " merely, leaving it to the wise gods to determine what " the good " for him may be; and in one prayer, which Plato puts in Socrates's mouth, almost all the best of Greek ideals and morality seems uttered. It is spoken not on the Acropolis, but beside the Ilissus at the close of the delightful walk and chat related in the Phcedrus.

" Beloved Pan, and all ye other gods who haunt this place, give me the beauty of the inward soul, and may the outward and the inward man be joined in perfect harmony. May I reckon the wise to be wealthy, and may I have such a quantity of gold as none but the temperate can carry. Anything more? — That prayer, I think, is enough for me."

city, each shaking in the air a red cloth in token of the bloody death to which the offender was devoted.

1 Xenophon, The Economist, xi, p. 8.

2 It was quoted later to us by the Emperor Marcus Aurelius, who adds, "In truth, we ought not to pray at all, or we ought to pray in this simple and noble fashion."

The Temples and Gods of Athens 227

Phormion and his party are descending to the city to spend the evening in honest mirth and feasting, but we are fain to linger, watching the slow course of the shadows as they stretch across the Attic hills. Sea, sky, plain, mountains, and city are all before us, but we will not spend words upon them now. Only for the buildings, wrought by Pericles and his mighty peers, we will speak out our admiration. We will gladly confirm the words Plutarch shall some day say of them, " Unimpaired by time, their appearance retains the fragrance of freshness, as though they had been inspired by an eternally blooming life and a never aging soul."*

1 Plutarch wrote this probably after 100 A.D., when the Parthenon had stood for about five and a half centuries.

CHAPTER XXI. THE GREAT FESTIVALS OF ATHENS.

198. The Frequent Festivals at Athens. — Surely our " Day in Athens" has been spent from morn till night several times over, so much there is to see and tell. Yet he would be remiss who left the city of Athena before witnessing at least several of the great public festivals which are the city's noble pride. There are a prodigious number of religious festivals in Athens. 1 They take the place of the later " Christian Sabbath " and probably create a somewhat equal number of rest days during the year, although at more irregular intervals. They are far from being " Scotch Sundays," however. Oh them the semi-riotous "joy of life" which is part of the Greek nature finds its fullest, ofttimes its wildest, expression. They are days of merriment, athletic sports, great civic spectacles, chorals, public dances. 2 To complete our picture of Athens we must tarry for a swift cursory glance upon at least three of these f§te days of the city of Pericles, Sophocles, and Phidias.

199. The Eleusinia. — Our first festival is the Eleusinia, the festival of the Eleusinian mysteries. It is September, the " 19th of Boedromion," the Athenians will say. Four

i In Gulick (Life of the Ancient Greeks, pp. 304-310) there is a valuable list of Attic festivals. The Athenians had over thirty important religious festivals, several of them, e.g., the Thesmorphoria (celebrated by the women in honor of Demeter), extending over a number of days.

3 It is needless to point out that to the Greeks, as to many other ancient peoples,—for

example, the Hebrews, —dancing often had a religious significance and might be a regular part of the worship of the gods. 228

The Great Festivals of Athens 229

days have been spent by the " initiates" and the " candidates " in symbolic sacrifices and purifications. 1 On one of these days the arch priest, the " Hierophant," has preached a manner of sermon at the Painted Porch in the Agora setting forth the awfulriess and spiritual efficacy of these Mysteries, sacred to Demeter the Earth Mother, to her daughter Persephone, and also to the young Iacchus, one of the many incarnations of Dionysus, and who is always associated at Eleusis with the divine " Mother and Daughter." The great cry has gone forth to the Initiates — " To the Sea, ye Mystae 1" and the whole vast multitude has gone down to bathe in the purifying brine.

Now on this fifth day comes the sacred procession from Athens across the mountain pass to Eleusis. The participants, by thousands, of both sexes and of all ages, are drawn up in the Agora ere starting. The Hierophant, the " Torchbearer," the " Sacred Herald," and the other priests wear long flowing raiment and high mitres like Orientals. They also, as well as the company, wear myrtle and ivy chaplets and bear ears of corn and reapers' sickles. The holy image of Iacchus is borne in a car, the high priests marching beside it; and forth with pealing shout and chant they go, — down the Ceramicus, through the Dipylon gate, and over the hill to Eleusis, twelve miles away.

200. The Holy Procession to Eleusis. - Very sacred is the procession, but not silent and reverential. It is an hour when the untamed animal spirits of the Greeks, who after all are a young race and who are gripped fast by natural instinct, seem uncurbed. Loud rings the " orgiastic" cry, "Iacche! Iacche! evoe!"

1 Not all Athenians were among the "initiated," but it does not seem to have been hard to be admitted to the oaths and examination which gave one participation in the mysteries. About all a candidate had to prove was blameless character. Women could be initiated as well as men.

There are wild shouts, dances, jests, songs, 1 postures. As the marchers pass the several sanctuaries along the road there are halts for symbolic sacrifices. So the multitude slowly mounts the long heights of Mount ^Egaleos, until — close to the temple of Aphrodite near the summit of the p ass — the view opens of the broad blue bay of Eleusis, shut in by the isle of Salamis, while to the northward are seen the green Thrasian plain, with the white houses of Eleusis town 2 near the center, and the long line of outer hills stretching away to Megara and Boeotia.

The evening shadows are falling, while the peaceful army sweeps over the mountain wall and into Eleusis. Every marcher produces a torch, and bears it blazing aloft as he nears his destination. Seen in the dark from Eleusis, the long procession of innumerable torches must convey an effect most magical.

201. The Mysteries of Eleusis. — What follows at Eleusis ? The " mysteries" are " mysteries " still; we cannot claim initiation and reveal them. There seem to be manifold sacrifices of a symbolic significance, the tasting of sacred "portions" of food and drink — a dim foreshadowing of the Christian sacrament of the Eucharist; especially in the great hall of the Temple of the Mystae in Eleusis there take place a manner of symbolic spectacles, dramas perhaps one may call them, revealing the origin of Iacchus, the mystical union of Persephone and Zeus, and the final joy of Demeter.

This certainly we can say of these ceremonies. They seem to have afforded to spiritually minded men a sense of

J We do not possess the official chant of the Mystae used on their march to Eleusis. Very possibly it was of a swift riotous nature like the Bacchinals' song in Euripides's Bacchinals (well translated by Way or by Murray).

'This was about the only considerable town in Attica outside of Athens.

remission of personal sin which the regular religion could never give; they seem also to have conveyed a fair hope of immortality, such as most Greeks doubted. Sophocles tells thus the story: " Thrice blessed are they who behold these mystic rites, ere passing to Hades' realm. They alone have life there. For the rest all things below are evil." 1 And in face of imminent death, perhaps in hours of shipwreck, men are wont to ask one another, " Have you been initiated at Eleusis ? "

202. The Greater Dionysia and the Drama. — Again we are in Athens in the springtime: " The eleventh of Elaphe-bolion" [March]. It is the third day of the Greater Dionysia. The city has been in high festival; all the booths in the Agora hum with redoubled life; strangers have flocked in from outlying parts of Hellas to trade, admire, and recreate; under pretext of honoring the wine god, inordinate quantities of wine are drunk with less than the prudent mixture of water. There is boisterous frolicking, singing, and jesting everywhere. It is early blossom time. All whom you meet wear huge flower crowns, and pelt you with the fragrant petals of spring. 2

So for two days the city has made merry, and now on the third, very early, "to the theater" is the word on every lip. Magistrates in their purple robes of office, ambassadors from foreign states, the priests and religious dignitaries, are all going to the front seats of honor. Ladies of gentle family, carefully veiled but eager and fluttering, are going with their maids, if the productions

Sophocles, Frag. 719.

2 Pindar (Frag. 75) says thus of the joy and beauty of this fgte: " [Lo !] *,his festival is due when the chamber of the red-robed Hours is opened and odorous plants wake to the fragrant spring. Then we scatter on undying earth the violet, like lovely tresses, and twine roses in our hair; then sounds the voice of song, the flute keeps time, and dancing choirs resound the praise of Semele."

of the day are to be tragedies not comedies. 1 All the citizens are going, rich and poor, for here again we meet " Athenian democracy " ; and the judgment and interest of the tatter-clad fishermen seeking the general "two-obol" seats may be almost as correct and keen as that of the lordly Alcmseonid in his gala himation.

203. The Theater of Dionysus. — Early dawn it is when the crowds pour through the barriers around the Theater of Dionysus upon the southern slope of the Acropolis. They sit (full 15,000 or more) wedged close together upon rough wooden benches set upon the hill slopes. 2 At the foot of their wide semicircle is a circular space of ground, beaten hard, and ringed by a low stone barrier. It is some ninety feet in diameter. This is the orchestra, the " dancing place," wherein the chorus may disport itself and execute its elaborate figures. Behind the orchestra stretches a kind of tent or booth, the skene. Within this the actors may retire to change their costumes, and the side nearest to the audience is provided with a very simple scene, — some kind of elementary scenery painted to represent the front of a temple or palace, or the rocks, or the open country. This is nearly the entire setting. 3 If there are any slight changes of this screen, they must be made in the sight of the entire audience. The Athenian theater has the blue dome of heaven above it, the red Acropolis rock behind it. Beyond the

1 It seems probable (on our uncertain information) that Athenian ladies attended the moral and proper tragedies. It was impossible for them to attend the often very coarse comedies. Possibly at the tragedies they sat in a special and decently secluded part of the theater.

8 These benches (before the stone theater was built in 340 B.C.) may be imagined as set up much like the " bleachers " at a modern baseball park. We know that ancient audiences wedged in very close.

8 I think it is fairly certain that the classical Attic theater was without any stage, and that the actors appeared on the same level as the chorus. As to the extreme simplicity of all the scenery and properties there is not the least doubt.

skene one can look far away to the country and the hills. The keen Attic imagination will take the place of the thousand arts of the later stage-setter. Sophocles and his rivals, even as Shakespeare in Elizabeth's England, can sound the very depths and scale the loftiest heights of human passion, with only a simulacrum of the scenery, properties, and me-

COMIC ACTORS DRESSED AS OSTRICHES.

chanical artifices which will trick out a very mean twentieth century theater.

204. The Production of a Play. —The crowds are hushed and expectant. The herald, ere the play begins, proclaims the award of a golden crown to some civic benefactor: a moment of ineffable joy to the recipient; for when is a true Greek happier than when held xip for public glorification ? Then comes the summons to the first competing poet.

" Lead on your chorus." 1 The intellectual feast of the Dionysia has begun.

To analyze the Attic drama is the task of the philosopher and the literary expert. We observe only the superficialities. There are never more than three speaking actors be-

iln the fourth century B.C. when the creation of original tragedies was in decline, a considerable part of the Dionysia productions seem to have been devoted to the works of the earlier masters, ^Eschylus, Sophocles, and Euripides.

fore the audience at once. They wear huge masques,

shaped to fit their parts. The wide mouthpieces make the trained elocution carry to the most remote parts of the theater. The actors wear long trailing robes and are mounted on high shoes to give them sufficient stature before the distant audience. When a new part is needed in the play, an actor retires into the booth, and soon comes forth with a changed masque and costume — an entirely new character. In such a costume and masque, play of feature and easy gesture is impossible; but the actors carry themselves with a stately dignity and recite their often ponderous lines with a grace which redeems them from all bombast. An essential part of the play is the chorus; indeed the chorus was once the main feature of the drama, the actors insignificant innovations. With fifteen members for the tragedy, twenty-four for the comedy, 1 old men of Thebes, Trojan dames, Athenian charcoal burners, as the case may demand — they sympathize with the hard-pressed hero, sing lusty choral odes, and occupy the time with song and dance while the actors are changing costume.

The audience follows all the philosophic reasoning of the

ACTOR IN COSTUME AS A FURY.

1 In the " Middle " and " Later " comedy, so called, the chorus entirely disappears. The actors do everything.

The Great Festivals of Athens 235

tragedies, the often subtle wit of the comedies, with that same shrewd alertness displayed at the jury courts of the Pnyx. " Authis! Authis!" (again! again!) is the frequent shout, if approving. Date stones and pebbles as well as hootings are the reward of silly lines or bad acting. At noon there is an interlude to snatch a hasty luncheon (perhaps without leaving one's seat). Only when the evening shadows are falling does the chorus of the last play approach the altar in the center of the orchestra for the final sacrifice. A whole round of tragedies have been given. 1 The five public judges announce their decision: an ivy wreath to the victorious poet; to his cfwregus (the rich man who has provided his chorus and who shares his glory) the right to set up a monument in honor of the victory. Home goes the multitude, — to quarrel over the result, to praise or blame the acting, to analyze with remarkable acuteness the poet's handling of religious, ethical, or social questions.

The theater, like the dicasteries and the Pnyx, is one of the great public schools of Athens.

205. The Great Panathenaic Procession. — Then for the last time let us visit Athens, at the f§te which in its major form comes only once in four years. It is the 28th of Metageitnion (August), and the eighth day of the Greater Panathenaea, the most notable of all Athenian festivals. By it is celebrated the union of all Attica by Theseus, as one happy united country under

the benign sway of mighty Athena, — an ever fortunate union, which saved the land from the sorrowful feuds of hostile hamlets such as have plagued so many Hellenic countries. On the earlier days of the feast there have been musical contests and gymnastic games much after the manner of the Olympic games,

1 Comedies, although given at this Dionysia, were more especially favored at the Lensea, an earlier winter festival.

although the contestants have been drawn from Attica only. There has been a public recital of Homer. Before a great audience probably at the Pnyx or the Theater a rhapsodist of noble presence — clad in purple and with a golden crown — has made the Trojan War live again, as with his well-trained voice he held the multitude spellbound by the music of the stately hexameters.

Now we are at the eighth day. All Athens will march in its glory to the Acropolis, to bear to the shrine of Athena the sacred " peplos "— a robe specially woven by the noble women of Athens to adorn the image of the guardian goddess. 1 The houses have opened; the wives, maids, and mothers of gentle family have come forth to march in the procession, all elegantly wreathed and clad in their best, bearing the sacred vessels and other proper offerings. The daughter of the " metics," the resident foreigners, go as attendants of honor with them. The young men and the old, the priests, the civil magistrates, the generals, all have their places. Proudest of all are the wealthy and high-born youths of the cavalry, who now dash to and fro in their clattering pride. The procession is formed in the outer Ceramicus. Amid cheers, chants, chorals, and incense smoke it sweeps through the Agora, and slowly mounts the Acropolis. Center of all the marchers is the glittering peplos, raised like a sail upon a wheeled barge of state — " the ship of Athena." Upon the Acropolis, while the old peplos is piously withdrawn from the image and the new one substituted, there is a prodigious sacrifice. A mighty flame roars heavenward from the " great altar "; while enough bullocks and kine have been slaughtered to enable every citizen — however poor—to bear away a goodly mess of roasted meat that night.

1 Note that this robe was for the revered ancient and wooden image of Athena Polias, not for the far less venerable statue of Athena Parthenos.

The Great Festivals of Athens 237

206. The View from the Temple of Wingless Victory.—We
will not wait for the feasting but rather will take our way to the Temple of Wingless Victory, looking forth to the west of the Acropolis Rock. So many things we see which we would fain print on the memory. Behind us we have just left the glittering Parthenon, and the less august but hardly less beautiful Erechtheum, with its "Porch of the Maidens." To our right is the wide expanse of the roofs of the city and beyond the dark olive groves of Colonus, and the slopes of ^Egaleos. In the near foreground, are the red crags of Areopagus and the gray hill of the Pnyx. But the eye will wander farther. It is led away across the plainland to the bay of Phaleron, the castellated hill of Munychia, the thin stretch of blue water and the brown island seen across it — Salamis and its strait of the victory. Across the sparkling vista of the sea rise the headlands of ^Egina and of lesser isles ; farther yet rise the lordly peaks of Argolis. Or we can look to the southward. Our gaze runs down the mountainous Attic coast full thirty miles to where Sunium thrusts out its haughty cape into the Mgean and points the way across the island-studded sea.

Evening is creeping on. Behind us sounds the great paean, the solemn chant to Athena, bestower of good to men. As the sun goes down over the distant Argolic hills his rays spread a clear pathway of gold across the waters. Islands, seas, mountains far and near, are touched now with shifting hues, — saffron, violet, and rose, — beryl, topaz, sapphire, amethyst. There will never be another landscape like unto this in all the world. Gladly we sum up our thoughts in the cry of a son of Athens, Aristophanes, master of song, who loved her with that love which the land of Athena can ever inspire in all its children, whether its own by adoption or by birth : —

" Oh, thou, our Athens I Violet-crowned, brilliant, most enviable of cities I"

THE END

Printed in the USA
CPSIA information can be obtained
at www.ICGtesting.com
LVHW081822041224
798309LV00009BA/458

* 9 7 8 1 5 3 7 6 1 8 3 6 4 *